Accepted

Endorsements

As an historian, I have studied this location and period in history for over a decade, and Paula Peckham's beautifully written novel brings both alive in a way that is as moving as it is authentic. I couldn't put this book down.
—**Alice Baumgartner**, author of *South to Freedom*

Paula Peckham is an extremely talented writer. Her beguiling style of writing places the reader directly into the heart of the story.

Each character is brought to life in original, unforgettable ways, as an unlikely romance springs up between two people who could not be more different.

Deep in the heart of Texas, suspense enters when already-loved characters find themselves in a dangerous realm of secrets.

Love, overcoming faith, and God's protection are all woven into this beautiful love story. This is one story you won't want to put down.
—**Anne Greene**, author of *For Such A Time: The Jarrett Ross Story*

Accepted is an unforgettable tale of love and loss, of faith and hope, set in 1860's San Antonio against the backdrop of slavery and the Civil War. Peckham has crafted a beautiful love story that will linger in your mind long after you close the book.

—**Nancy Lavo,** author of *The Place Where You Belong*

Accepted

PAULA PECKHAM

ELK LAKE PUBLISHING INC.

PUBLISHING THE POSITIVE
Plymouth, Massachusetts

A Christian Company
ElkLakePublishingInc.com

Copyright Notice

Cover and Interior Design: Derinda Babcock, Deb Haggerty
Editor(s): Cristel Phelps, Deb Haggerty

PUBLISHED BY: Elk Lake Publishing, Inc., 35 Dogwood Drive, Plymouth, MA 02360, 2023

Library Cataloging Data

Names: Peckham, Paula (Paula Peckham)
Accepted / Paula Peckham
316 p. 23cm × 15cm (9in × 6 in.)

ISBN-13: 9798891340206 (paperback) | 9798891340213 (hardcover) | 9798891340220 (trade paperback) | 9798891340237 (e-book)
Key Words: Christian historical romance; San Antonio, Texas; Underground railroad; independent woman; dyslexia; farm, farming, farmer; donkey, animal rescue

Library of Congress Control Number: 2023947123 Fiction

Dedication

I dedicate this book with much gratitude to my mother, Sandy Babb, who taught me to love, not only with her words, but also with her excellent example. Thank you, Mama, for showing us how it's done.

Acknowledgments

Many thanks to all who helped me with the research about the Texas Underground Railroad. Special thanks to Alice Baumgartner, whose book, *South to Freedom,* opened my eyes to a reality I wasn't taught in my high school history classes. Thanks also to Kenneth Stewart, director of the San Antonio African American Community Archive and Museum for answering my questions and providing the DVD, *Just a Ferry Ride to Freedom.*

Thank you to my husband, John, who plans the research trips for every book and who found the cotton gin museum of all things.

As always, grateful acknowledgment to my critique partners who smooth the rough edges. Nancy, Teresa, Peggy, Connie, Ally, Emilee, Joy, Cathy, Deena, Cheryl, and Jodi. The writing life is much easier—and much more fun— with you in it.

Finally, to Kathy and Ronda for your constant encouragement and cheerleading. You never let me fail to believe in myself. Love you more!

Chapter One

SAN ANTONIO, TEXAS—SPRING, 1864

They wasted time with every moment they stood idle.

Jonathan Campbell squinted one eye and peered at the cloudless sky. Mr. Nelson, from the feed store in San Antonio, should be along directly. Jonathan had placed his order for corn and cotton seed back in March, and they were due to arrive today. He sucked his teeth, impatience building. The store owner's offer to deliver surprised him, but he was glad enough to accept the help that saved him from making a trip to town. The urge to start made him antsy. Where was the man?

With one knee pressed into the damp ground, he stretched his tight back with a groan. Sweeping his hat from his head, he wiped his sleeve across his brow. The sun's rays brought welcome warmth after a frigid February and a rainy March, and he had worked up a sweat. Long, straight furrows gave testament to the labor he and the two farmhands had completed so far. The week had been productive. Preparing the soil to receive seed, helping along the life cycle established by God, spoke to a spot deep in his soul.

He gave the wrench he gripped in his sweaty hand one last yank and glanced up at the young man, who waited for him to work his magic with the plow. The hired hand had phenomenal skills with horses, but mechanical things reduced him to fumble fingers. "Try now, Teddy. I think it's ready to go."

Teddy grinned. "Is there nothing you can't fix?" He popped the reins against the back of the draft horse, urging him on with a click of his tongue. The animal's enormous hooves dug into the ground, and the machine lurched into motion. The depth wheel rotated easily now, silver metal from the plowshare glinting in the sun.

A pleased smile broke across Jonathan's face as the rich, brown earth appeared. God made Adam from the dust of the ground. If only creating came that easy for him. Unfortunately, his took nothing but honest, hard work. Ah, well. When God made him, he added an extra pinch of *farmer*. He loved this life.

He stood and tugged his hat back down, then dusted his hands together. Halfway across the field, Ernest drove a team of mules, working his half of the acreage. The older man worked too far away for Jonathan to see, but he imagined the wicked grin that probably crossed his face. Teddy's delay gave Ernest a jump on their progress.

Neither helper said anything aloud, but the farmhands competed to see whose team would finish first. Each stood convinced his choice of work animal ranked superior to the other. Teddy had fidgeted, casting anxious glances toward the opposite side of the field as he waited for Jonathan to fix the broken plow.

Ernest preferred working with the lean mules. Teddy loved the big draft animal. Jonathan preferred the animal that cost the least to feed and care for. At present, the contest measured in at a draw. Both required shoes to protect against stony sections of land, both required feed during the winter. But both pulled their weight. Neither pulled particularly at his heartstrings. They were animals. Property. They had a job to do. And right now, that job meant getting this pasture ready for planting.

"Jonathan." Belle's voice carried across the field. He turned with a smile to greet his little sister.

She tramped over the plowed furrows, stepping up and down between the rows of dirt. A hamper banged against her knee as she came his direction, fingers wrapped around the handle.

Jonathan met her halfway.

"What've you got? The way you're lugging that basket around, it must weigh as much as you."

"Ma's seen the way y'all eat when you come for lunch at the house. She packed enough for an army, so far as I'm concerned. You'd never know there's only three of you."

Jonathan laughed as he reached for the food. He rubbed his hand over her head, callouses on his palm snagging against her smooth blonde hair, pulling strands from her tidy braids.

"Stop." Belle yanked her head away with the injured tone only a thirteen-year-old could affect. She smoothed her hand against the braids, darting a quick glance toward Teddy.

"Whoa there, missy. Don't bat those big blue eyes at the hired help." Jonathan cocked a warning eyebrow at her.

Belle turned as red as a tomato. "What—?" She stammered to a halt. "You're stupid."

Jonathan moved to block her view of the strapping young man walking behind the Percheron. "We've got work to do. Thanks for lunch. Head on back and see if Ma needs your help."

Belle narrowed her eyes. "I don't answer to you. Just 'cause Pa died doesn't mean you get to boss everybody around."

"That's exactly what it means." Jonathan held up a hand, a peace offering. "But my apologies." He waggled his fingers toward the house. "Unless you plan to drive a plow, you're in my way."

Belle stuck out her tongue. Then, with a last glance toward Teddy, she whirled around, braids flying.

Jonathan chuckled as she stomped off. Indignation vibrated through every step.

Both teams turned the corner at the far end of the seventy-five-acre field and headed his way. He whistled to catch the men's attention and swung the basket through the air. "Lunchtime, boys," he hollered. A field this large took a while to prepare, and they were on a schedule. But they had to stop to refuel now and again.

By the time they reached him, he had the contents spread across the ground. Six sandwiches, made with thick pieces of homemade bread and a hefty slice of ham, came wrapped in a dishcloth. A glass jar held fermented sauerkraut Ma'd put up last fall. Jonathan shook out equal portions onto tin plates he found in the basket's bottom. One jug held milk and a second carried water from their well. A plate of cookies lay on the bottom of the basket, a sweet dessert to finish the meal. When the men joined him, Jonathan bowed his head and gave thanks for the food.

They sprawled on the grass, enjoying the chance to rest. Life burgeoned busily around them as spring woke the earth. Mockingbirds sang, trilling through their repertoire of borrowed tunes. Bees hummed over early spring wildflowers, gathering nectar and pollen as they went. A breeze ruffled Jonathan's hair as he leaned back on one hand, chewing with contentment. He could spend the rest of his life taking care of this farm and be completely happy.

They wolfed down the meal, taking turns drinking from the jugs. Ernest smacked his lips over the sauerkraut. "Not as good as my *mutter* used to make, but this is *gut*."

Jonathan cocked an eyebrow at the older German, grinning. "I'll let Ma know she's earned your stamp of approval."

Teddy brushed crumbs from his mouth. "What's next, boss?"

Jonathan flinched at the title. He wasn't ready to fill his pa's shoes.

The young man reached for a second cookie. "Are we gonna do an extra field of cotton this year after we get the corn in?"

"Yes. The seed arrives today. I want to turn the sod in that section on the other side of the creek. We'll plant cotton there. Last time I visited Galveston, I saw cotton bales lined up from one end of the port to the other. Rumor has it the armies want to buy every bale they can find to make uniforms for the dad-blasted war, but Union soldiers are blockading the port. Corn will always be our money-maker, but cotton prices may go up this year."

Ernest sighed. "Plowing a new field is such a beating. We could build anything under the sun with that sod. It's tough as nails." He glanced at the team of mules grazing nearby. "My boys'll need an extra helping of feed tonight."

Teddy snorted. "Benny's strong enough to do it. And he won't need no extra feed, neither."

Ernest glowered. "I never said the mules couldn't. But they'll deserve a reward for good work."

Jonathan stood, ending the argument before it started. "Back to work, fellas."

Benny nickered, perked ears facing forward as he stared toward the farmhouse. Jonathan turned, following his gaze.

"Here we go." He rubbed his hands together in pleased anticipation.

Mr. Nelson's wagon rumbled down the drive. Jonathan walked to meet the man. Seed bags filled the wagon bed, piled in orderly rows.

He frowned. Lots and lots of rows. Maybe the man would make another stop after dropping off his part of the purchase.

Jonathan doffed his hat, extending his hand for a greeting. Mr. Nelson pumped it, well pleased to deliver his bounty.

"Afternoon, Mr. Nelson. You're here just in time. I'm gonna start in behind these men and plant while they finish plowing. I think we can finish today."

Mr. Nelson hitched his thumb over his shoulder toward the bed of the wagon. "You're gonna need more land plowed if you plan to use all this. Had to deliver this one myself. Didn't want to put the responsibility of carrying back such a large payment on a stock boy." He gazed over the partially plowed section. "But another reason I offered to deliver the seed is so I could check out what betterments you must've done on the property. For sure, this little field ain't gonna use the whole order. It's a sight more'n what your pa ever ordered."

Ernest and Teddy approached the wagon.

A sick feeling curdled in Jonathan's stomach. He peered at Mr. Nelson, wanting to ask, but afraid of the answer. Had he ordered all that?

"Golly." Teddy whistled. "What're we gonna do with this much seed?"

Mr. Nelson sent a shrewd gaze toward Jonathan. "I wondered that meself. There's enough in the wagon to plant that field ten times over. Can't say as I've ever filled an order for ninety-two bags of corn seed before. And cotton on top of that."

Ninety-two! Jonathan swallowed bile. He didn't order ninety-two bags. He had filled out the slip in the store requesting twenty-nine. Sweat trickled down his spine. God, not again. Why did this happen to him? How could he ask Mr. Nelson without the hired hands overhearing?

"Er, could I see that order?"

"O' course." Mr. Nelson rummaged under the seat.

Jonathan turned to Teddy and Ernest. "Let's get those plows moving, men. We're wastin' daylight."

"Ain't you gonna need some help unloading?" Teddy's wondering gaze remained focused on the excess in the bed of Mr. Nelson's wagon.

"I wouldn't send 'em off just yet, son." Mr. Nelson handed the order slip over with a flourish. "I spent more time than I wanted loading this all by my lonesome."

Jonathan scanned the order. His handwriting filled the page, big as day. Ninety-two. His skin flashed cold with shock. He couldn't pay for this.

Ernest nudged him with an elbow. "What're your big plans there, Jon? You've been keeping secrets from us. Are we plowing under more pasture?" He slapped a congratulatory hand on Jonathan's shoulder. "I always thought your *vater* could do so much more with this place. I'm glad to see you branching out. Come on, Teddy. Let's store the bags in the barn." He smiled up at the shop owner. "If you'll step down, Mr. Nelson, I'll drive *da* buggy closer. You can go wit' Jon to the house to settle up."

"Wait, Ernest. Hold on." Jonathan scrubbed a hand across his face. "Mr. Nelson, I'm afraid there's been a mistake." Heat creeped up his neck, and the tops of his ears burned. "I don't suppose you can take any of this back? Sell to another farmer?"

His gut churned at the sight of Ernest and Teddy's confused faces. Slowly, their proud excitement trickled away, replaced by doubt.

Mr. Nelson sobered. "Son, I'm sorry. I pay cash for my orders. I can't get that money back. And everyone bought their seed weeks ago, same as you. I cain't think of a soul who hasn't come to see me already. I might can—"

"Don't worry about it, Mr. Nelson. I, uh … I've been thinking about expanding but hadn't quite made up my mind. I guess my imaginings got the drop on me and I ordered without paying attention. This delivery pulls the trigger for me, eh?"

Did that sound like a big lie? Sure felt like one sayin' it. *Please forgive me, Lord.*

Based on the skepticism in Mr. Nelson's eyes, the answer was yes.

Jonathan pushed on. "Go ahead, you two. Haul this to the barn. We've got a lot to do this spring." His voice sounded too hearty. Time to rein in his enthusiasm. He plastered a fake smile on his face and gestured for the shop owner to precede him as he turned toward the house. "If you'll come with me."

He pushed the front door open, praying he wouldn't run into Ma or his three siblings as they headed to his father's office. The long hallway that split their home into two halves stood empty. Female voices drifted from the kitchen at the back of the house, where the clank of dishes told Jonathan things were being washed or cooked. Good. Work there occupied Ma and Belle. He wouldn't run into them.

Now if he could get through this meeting without either brother barging in. The older one had enough savvy to pick up on the fact something was wrong. Too bad his move to Waco to attend Baylor University wasn't until the fall.

Jonathan didn't worry about crossing paths with the youngest. If the world around him didn't involve fishing, the eight-year-old couldn't be bothered to notice.

The house rested, quiet. He might get out of this with no one the wiser. Walking quickly, he turned to his left. "This way."

Once inside the small room, Jonathan moved to the desk. "Sit, please." He pulled open a drawer and withdrew a box, then plopped into the creaking chair with a sigh.

"I'm gonna shoot straight with you, sir. Didn't want to say anything in front of my men, but I made a mistake on that order, as I'm sure you cottoned to by now. I don't expect you to take on responsibility for my error, but I need a little time to get funds together. I have enough here to cover what I *thought* I'd pay you today. I have to go to the bank for the rest. Can you give me a day or two?"

Mr. Nelson gazed at him with kindness. "What a sorry mess, Jonathan. I can give you till Friday, but that's all. Bills of my own sit on my desk, waiting to be paid."

"Understood, sir. Friday'll be great." Would he have enough money?

"Son, if ya don't mind my asking, how'd you make such a mistake? What were you thinking?"

Heat flared on Jonathan's neck for a second time. "It's hard to explain. I've struggled with this for as long as I can remember. Sometimes letters and numbers get jumbled in my head. I can usually work around it, but this one slipped through." His gaze focused on the scarred surface of the desk, and he forced words past his embarrassment. This had been his burden to carry since first learning to read. He glanced up. "Please, sir, keep this to yourself. I—"

Mr. Nelson held up a hand. "Your secret's safe with me. Wish I could do more to help you. Now that I know, you place your order only with me, not with that dunderhead boy I hire to help during the busy season. He didn't know any better. I coulda stopped this if I'd taken the order myself." He paused, regret filling his face. "If anyone else places an order for seed, I'll sure let you know."

Jonathan stood and handed the money over. He shook the older man's hand, worry dogging his heels. "Thank you, sir. I appreciate it. And I'll be along Friday with the balance."

I hope.

Chapter Two

Quenby Martin sat in the pleasant parlor, wishing to be anywhere but there. Her mother sat beside her, bookended by Quen and her younger sister, Prissy. Mother chatted with their hostess, the widow Mrs. Tara Lancaster.

"Tea is still such a pleasant treat after all those years on the coast of Nigeria." Mrs. Martin smiled at Mrs. Lancaster over the fragile teacup in her hand. "As the missionary's wife, I tried to set an example of acceptance by partaking of everything they offered. However, the plants used for their teas don't hold a candle to what I grew up drinking in America. This is chamomile if I'm not mistaken." She sipped, closing her eyes to savor the hot liquid. "Isn't this delicious, Quenby and Prissy?"

"Oh, yes. Delicious." Excitement bubbled in every syllable Prissy uttered. She adored these engagements with all the enthusiasm an eleven-year-old could muster.

"Hm-mm." Quen glanced down at her half-full cup. The tea tasted nice, but Quen would bet one of her prized books Mother's excitement had less to do with the delicious herbal tea and more to do with a chance to get out of the house.

Mother seemed to struggle with their change to a new life in San Antonio. Coming to Galveston in 1861 had been hard enough. At least then, Father had secured the position as head pastor. Being forced by the war to move to San Antonio had been far worse. For the first time since Quen was five years old, her father didn't hold a place of prominence in society. The lack of social standing took its toll on her parents. Mother no longer reigned as queen bee, invited to all the parties. The Martin family was merely one of the crowd here in San Antonio. Relief flooded Quen, however. No more social duty.

Mrs. Lancaster had issued her invitation to the Martin ladies to join her for an afternoon social. She approached them the first Sunday Quen and her family attended the Baptist church. Mother accepted with gratitude and the overture thrilled young Prissy. Quen preferred to explore the town. Mother didn't give her the choice.

"You lived in Africa prior to moving to Galveston?" Mrs. Lancaster offered a plate of scones. "Tell me more about life in Nigeria. I've visited Galveston several times to enjoy the seaside. However, I've never stepped foot in Africa. I'd love to know all about it." She nibbled a bite from a cookie. "Moving your family across the Atlantic seems a rather extreme choice. What convinced you to do that?"

Mother stretched her lips in a thin facsimile of a smile. "Well, one does what the good Lord leads one to do."

Quen snorted softly at her mother's comments. Or what one's husband and father demands, family's desires in the matter notwithstanding. The good Lord hadn't led *her* to Africa. She'd gone dragging her heels like a stubborn little donkey. What if Mother would've insisted they stay in Pennsylvania? She darted a quick glance at her parent.

No, that would never have happened. Father ruled his home with one hand clutching his Bible and the other clutching control. Quen shook her head at the preposterous idea her mother would go against his wishes. When pigs fly. She stopped her sigh mid-breath when she caught Mrs. Lancaster's smiling gaze focused on her. Quen blinked.

Had she revealed her thoughts?

The rigid posture she'd learned to hold as a child relaxed when Mrs. Lancaster turned back to her mother.

"I'm curious. How did you spend your days?"

"The first thing we did, of course, was build a church." Mother warmed to the subject. "We followed with a clinic where I focused on the physical health of the mothers and newborns of the families we served. Our final project was a school, so we could teach the children reading, writing, and mathematics."

Quen's boredom dissipated, and she jumped in. Teaching at the school had been her crowning accomplishment. "There were nineteen children, spanning from age three to my age— nineteen. I taught them to read from the Bible. One of my favorites, Ndidi, had the adorable habit of—"

"I'm sure Mrs. Lancaster is not interested in that." Mother interrupted. "She doesn't want to hear the name of every child in the village." She smiled and straightened her spine. "My husband preached every Sunday, of course."

Quen swallowed her words. Why did Mother always brag about him? His success didn't determine her worth. Quen would stand on her own two feet as she made her way through life, thank you very much.

Mrs. Lancaster arched an eyebrow. "How nice." She turned to Quen. "*You* were the teacher? Utterly fascinating. You would make a spectacular addition to the school in San Antonio. Think of the stories you could weave into your lessons from your experience abroad."

Startlement flashed over Mother's face.

"Well-bred young women do not need to work. Besides, Quenby spent all her educational years in a one-room hut halfway across the world. She has no official training. I'm sure the school here would find her lacking. God will reveal to us what Quenby's purpose in this lifetime will be."

Quen took a deep breath but said nothing. God hadn't revealed much of anything to her except how to pretend her family lived a perfect and happy life. Perhaps God only spoke to men. Certainly seemed that way in the Bible, where women were relegated to less-than-desirable roles.

Mother cleared her throat, then picked up the previous thread of conversation. "The tribal leaders were called kings. It's funny to think about now. Our house was just as fine as the homes of the kings." She took another sip of tea. "We enjoyed a very exciting life."

For once, Quen agreed with her. When she finally got used to Africa, life *did* excite her. She enjoyed a level of freedom in Nigeria that disappeared once she stepped on American soil again. She missed playing an important part in the lives of people around her, lives she could help. The families they'd served accepted her. She'd been loved and important, like she had a purpose.

"What made you leave?" Mrs. Lancaster peered with interest over the rim of her cup.

Mother sighed. "The Baptist Conference called us home. The threat of war in America made funding insecure. We needed to travel while circumstances remained safe."

Mrs. Lancaster turned to Quen. "How old were you when you left America?"

"Five. Leaving Philadelphia terrified me at first. I didn't want to go without my grandparents or my friends."

"You did just fine, Quenby. There's no need to be dramatic." Mrs. Martin's interjection held the faintest hint of disapproval.

Quen returned her gaze to her hands clasped in her lap. Fervid prayers begging to stay where things were familiar had gone unnoticed and unanswered. Leaving everything she knew in Philadelphia had broken her heart. But Nigeria had slowly put the pieces back together again. She grew to love living there. Then the situation had reversed. Leaving Africa felt like leaving a piece of her soul.

She subsided, leaning against the back of the chair. Glancing out the window of Mrs. Lancaster's parlor, she drew a comparison in her mind. The wide dusty road cut a slash of brown between white stuccoed walls and weathered wooden buildings. Living by the ocean in Galveston had been an interesting change, but the humid port offered little once one left the shore. So far, life in Texas paled in comparison to the vibrancy of Nigeria. Here, noises were ordinary, everyday. An unexciting rumble of passing buggies and the sound of too many voices replaced the soothing susurrations of the waterfall behind the school, the constant cooing and calling of brightly colored birds, and the lyrical voices of the Nigerian women.

No more being in charge of a classroom full of enthralled children eager to learn. No more hikes through lush, green forests. No more assisting the little old man who owned the store in Galveston. *I have nothing to do here.*

A servant girl returned to the parlor with a fresh pot of tea. Quen was unable to keep her gaze from the young woman. Being waited on by an enslaved person was a disquieting experience. It unnerved her.

In Nigeria, everyone around her had black skin. They hadn't served her. Hadn't seemed *less than*. Mrs. Lancaster showed only kindness to the girl, but Quen had seen other Blacks in the fields on their journey through Texas to reach San Antonio. There'd been no compassion in the White men on horseback. Threats coiled in the whips looped over their saddle horns, in the rifles that lay across their laps. Life for a Black person in Texas seemed vastly different from what she'd witnessed in Africa.

"These are the most delicious little biscuits." Prissy took a delicate nibble. "We visited with the Thompson family last week. She served tiny sandwiches made with cucumber slices. And a whole plate full of these same biscuits with a little jar of orange jelly."

"In point of fact, these aren't biscuits." Quen looked at her younger sister with annoyed fondness as she wagged one of the delectable treats at Prissy's face. "And Mrs. Thompson didn't serve hers with jelly. These are scones, and the jar held marmalade."

Prissy narrowed her eyes. Quen half-expected her to stick out her tongue. She'd been teaching Prissy since she could walk. She struggled to stop now.

"Whatever they were, they're delicious." Prissy turned her nose up and faced away.

Quen snorted. Her little sister's nickname suited her well.

"Honestly, Quenby. This habit you have of correcting ..." Mother sent a pained smile toward Mrs. Lancaster in silent apology. She patted Prissy's arm. "Continue, daughter."

Quen's grin faded. She bit back a defensive retort.

Prissy's face lit as she described every bite of what she'd enjoyed at Mrs. Thompson's tea. She eyed the plate of scones with longing. "May I have another?"

"One accepts what is offered." Mrs. Martin gently remonstrated. "One doesn't ask. Besides, you don't want to ruin your pretty figure."

Quen waited until Mrs. Lancaster captured her mother's attention again, then leaned back and tapped Prissy's chair. When she glanced over, Quen slipped her an extra scone from her plate. Her sister's eyes widened with mischief, and she darted a look at their mother as she reached for it. Straightening, she flipped her blonde hair, curled in perfect long ringlets, over her shoulder. Her blue eyes sparkled.

Lifting a hand, Quen absent-mindedly patted her own brunette length, currently balanced in a precarious bun on the back of her head. She had stopped concerning herself with the inevitable comparisons of their appearances about six months after Prissy's birth. Her sister truly shone with beauty, just like their mother.

Prissy and Mother seemed to belong to a private group—one she'd not been invited to join. The words to justify her feelings appeared when a fellow passenger on the ship back to the States shared a Danish fairy tale book with her. The ugly duckling could be her. Unfortunately, her swan stage seemed reluctant to appear. She took after her Puritan father's side of the family. Long, straight hair, void of curl. A long, straight nose her father insisted was patrician. Long, straight body. Blue-eyed, blonde-headed Prissy outshone her with ease.

She gave the bun on her head a little shove. A pin ejected itself from a heavy, gleaming coil. Quen gasped and tucked her hand back on her lap. The whole, heavy mess was about to tumble down. She closed her eyes with resignation. Why bother?

"Knowing you enjoy the scones will please Missouri." Mrs. Lancaster held out the fresh teapot, refilling Mrs. Martin's cup. "She's learning to be quite the baker. Her first attempts were simple desserts, but she's progressed more rapidly than I believed possible. Her next project is to tackle breads."

Quen cocked an eyebrow. Missouri must be the name of the young Black girl. Learning to bake ... interesting. She'd like to learn alongside her.

Mrs. Martin gave a dramatic sigh. "In Nigeria, we couldn't get a decent loaf of bread to save the day. Between puff-puff fried bread and the sour foo foo bread—"

That did it. Quen couldn't pretend to be interested in a recipe for the sour spongy bread the villagers cooked every day. She slid her gaze toward the doorway. She'd spotted the library in the room beyond almost the moment they sat down. All that literary potential drew her like a magnet. She stood, placing her teacup and saucer on the small table in front of them. She smoothed her hands across the flat front of her pinstriped skirt and meandered toward a mirror, patting at the tentative bun. Perhaps she could convince Mother she only checked her appearance. That would make her happy.

She used the reflection in the mirror to gauge the interest level of her mother. Satisfied she was not the object of her speculation, Quen inched closer to the library, pausing at a painting on the wall. Would they notice if she slipped away to the tantalizing room? She stopped in front of the gilt frame, pretending to study the canvas.

"Such a skillful use of backlighting." She acted the part of a besotted art student.

Mrs. Lancaster appeared noiselessly at her elbow.

"William Sidney Mount painted this in 1831." Mrs. Lancaster's cultured tone rang with smooth confidence. "The title is 'Dancing on the Barn Floor.' My husband, God rest his soul, loved imagining himself as a down-to-earth, common man, in touch with the ordinary world around him. I purchased this as a gift for our first wedding anniversary."

The woman paused, then tilted her head in a slight nod toward the library. Eyes sparkling with humor, she turned back to the others. She swept forward, resuming their conversation and providing the perfect shield for Quen to slip away.

A broad smile split Quen's face. Mrs. Lancaster took charge with practiced skill and drew her other two guests in.

Her heart warmed to the widow. She'd made no new friends since their arrival from Galveston and had ample time on her hands. Hardly any furniture or household goods had arrived yet on the train. No art supplies, no piano.

No books.

She turned back to the library. Sighing with pleasure, she entered the room. She drew a deep breath, enjoying the dried, musty smell of the pages and book binding glue, the particular odor of leather covers. Trailing her fingers along gold-embossed spines, she took her time exploring. Charles Dickens, Herman Melville, Jane Austen. The letters impressed onto the spine of a particular favorite—Henry Wadsworth Longfellow—drew her fingertips. The conversation in the other room faded from her consciousness, replaced by words from the beloved poet as she traced his name.

"Ye who believe in affection that hopes, and endures, and is patient,

Ye who believe in the beauty and strength of woman's devotion ..."

Her heart gave a lonely thump. Finding a man worthy of devotion seemed highly unlikely. Pushing away images wrought by the poem, she sighed and continued to "take her turn about the room," amusing herself by quoting Miss Bingley from *Pride and Prejudice*. She focused her mind on the problem of plotting how she could finagle another invitation to Mrs. Lancaster's house. Perhaps she could put up with banal conversation if she would gain access to this library.

Maybe San Antonio wouldn't be so bad after all.

Chapter Three

Jonathan turned away, unable to meet the banker's questioning gaze any longer. "Thanks for your help, sir. I'll be in touch." He retreated outdoors where the morning sun warmed the air.

Sickness roiled in his stomach. What should he do?

He stood on the broad wooden sidewalk in front of the bank, disregarding the traffic flowing around him. Women paced by—parting around him like water flowing past a large rock in the river. Wagons rumbled in the street, and Texas Rangers and cowboys trotted by on horses, stirring up dust. Dogs barked, neighbors called to one another. None of the noises mattered, merely background to the conflict raging inside.

If he withdrew the remaining balance owed to Mr. Nelson, his family would have next to nothing left in the bank until harvest. How would he pay the hands? What if he needed to have the vet out to the farm? Ma would need dry goods—coffee, flour, salt.

His brother Herschel had talked nonstop for the past few months about going off to college in the fall. Jonathan wanted to do nothing to dissuade that. The war loomed ever closer. He did *not* want Herschel to enlist. Whatever was necessary to get him enrolled instead, he wanted to do.

Belle grew like a weed, more than just up, and her bodices strained at every seam. Little Bay could get by wearing Herschel's hand-me-downs, but shoes were probably a necessity.

The farm provided a good living, but draining all the cash at once? Had a similar situation ever forced Pa into this decision?

He took his hat off, closed his eyes, and tucked his chin to his chest. God would get them through this. True, his error had placed them in this situation, but the mistake didn't come from laziness or lack of care. All things worked to the good for those who loved the Lord. The situation would be all right. Somehow.

A polite cough interrupted his musing, pulling him from his thoughts. His best friend, Manny Blair, stood before him.

"Hello? Cat got your tongue?"

Jonathan blinked, bringing his focus back to Commerce Street. He drew a deep breath and stared back.

"Hey." Manny frowned. "What's up, *amigo?* Something wrong?"

He managed a strained smile. "I'm OK. Just trying to figure something out."

"Really, Jon?" Manny's skepticism was obvious. "I can probably count on one hand the number of times I've seen you down. What's going on? How can I help?"

Jonathan snorted, shaking his head with disgust. "I made a mistake with my bank account. I'll figure things out."

"Show me your books. I'll help you find where you went wrong."

He glanced away. It didn't sit right to lie to Manny. Couldn't look him in the eye as he forced the untruth past his lips. He rubbed a finger against his eyebrow. "I don't keep books. It's all in my head."

Manny stared. "That's the stupidest thing I've ever heard. Who doesn't keep books?"

Jonathan's face heated. It *was* the stupidest thing. Everyone knew a farmer had to keep books. His father had a journal for each year, going back decades. How ridiculous to say otherwise. He couldn't believe Manny fell for the fib.

"This calls for discussion." Manny glanced across the street to the Menger Hotel. "I left Abby in the dining room, enjoying some peace and quiet without babies over a cup of coffee and her book. It'll be a treat for her to stay as long as she can." He clapped a hand on Jonathan's shoulder. "We'll figure out how to fix your problem. I'll let her soak up her alone time a little longer and treat you to a cup of Arbuckle's at the cafe."

Bustling activity along the main street through town brought a smile to Quen's face. Quite a contrast to the ocean breezes and cries of seagulls she'd experienced in Galveston. Nature's songs were overlaid, drowned by the noise of busyness. Rattling carriages, rumbling wagons, and jingling harnesses all crowded the air. She stood against the wall of the Roberts's Steam Bakery, enjoying the scent of freshly baked bread, and simply watched.

The batwing doors of a saloon across the road swung open, and a man stepped through. He paused, tugging his hat onto his head, then stepped down the stairs to a horse at the hitching post. He reached up to clap his hand against the roan's neck, and his mouth moved as he spoke to the animal. The breadth of his shoulders, narrowness of his waist, and length of his legs drew Quen's attention. Her fingers fluttered at her collar as she let her eyes linger.

When she gazed again at his face, her breath hitched on a gasp. Amusement crinkled the corners of his brown eyes, which stared at her as frankly as she had apparently studied him. Heat burned the tops of her ears. Good heavens. He caught her staring like a loose woman. If she hurried down the sidewalk, would he think she ran away?

"Hey, Samuel." A man's voice called out, and the handsome stranger turned away, breaking eye contact. Quen drew a breath, unaware until that moment she'd been holding it.

"Miss Quenby Martin!"

Mrs. Lancaster's cultured tones caught Quen by surprise. She turned.

The widow had come from inside the bakery and now moved toward her. Confidence exuded from her long strides and erect posture. Missouri walked at her side, small packages in her arms. One held items from the bakery, and the smell of bread tantalized even more up close. Mrs. Lancaster approached with a smile, her skirt floating with each step, the perfectly measured hem just missing the ground.

Quen swept the older woman with an appreciative glance. Prissy would ask for every detail. A sash of velvet, probably as soft as a lamb's ear, wrapped around Mrs. Lancaster's still-thin waist. A row of tiny pearl buttons marched from her elbow to her wrists, glittering in the pale spring sunlight as she waved. Mrs. Lancaster's eyes twinkled from beneath a dark net veil attached to a small, black top hat. Quen admired her style immensely.

"Dear girl. How are you?" Mrs. Lancaster pulled her near for a quick buss on the cheek. The widow straightened and glanced over her shoulder at the girl behind. "Missouri, you remember Miss Martin?" She faced Quen again, one eyebrow cocked. "I believe she coveted our library." Laugh lines deepened around her eyes.

Quen disguised her embarrassment with a clearing of her throat. "Mrs. Lancaster, what a pleasant surprise. Please, call me Quen." She turned to the girl. "Hello, Missouri. Nice to see you again."

Missouri ducked her head with a shy smile. Freckles dotted her nose and cheeks. Quen smiled. Few people in Nigeria had freckles. Their appearance always seemed to give the faces a friendly feel.

Quen glanced at the bags in her hands. "I see you've been shopping. Does that bread taste as delicious as it smells?"

"It is marvelous." Mrs. Lancaster placed a hand on Quen's forearm. "I'll send some along with you. I'll get fat if I eat it all. But now, please accompany us to the Menger Hotel for an afternoon refreshment. You and I didn't enjoy as much conversation at our last visit as I would have liked."

Quen pushed aside doubt flooding her at the prospect of holding up her end of a conversation about scones or bread. She focused instead on the possibility of another stroll along Mrs. Lancaster's bookshelves. Pleased anticipation quickened her pulse at the prospect.

"That's very kind of you, Mrs. Lancaster. I'll struggle to repay your kindness and hospitality if you continue to entertain me like this. I'm in your debt."

"Nonsense." The smooth voice disregarded Quen's attempt at propriety. "Let us not stand on ceremony. I'm a nosy old bird with nothing else to do, and I'm interested in your life in Nigeria. I have no doubt your day-to-day activities were, hmm ..." She paused, placing a gloved fingertip against her lips in a thoughtful move. "... shall we say, less fervently coordinated there by your Baptist father than they are now. I'm sure I would have preferred Africa. More freedom. I want to learn about your experiences."

Quen froze. How could Mrs. Lancaster possibly understand so much about their family following one afternoon tea? Her estimation of Mrs. Lancaster as nothing more than a wealthy socialite took a slight turn. Who *was* she?

"It's settled, then. Come along. My carriage is down the way. How did you arrive here?" She glanced around the bustling activity in the streets as if expecting to see a horse-drawn carriage with Quen's name emblazoned on the side standing by.

"Oh, ma'am, I walked." Quen's tone matched Mrs. Lancaster's with its frankness. "Our house is nearby, and I enjoy watching people. I'm still learning my way around, and it's easier to explore on foot." She shrugged.

Mrs. Lancaster appraised her. "My. How industrious. Perhaps we should follow your example. We can place our packages in the carriage."

Quen blinked. She shot a glance at Missouri. Was the girl as startled by the sudden change of plans as she was? Missouri's indulgent smile said otherwise. Good humor glowed from her dark eyes as she gazed at the older woman with fondness.

Quen grinned at Mrs. Lancaster. "If that's what you want to do, I'm pleased to join you. Perhaps you could be so kind as to point out the town as we pass by." She darted a glance across the street, but the long-legged mystery man no longer stood there.

Mrs. Lancaster pulled Quen's hand into the crook of her arm and strolled as if she promenaded along a sidewalk in London. Quen slowed her quick, got-things-to-do pace to match the widow's, enjoying the sway of their skirts as they meandered. She drew a deep breath and exhaled slowly, relaxing into the older woman's company.

Mrs. Lancaster was going to be *fun.*

"This is the General Land Office. Should you decide to take up homesteading, this is where you'll come to claim your land."

Quen laughed. "I don't believe I'm the homesteading type, ma'am."

Mrs. Lancaster tilted her head close to Quen's, as if she had a secret to tell. "Never say never, child. Life will surprise you. You may very well find yourself saying and doing things you never thought possible." Her eyes narrowed with mischief.

Mrs. Lancaster continued, narrating the history of each store with a steady stream of facts as they passed. "Now, this one will become a favorite, I'm certain." Mrs. Lancaster paused in front of a storefront with *Solomon Deutsch & Co.* painted in curling script letters across the window. "Dry goods, clothing, canned goods ... if you need it, Solomon has it. Let's go inside."

There was, indeed, a bit of everything in the store, every shelf, nook, and cranny stuffed full. The variety stunned. Mrs. Lancaster plucked a card of ribbon from a bin with a pleased exclamation. "This will match my blue riding habit perfectly, won't it, Missouri? And look." She gave a single, pleased clap when a store clerk placed a sign in the bin as they watched. "It's on sale."

Missouri merely nodded her agreement. Quen was about to comment on the shade of blue when the wording of the sign caught her eye.

Ribbon For Sell, 2 days only

"Pardon me, sir." She tapped the young man on the shoulder as he turned to walk away. "I'm sorry, but you've made a mistake."

The clerk turned back to her. "It's no mistake. Them ribbons are for sale."

Quen drew a patient breath. "Yes, I see they are for sale. In point of fact, that is the problem. They are for *sale*."

"Right." He squinted at her. "Them's for sale."

She smiled. How to help him understand? "Indeed. However, your little sign here says *sell*. S-E-L-L. The word following a preposition must be a noun." She tipped her head. "Or a noun phrase. You've written a verb." She smiled with bright encouragement. "You've made a mistake."

The clerk frowned at her and walked away, shrugging his shoulders.

Mrs. Lancaster cleared her throat. "Come, dear." She took the moment to steer Quen toward the cash register.

Jonathan and Manny stood in Mr. Solomon's store, waiting for Casper Solomon.

"I'm telling you—Casper was always good at math in school. He keeps the books for his father. If he can manage everything that comes through this store, he can straighten out the confusion with your account." Manny had the patience of Job, waiting for the man to emerge from the storeroom.

Jonathan, unfortunately, was less calm. Manny had lit upon the idea of enlisting Casper's help over their cups of coffee. He couldn't bring himself to explain the situation to his friend, especially not here. He prayed Casper wouldn't have time to spare, and he could escape this situation with Manny none the wiser. No one—no matter how good he was with numbers—would find any hidden money tucked away behind an incorrect sum in a ledger. He hadn't missed carrying a one while balancing the books.

A throaty laugh caught Jonathan's attention, announcing the amused person as effectively as a butler calling out the name of a visitor in a grand hall. Mrs. Lancaster entered the store with her servant, followed by a girl he didn't know. The young woman walked with the widow to a barrel full of sewing notions, where they paused and poked around. His gaze tracked down her long, lean body. She was a tall one, that was for certain. His examination froze when she opened her mouth and spoke.

"I'm sorry, but you've made a mistake."

Hackles raised, and a shudder traveled through his bones when that know-it-all tone of voice pierced Jonathan's eardrum. Her tone sounded exactly like one that had haunted him in school.

"Criminy. It's Nell Rogers all over again."

Manny glanced over. "Nell? That isn't Nell."

"Might as well be. Don't you remember how snooty she was about being so much smarter than everyone else?"

"I don't remember that." Manny frowned.

Heat crept up the sides of Jonathan's face. *That's because you could read, just like the rest of them.* "Well, that girl sounds like her to me."

He eavesdropped on the conversation with the horrid fascination of someone who has come upon an accident. The tone of her voice as she corrected the poor clerk set his teeth on edge.

He shuddered again. Lord, spare him. The older lady stepped up and guided the young woman to the register. They paid for the card of ribbon and left while Jonathan stood, nerves rattling in his stomach about how he would explain things to Casper. God would guide his steps. If Casper was available, the Lord would give him words to say. If not …

Please be too busy to see us.

Casper finally rushed out, clearly harried.

"Sorry, *amigo*. The coach delivered today, and I had to check the stock against the list. How can I help you?"

Jonathan stiffened when Manny turned to face him. He twisted his hat nervously, as if he could squeeze the words he needed to say from it. He waited for direction from above. Would he have to tell his secret, or would God send him down a different path? After an awkward moment of silence, Manny stepped in. "Jonathan's having trouble getting the numbers to add up in his bank account. We thought you could help."

Casper shook his head. "Sorry, friend. *Vati* has me hopping. I can barely keep up with what I've got here. I wish I could carve out the time."

A bellow came from the storeroom. Casper shot a frazzled glance over his shoulder, then faced the friends. "Gotta go. Hope you figure everything out, Jonathan."

He turned and trotted back the way he'd come.

The breath Jonathan held let loose with a whoosh. That door had definitely shut. He jammed the abused hat back on his head, whirled around, and stepped quickly out the front door.

Manny joined him. "Well, that was a bust. We gotta think of something. Do you mind if I talk to Abby about it?"

Jonathan snorted. "Sure. The more, the merrier."

He flushed as Manny's gaze searched his face. The lie suddenly was too much to carry. Speaking it showed disrespect to God and his best friend. "Manny, it's not that I can't do the sums. I do keep a ledger. Everything gets written down, just like Pa did. It's only ... sometimes words and numbers mix up in my head." He punched a fist into his other hand. "I know how to farm. I can do it. It's just this stupid thing ..."

Compassion softened Manny's gaze. An idea brightened his face. "Can your mom do the books?"

"I don't want to ask her. Some days, she is so sad about Pa dying, she can hardly get out of bed. Plus, she's got her hands full taking care of Belle and Bay. Pa always handled the finances. I hate to dump another responsibility on her."

Manny clapped a hand on his shoulder. "We'll figure something out. Don't worry."

Jonathan turned and stared across the street at the bank. There was nothing for it. He'd have to withdraw the money to pay Mr. Nelson. The sick feeling that'd ridden around in his stomach since earlier in the week intensified. What would they do after that?

Adding to his worry was the uncertainty of how the War Between the States would affect Texas. Most Texans wanted little to do with the fighting. Small farmers didn't have a dog in that hunt and simply wanted to tend their land and protect their homesteads from the occasional Comanche incursion. Jonathan's future trembled on the edge of a precipice. He sent a silent prayer.

Father, I know you have plans for me. I trust you to show me what to do.

Chapter Four

Quen waited with Missouri while Mrs. Lancaster paid for her ribbon. The women exited and continued down the sidewalk.

"Here we are. I love the restaurant at the Menger Hotel." Mrs. Lancaster steered them toward the building on the corner.

Quen eyed the front. Enormous wooden doors welcomed visitors. Elaborate balconies offered a place to enjoy sunrises, a hot mug of coffee in hand.

They entered the main foyer. She sucked in a breath at the floor covered in a gorgeous mosaic pattern and windows reaching to high ceilings. Natural light streamed in, highlighting every crafted detail.

"The chef bakes delicious little hard cookies called biscotti. They're perfect for dunking in your coffee. You must try them, Quenby. It'll be my treat." Mrs. Lancaster grimaced at her feet. "While I admit these boots are attractive, they pinch my toes. Since I cannot pull them off in mixed company, I'll do the next best thing and get off my feet. Come. Let's have a sit-down." She tugged Quen through the doorway to the dining area and beckoned a waiter with an imperious wave.

"Charles, if you would be so good as to show us to my regular ta—oh! Never mind. Please seat us over there." Mrs.

Lancaster turned to Quen, excitement flashing in her eyes. "Quenby, I want to introduce you to a most singular young woman. You simply must meet Mrs. Abigail Blair."

The waiter reversed direction with a smooth turn on the ball of his foot. He led the way to a table topped by a gleaming white cloth where a young woman sat alone. A cup of coffee cooled in front of her as she read a book.

"Abigail, what a pleasant surprise to find you here." Mrs. Lancaster bustled over.

The woman placed a marker between the pages, then rose from her seat to embrace the widow. Mrs. Lancaster rested her hands on Abigail's shoulders. "You look quite well. You must be getting more rest these days." She turned to Quen. "She has two beautiful babies. They were a Christmas present over a year ago." She faced the young woman. "They must be walking now. Where are they?"

Abigail glowed with pride. "They're with Yaideli. It's so nice having Manny's grandmother close. She loves watching them. Such a blessing for us. And, yes, they were the best Christmas gift I've ever received."

Quen slid into the chair Charles offered her, hiding her glance beneath lowered lashes, comparing the new mother's slim silhouette with her own. She would never have guessed the slender woman had given birth, especially to twins. Keeping her expression composed became a struggle as she took in the other's appearance.

Abigail seemed about the same age as Quen, but there the resemblance ended. She wore her hair in a thick braid that hung straight down her back. No frilly embellishments softened her profile. Instead, her unfashionably tanned face and a light coating of freckles painted her with natural attractiveness.

But the real shocker was her attire. She sported a pair of men's dungarees. Even her shirt, made of a work-softened, pale blue cotton, appeared to have come from the church mission bag. Rolled-back sleeves revealed slim, tanned forearms. However, despite her manly outerwear, feminism shone through. Her dainty hands had long, slender fingers, and rosy lips turned up in a smile. Her eyes twinkled with welcome.

Mother and Father would detest her. The appeal of gaining her friendship instantly increased. *I bet she does exactly what she wants to do with her life. And she probably doesn't sit there like a lump on a log while her father lectures for hours on end about her sins and shortcomings.* Her gaze roamed over Mrs. Abigail Blair—wife, mother, and breaker-of-molds extraordinaire—admiration glowing from her eyes. She probably didn't take sass from anyone.

Mrs. Lancaster sat and tucked her feet under the concealing cover of the tablecloth. She sighed with satisfaction.

"Ah, that's better. My feet are happy." She eyed the young woman with the book. "Abigail, I want you to meet my new friend, Quenby Martin." Mrs. Lancaster made the introductions. "Quenby and her family recently moved here from Galveston, and we must find her a friend closer to her own age. No one wants to tag along behind a doddering old fool like me."

Quen murmured a disagreement, but Abigail tossed her head back and laughed out loud.

"Mrs. Lancaster, you know full well you leave the rest of us in the dirt." Abigail turned to Quen and extended a hand. "Hi, please call me Abby. No one calls me Abigail except my friend Lawrence." She shot a smile toward the widow. "And Mrs. Lancaster."

Quen shook the proffered hand, finding Abby's grip warm and firm. She returned the young woman's smile. A thrill of excitement buzzed through her at the thought of gaining a new friend. Especially one who promised to be so interesting.

"How are you, Missouri?" Abby faced the girl standing at Mrs. Lancaster's shoulder. "The last time I saw you, you were tugging the halter of a very cranky donkey toward Mrs. Lancaster's place." Her gaze flicked to the older woman, then back. "How is that working out?"

"That crow bait does nothing but kick up a row, ever' chance he gets," Missouri said.

"Now, Missouri. You hobble your lip. Mortimer is just as fine as cream gravy." Mrs. Lancaster tugged her linen napkin into her lap while she peered down an autocratic nose. She gave a tiny sigh. "It has recently come to my attention that a donkey, despite being in possession of a pleasant home, can find himself in mischief if he is in want of a companion. 'Tis not a slight on his character." A sharp nod emphasized her opinion. "He's merely lonely."

Missouri snorted. "Lonely, my foot. That old nag likes to make trouble."

Abby burst out laughing again. "*Mortimer*? That name sounds too fancy for a burro. Oh, Mrs. Lancaster. Whatever possessed you? And who told you he acts up because he wants a buddy?"

"If you must know, Caleb shared that wisdom with me. I trust him implicitly. If he says Mortimer needs a friend, then Mortimer needs a friend." Mrs. Lancaster turned her face away, nose in the air, and gestured to the waiter. "We'll speak no more about it. Poor Mortimer is being slandered."

"Slaughtered, you say?" Hope rang in Missouri's voice.

"Caleb would be most disappointed in us if we failed to rehabilitate Mortimer." Mrs. Lancaster's no-nonsense tone of voice clarified the donkey would live to see another day.

Quen's gaze bounced between Missouri, Mrs. Lancaster, and Abby. "Caleb sounds wonderful. Who is this paragon? I'd like to meet him."

"He owns a small piece of land outside the city. I consider him an expert on all things dealing with farming, animal husbandry, and the sort. I've known him for quite a while, and he has never failed me with a bad piece of advice." Mrs. Lancaster seemed happy to change the conversation from the disparaged donkey. "Missouri, you could use a rest. You seem as cranky as our dear Morty. Charles, please pull an extra chair over. I feel ridiculous with her looming over my shoulder."

The waiter coughed, his gaze darting toward a table of men near the center of the room. "Mightn't she be more comfortable sitting out back with Hettie, ma'am? We don't serve ... her kind here."

Mrs. Lancaster's expression turned glacial. "Why, Charles. I'm not asking you to *serve* her. I'm asking you to *seat* her."

The waiter winced as he received the chilling blast. He turned to reach for a chair.

"I'll serve her *myself*." Mrs. Lancaster uttered the sentence with an air of absolute conviction, accompanied by a challenging stare directed at the table in the center of the room.

Quen's breath caught, and her heart pounded. Seeing Missouri treated poorly recalled further indignities she had witnessed since moving back to the States. Her experience in Nigeria had been just the opposite. She had been the outsider there, the different one, but all had accepted her.

The men in question muttered among themselves, but none contested the widow. Quen's admiration for Mrs. Lancaster soared.

The waiter's arrival with a tray holding a steaming pot of coffee and two small, white cups broke the tension. He placed the dainty mugs in front of the two women and topped off the coffee in Abby's. He then set the tray of biscotti in the center of the table.

Mrs. Lancaster stopped him. "And another cup and saucer, please." She tapped the table in front of Missouri with her index finger. Her light tone belied the granite in her gaze. The waiter turned without a word to do her bidding.

Quen reached for a biscotto. She studied the hard rectangle with doubt. One could crack a tooth. Mrs. Lancaster had no such qualms. She dipped one into her coffee, then tapped the extra drops off and nibbled a corner. Bliss crossed her face as she chewed. She passed the tray to Missouri.

"I taste almonds. Don't you, Missouri? Perhaps we can speak with the chef. How wonderful if you could learn to make these at home."

The conversation in the middle of the room grew agitated, water boiling over in a pot. The word "war" rose above the rumble of voices.

"Those dang bluecoats have taken up residence in the Gulf. You'd think after two years of bringing that war this far West, they'd have moved on."

"They've all but strangled the import and export of goods. I cain't sell my cotton. Lee thinks he's weakening the Confederate army."

The men's anxiety and anger appeared directed at the idea they were being told what to do and how to live their lives.

Abby narrowed her eyes at the men, then changed the subject, transferring her gaze to Quen. "You recently moved here from Galveston? Were you born there?"

"No. I was born in Pennsylvania, but I've spent most of my life in Africa. My father took a position as a missionary in Nigeria. The Baptist Church funded us. They called us home in 1861 and sent us to a fledgling church in Galveston." The table where the men still conducted their heated conversation about the conflict drew her gaze. "Then the War Between the States began. When the Union Army blockaded the ports, life became difficult. The army allowed no goods in or out of the city. Father reached out to a distant family member who lives in Austin, asking if he knew of a different church in need of a pastor. The cousin directed us here." She glanced at Missouri. "Texas differs greatly from Nigeria, to be sure."

"Fascinating!" Abby leaned forward. "Tell us more about life in Nigeria. What was the weather like? What did you do? What kinds of animals were there?"

The waiter returned, interrupting the barrage of questions. He placed a cup and saucer in front of Missouri, then stepped quickly away.

Mrs. Lancaster listened with avid attention as she poured coffee for the girl.

Quen smiled as memories flooded her mind. "Interesting animals were always just out of sight in the nearby trees. I woke to the friendly chattering of monkeys each morning."

"Monkeys? Oh, my." Mrs. Lancaster raised her eyebrows.

Quen pictured the home where they'd lived. "Red-throated bee-eaters, with shimmering green feathers, nested in holes in the ground in front of our home. Their colony filled the afternoon air with music."

Her voice rose with excitement as she warmed to the subject. "I used to get a shiver down my spine at night when laughing cackles from hyenas started. Or sometimes, deep, rumbling growls from roaming lion prides would roar through the evening air."

Abby gasped. "Lions? Gracious."

"Simply fascinating." Mrs. Lancaster placed her cup on the saucer with a decided clink. Her face changed. She suddenly seemed all business. "So, tell us, Quenby. What are your plans now you're in San Antonio?"

Quen toyed with the spoon in front of her. "Finding a job is top of my list. I'm used to working, and I'm bored with nothing to do. I would like to have financial independence too." A vision of a long, dreary life flashed through her mind. She simply couldn't live like her mother had. If being the daughter of a man like her father was tiresome, she could only imagine what being the wife of one would entail. Longing for a different life beat in her chest like the wings of a trapped bird.

"What do you enjoy? What are you good at?" Abby prodded.

"In Nigeria, I taught children at the school. And I enjoy working with numbers. The job of handling our finances while we were there belonged to me. I snuck away to perform that same work for an elderly gentleman in Galveston who owned a store. He was our neighbor. Of course, he kept my association with him quiet. His eyesight was failing, and he feared he was being taken advantage of. Despite the handicap of my gender, I think I make a quite respectable accountant."

Abby cocked her eyebrows at Mrs. Lancaster. "Do any of your hoity-toity friends need help with their household books?"

Quen gasped.

Mrs. Lancaster gave Abby a stern look. "That is an outrageously cheeky thing to say, child." A considering expression crossed her face. "I'll have to ponder that. It's possible."

Abby barely hid her grin behind a napkin. Quen met Missouri's resigned gaze across the table.

The young woman shook her head. "Never leave these two alone together. They're trouble."

Mrs. Lancaster sent an arch glance to her companion while Abby laughed again. The front door opened, allowing noise from the street to enter the quiet dining room.

Abby smiled. "Ah, there's my Manny. I better go." She picked up her cup and took one last swallow, blotted her lips, and placed her napkin on the table. She tucked the book she had been reading under her arm and moved to stand behind Missouri's chair. "Quen, it was a pleasure." She nodded to Mrs. Lancaster and Missouri. "Ladies, I enjoyed it, as always. Missouri, give Mortimer my best."

She paused. "Quen, please leave your address with Mrs. Lancaster. I'd like to come visit at your new home and have you out to our place when you have time. One can never have too many friends."

Abby walked toward the gentleman in question. Quen found him as surprising as Abby had been. He wore his long black hair pulled back into a silky ponytail, revealing scars that covered the right side of his face. He took Abby's hand in his as she gazed up at him with a loving smile. The absolute unexpectedness of them both fascinated Quen.

"How long have they been married?" She winced as the wistful words reached her own ears. She peeked at Mrs. Lancaster and Missouri to see if they heard it too.

With an artless and searching expression, Mrs. Lancaster studied her. "About a year and a half. And never were two people more deserving of their happiness. That union pleased me." Her eyes narrowed. "But let's not talk about them. We need to find you a job."

Jonathan turned at the sound of a shout. Manny led Abby across the busy street. Soon, they stood in front of the hitching post where he waited with his horse, Cisco.

"Hey, Jonathan." Abby smiled, her greeting light and friendly. "I didn't realize you were in town today. What a happy coincidence. Had some business to take care of?"

Jonathan nodded, but his lips pressed into a thin line. He darted a glance at Manny, but his friend's face gave nothing away. Jonathan loved Abby. She'd probably have something figured out in no time, but exposing his shortcomings still rankled.

Manny unhitched Abby's horse, Bird. He held the reins while she mounted. "Let's go get the babies. If we leave them too long at Yaideli's, I'm afraid she won't give them back." Manny turned to his friend and stuck his hand out.

Jonathan shook the proffered hand.

He pulled himself into Cisco's saddle, then tipped his hat to the couple. Jonathan turned the horse with a nudge and headed toward home. Thinking of the approaching conversation with Ma made his stomach turn.

I'm counting on you, God. Please show me what to do next.

Chapter Five

Jonathan carried his plate to the sink where his mother washed dishes. He pressed a kiss against her temple. "Supper was good, Ma. Thank you."

Ma's eyes crinkled in a tired smile, and she placed her palm against his cheek. "That's a kind thing to say, son."

He glanced out the window over the washbasin, peering through twilight-stretched shadows in the yard behind the house. If only he could find answers there.

The scent of warm cornbread, baked from the previous year's crop grown on their farm and soaked in melted butter, hung in the room. *I hope everyone else enjoys this as much as I do. We're gonna be eating an awful lot more come fall.*

Ma squinted as she studied him. She leaned back against the large white farm sink, slipping her hands into her apron pockets. "Something's bothering you. A mother knows her children, especially the first. You're the most content of the four. I notice when your light dims."

Jonathan started to disagree but snapped his mouth shut at the look in her eyes. He glanced over his shoulder at his brothers and sister, sitting at the table finishing their supper. Nerves assailed him, clenching his gut.

"Ma, can I talk with you? Alone?"

She arched an eyebrow before turning to the younger children. "Belle, when y'all are done eating, you and Bay finish washing dishes. Herschel, you'll head out to the barn to start the evening chores."

A chorus of "yes, ma'ams" answered her directives. They continued their conversation.

"Why don't we sit in the study?" Ma waved a hand in the direction of the doorway.

Jonathan gulped past the lump in his throat. Might as well. That way, he'd confess to both parents.

All three of them—Ma, Jonathan, and the memory of his father—cramped the room. She seated herself in the creaky chair behind the desk his pa had used. Her hands slid along the cracked leather arms with a sad caress.

Pa's strong presence filled the room. At times, thinking of him there comforted Jonathan. Other times, the imagined company made him sad. Watching the lonely gesture Ma made caused an ache in his chest. He turned away and stared out the window, his hands shoved in his pockets to still their trembling.

"Son, sitting on this egg isn't going to hatch it. What's wrong?"

Jonathan faced her and drew a deep breath. "I made a mistake ordering the corn seed. We ended up with more than I intended."

"That's not so bad. We can plant more, or we can save the seed for next year. If we keep it cool and dry, it'll hold." Ma frowned at him, worry at what still bothered him shadowing her eyes.

"Yes, we can do both those things." And more. A picture of the heavily laden wagon filled his mind. "We'll have to be miserly with the money."

Her eyes widened. "Oh. I see. For how long?"

He cleared his throat. "Um, pretty much until the harvest comes in."

She was unsuccessful at disguising her gasp. "That's the entire summer. I don't understand."

The hurt and confusion on her face made him cringe. He'd failed her. He'd failed them all. *Pa, I'm so sorry.*

"The situation may not be as bad as I think. Better to be safe than sorry, right? I've got plans in the works. In fact, I might straighten things out in a week or so."

The desire to erase the concern from his mother's face overrode his honesty. He was helpless to contain the lies.

She placed her hands in her lap. "Well, then. Not to worry. I have faith in you. You got me all stirred up for nothing."

The panic that had lived in his gut since the seed delivery screamed like a mountain lion. He gritted his teeth and forced a smile. "I'm sorry. It's just ... could we not spend any money for a few days? Until I get this fixed?"

Ma shrugged as she stood. "There's nothing that can't wait a week or two. The pantry is stocked, and you said last week we have enough feed to tide the cows over till the grass emerges. Don't worry about a thing." She smiled and left.

He slumped against the windowsill as her boot heels tapped their way back to the kitchen. Groaning, he lowered his head to his hands. His father's and grandfather's old journals filled the bookshelf beside him. He drew his hands down his face, scrubbing the day's growth of whiskers, and with a sigh, reached for an older book. He'd find some ideas his grandfather had used when he first started the homestead. They must've had other means of income before the farm provided today's living.

He sat behind the desk and placed the journal face up. With grim determination, he leafed through the pages until he found entries for spring. Concentrating fiercely, he stared at each word, willing the spidery, cursive letters to make sense.

March 5, 1826

Plow. Trick. Garden.

"No, that can't be it." Jonathan rubbed his eyes. "I've never heard of a trick garden."

Plow. Trick.

A bird chattered angrily outside the window. A flash of bright blue feathers darted past, and while Jonathan watched, a jay swooped dangerously close to the family cat. The cat's mouth opened in a silent *meow* as it ducked low every time the bird dove. The animal crouched, its tail snapping with indignation, eying the jay with murderous intent clear in its eyes.

Jonathan smiled, then his attention wandered back to the office. He glanced down and smacked his forehead with the heel of his hand. Focus.

Plow trick ...

No.

Truck.

Truck. Garden.

"Stop splashing me." Bay's voice raised in complaint from the kitchen.

Jonathan looked toward the door, waiting, expecting Belle's reply. She didn't disappoint.

"I didn't splash you. You didn't turn the glass over to drain the water. It's your fault."

Concentrate! He pressed the heels of his palms against his eyes.

Plow. Truck. Garden. For. Blowgreen.

What? Blowgreen?

Jonathan sighed. A memory of his father's voice discussing plans while they sat at the kitchen table in the evening, sipping cups of coffee, entered his mind. What did they plant first? Carrots, onions, potatoes, garlic. He pictured a different scene. His dad had the plow hitched to the stocky Percheron, his heavy bulk leaning into the reins. Together, man and beast turned the rich brown earth into neat rows.

He started over.

Belowgreen. Below ...

"Belowground." He announced the word with enough emphasis to compete with the judge naming the winning entry of blackberry jam at the fair.

Crops.

"Plow truck garden for belowground crops. Hah!" Jonathan slapped both hands against the desk in triumph. "Time to plow the small garden beside the barn."

The words on the page lay harmless. Understandable. They had lost their power to intimidate. Just an ordinary string of letters now. The triumph died as quickly as it came. He'd burned through five agonizing minutes on six stupid words. He thought of all the tasks he had waiting. Better uses of his time surrounded him on all sides. He flinched as shame flooded his heart.

Jonathan pinched the bridge of his nose. If he believed in curses, he'd wonder who had placed one on him. How could the words be different now than five minutes ago? Gritting his teeth, he leaned forward and forged ahead. He must discover a viable method of bringing in some money.

Quen startled at the sound of a firm knock on the front door, the newspaper with its want ads drooping in her hands.

"Who could that be?" Mother stiffened in her chair by the window. Her needlework dropped forgotten into her lap. She patted her hair with concern, sweeping a critical glance around the room. "Quenby, answer the door."

A surprised "Oh!" escaped her at the sight of Abby's smiling face on the opposite side of the threshold. "How delightful! Come in." Quen stepped back and pulled the door all the way open, waving an arm in invitation. "Mother," she called to the other room, "my new friend I told you about is here."

Quen led Abby through to the parlor. Mother's gaze roved up and down Abby's pants-clad legs and horror showed on her face. Her outrage struck her dumb.

Quen swallowed her nerves, rushing to fill the silence. "Abby, this is my mother, Mrs. Martin." Her words stumbled to a halt. Impossible to disguise her mother's disapproval.

Abby sent a calm smile toward Quen's mother, appearing as unruffled as the cat perched like a loaf of bread on the sunny windowsill. "Good morning, Mrs. Martin. Pleased to know you. What are you working on? My mother used to do needlework all the time."

Flustered, Mother picked up the wooden hoop in her lap, then seemed to remember Abby's appearance offended her, and dropped the needlework back down. Her mouth moved, but no words emerged.

"Manny sent me to town to get a piece for the plow, and I thought I'd stop by to visit my new friend." Abby barged right through the awkward silence—her voice cheerful. She turned to Quen. "Care to join me at the hotel dining room for a cup of coffee and whatever breakfast breads they have left from this morning? They sell them for half price after the morning crowd leaves."

Quen leaped at the chance to escape. "That sounds wonderful. If you want to wait outside, I'll grab my wrap." Mother would require mere moments to regain her aplomb. She feared whatever words might come next.

Abby grinned, a mischievous glint shining from her eyes. "No hurry. I'll chat with your mom while you fetch it."

Quen chewed her lower lip, then whirled and dashed to the back of the house. She snatched a shawl from her wardrobe and raced back to the room. Would Mother freeze the young woman with icy silence?

Abby's laughter greeted her disbelieving ears. Quen slowed, trailing her hand along the wall, straining to hear what she said.

"Oh, me too, ma'am." Abby spoke as comfortably as if she had known Mother all her life. "Now that I'm a parent myself, I'm more aware of the importance of raising my children well. You've obviously done a fine job raising Quen to be a woman who knows and follows her own mind."

Astonishment froze Quen in her tracks. Gathering herself, she entered the room, hurrying as if she'd just returned.

Mother paused, indecision wrestling with pride on her face, then nodded toward Abby with a genteel gesture. "Thank you for your kind words. One does what one can."

A snort escaped before Quen could stifle it. Not exactly a ringing endorsement. She covered her mouth with her hand and faked a cough to disguise the sound.

"Would you like me to stop at the bakery Mrs. Lancaster showed me?" Quen said. "I can bring home a fresh loaf of bread."

Faint disapproval appeared on Mother's face. "Of course not, Quenby. As your beloved Thoreau says, 'wealth is the ability to fully experience life.' Why spend our coin on something we can do ourselves—and with pride and enjoyment for a job well done? We are fully capable of baking our own bread."

Quen swallowed defensive words and pasted a smile on her face. "Right you are. I'll be happy to help you with the task when I return."

Seated in the long dining room of the Menger Hotel, Quen sipped her coffee, then stirred in a spoonful of sugar. "Where are your beautiful children I keep hearing about?"

Abby smiled, pride and love glowing from her face. "They're with Manny." She grimaced. "Robby is sick. He's turned into a snot volcano. He's cranky, doesn't sleep, and is no fun to be around. Manny told me to come to town for the plow part, said he'd stay with the babes so I could have a break. It's just me and my mare, Bird, today, like old times."

She beamed when she talked of her family. Quen swallowed the envy choking her. Had anyone ever been so totally over the moon about her?

Both women leaned back in their chairs when the waiter returned bearing a platter with a wide variety of pastries and breads. Quen laughed. "My goodness. You didn't do this justice when you described 'leftover breads.' This is amazing." She selected a muffin.

Abby chuckled. "I love eating here. We don't come to town often, and it's a treat to stop in."

"It's a treat for me too." Thoughts of her own life sobered Quen. "How did you charm Mother out of saying something rude earlier? I feared leaving you in the room together."

Abby chuckled. "She wasn't that bad. I know my choice of clothing gives people a start. They need time to get used to me. If she raised you to be the person you are, there must be some benevolence inside her somewhere."

A rueful smile tugged at Quen's mouth. "My mother can be difficult to please."

Abby pulled a face, sympathy softening her eyes. "Don't all mothers have high expectations for their children?"

"I suppose." Quen drew circles on the snowy tablecloth with her spoon. "Sometimes meeting them has seemed impossible." She snorted. "My sister Prissy doesn't seem to have the same problem."

"How old is she?"

"Eleven, and she is funny and beautiful. She's practically perfect."

Abby narrowed her eyes. "No one is perfect."

"Tell my mother that." Quen's voice was low. She shrugged. "I try to understand. Mother had a lot of trouble when we arrived in Africa. I didn't realize what was happening, but my Auntie Aduka explained it." Quen glanced around the nearly empty dining room. At this late hour of the morning, they were almost alone. "She suffered several miscarriages."

Abby sucked in a breath. "Oh no, how horrible. What an awful thing for all of you to endure. I had morning sickness for months with mine. That time was awful, but I'm grateful both babes arrived healthy."

Quen flinched. "I know next to nothing about that part of a woman's life."

Abby laughed. "They don't tell us anything, do they?"

"They certainly never told me. My Nigerian aunties finally explained to me enough about what Mother was going through for me to understand. All I really knew for sure was she was unhappy, and I could do nothing to make her better." Quen gazed toward the window, watched people walking by. "We went to Africa to serve God. I never saw him there, though." Her voice trailed off when memories flooded her mind.

Bringing herself back to the present, Quen met Abby's frown with a straightening of her spine, forcing thoughts of self-pity from her mind. "Prissy's birth healed us all. My mother became happier, so I did too. But I've always been sad Prissy brought a smile to her face when I couldn't. I just wasn't good enough."

Abby stood and moved beside Quen's chair. She leaned over and hugged her. "I'm sorry. Hopefully, you've learned by now you *are* good enough. God made us in his image. You're exactly what you're supposed to be."

Quen's mouth twitched. She wasn't sure God had anything to do with making her. Never saw much evidence of that. She laughed self-consciously. "I tell myself I'm good. Some days, I actually believe it."

Abby returned to her seat. "Well, then. That's that. Speaking of bringing value ..." Her voice was matter of fact. "We need to find you a job. Last time we spoke about this, you mentioned being good with numbers and finances. I know someone who can use your help."

Chapter Six

Jonathan walked out of the barn into the morning sunshine. Brisk air raised chill bumps on his arms. Spring heralded the coming summer heat, but nights were still cool. He sighed with pleasure, and gratitude swelled his heart. "Bless you, Father, for this day."

Cows lowed from the pasture behind the barn, waiting for hay to be tossed their way from the large pitchfork Herschel wielded. The zing of milk squirting into a metal pail called out a cadence from inside the barn. He pictured Belle sitting on a stool, leaning her head against a warm flank. To his right, Bay fussed at squawking chickens, competing for the feed he scattered on the ground in their coop.

Jonathan wiped his hands with a dirty rag. He didn't mind the problems that came with plowing time. He enjoyed tinkering with mechanical things. His brain knew what to do. No dancing letters or tricks of vision.

He smiled when Manny approached on his gelding, walked out to meet the trotting horse.

"Hey, amigo. What brings you here?"

Manny dismounted. He tossed an arm across Jonathan's shoulders. "I, being the excellent friend I am, have good news for you."

Jonathan cocked an eyebrow with good-humored skepticism. "Oh? And what might that be?"

"Abby found you a bookkeeper. Do you know Quen Martin?"

A spurt of anxiety curdled in Jonathan's stomach. He kept his expression neutral. "Quinn Martin? Nope. Never heard of him."

Manny started to speak, then grinned.

Jonathan frowned. *He's up to no good.*

"Quen has experience keeping finances. Abby did an impromptu interview in town yesterday, and she thinks Quen can help you."

"I don't know. I'm not real fond of the idea of some stranger poking around in our business. Things are working out." Jonathan trained his gaze on the rag in his hands, paying close attention to the grease under his fingernails.

"That's a big ol' pile of cow patty." Manny gave Jonathan a frank look. "What *things* are different today than the other day in town? How are they better?"

Jonathan's face heated. "I talked with Ma. She understands we need to pinch pennies for a while." The half-truth tasted bitter in his mouth.

Manny huffed. "You said that whole dang wagon was full of seed, Jon. You gonna plant every acre on your property? Who's gonna plow it? Tend it all?" He cocked his head. "What's your real plan?"

Jonathan swallowed. "So, I don't have every detail worked out."

Manny crossed his arms across his chest. "I'm bringing Quen out to meet you. Together, y'all will figure out what can get you over the hump this summer."

"Who is this guy? How does Abby know him?"

Manny chuckled. "Quen is new in town. Mrs. Lancaster introduced them. You know you can trust Mrs. Lancaster."

Jonathan narrowed his gaze. "I don't trust the look on your face."

Manny clapped him on the back. "Relax. This is gonna be great."

Quen struggled to sit still. Abby sat on the wagon bench next to Manny with Quen squeezed in at the other end. Each woman held a squirming toddler on her lap. Bird pulled the wagon down the empty road, ears perked, tail swishing as she trotted along.

"What are these beautiful flowers?" Quen pointed at the passing field, a carpet of navy as far as she could see. Bree gurgled, reaching a chubby fist as if to grab one.

Abby stretched to move her chin out of reach of Robby's sticky fingers. "Those are bluebonnets. They're one of the first flowers to show up once winter gives way to spring. They're lovely, aren't they?" She spoke past the little fingers clamped on her bottom lip.

Manny glanced at the pasture. "*En Español*, we say *el conejo*."

Abby squinted. "The rabbit?" She covered Robby's hand with hers, then pretended to nibble on his fingers. "Why on earth do you call them that?"

He laughed. "The white petals at the top of the blooms resemble the cottontail of the rabbit."

Abby frowned at the field. "If you say so." She turned to Quen. "I believe bluebonnets in the spring are one of God's best gifts to us. Don't you agree?"

Quen's grin became forced. God's gifts stopped coming long ago. He didn't pay attention anymore. Bree waved her hand in the air as if she greeted the passing flowers.

"Look." Abby pointed down the road, drawing Quen's attention from her musings. "Mrs. Lancaster and Missouri."

Quen followed Abby's gaze.

Mrs. Lancaster perched on a sidesaddle, holding the reins of a honey-colored palomino in one hand, and a parasol to shield her face from the sun in the other. Missouri waited alongside her on a smaller bay mare. A Black man stood at the gate to a small farm, gripping the bridle of Missouri's mount in one hand, stroking the mare's nose, looking up at the women. The threesome appeared deep in conversation.

Bird whickered, drawing their attention. Missouri glanced away, wiping at her eyes. Mrs. Lancaster folded a small piece of paper and slipped it into her glove. Quen frowned at the furtive movement. The man dropped his hands to his side and stepped back, turning a genial face in their direction. His brown skin gleamed in the sunlight. Unexpected freckles scattered across his nose and cheeks.

Manny pulled Bird to a stop. He doffed his hat. "Morning, ladies. Caleb."

Quen started. This was Caleb?

Mrs. Lancaster chuckled. "You seem surprised, Quenby Martin."

Quen's ears grew hot with embarrassment, pushing away her questions. She darted a quick look at the man.

His wide smile brightened his eyes. He glanced at the widow.

"What have you been saying 'bout me, Miz Lancaster?"

His drawl sounded very Southern to Quen's Northern-born ears.

He tucked his thumbs behind his suspenders. "Am I not what you expected, miss?"

Quen opened her mouth but failed to find words.

Abby took pity on her, amusement dancing in her eyes. "Caleb is our local authority on all things farming. He owns this farm." She introduced Quen.

Quen recovered her composure. "I'm pleased to meet you, Mr. Caleb."

"Ah, now. Nobody calls me mister 'round here, Miz Quenby. I'm just Caleb." He nodded his head toward her, friendliness beaming from his eyes.

"What are y'all up to?" Abby glanced from one face to the other. "Is Caleb trying to convince you to take another donkey, Mrs. Lancaster?"

"I have exactly the number of donkeys I desire, Abigail Blair. I needed to speak to Caleb about Mortimer's care, however." The humor in Mrs. Lancaster's voice ruined her haughty act. "What, pray tell, are the three of you doing? I see young Roberto is feeling better."

Abby heaved a theatrical sigh. "*Gracias a Dios.* If I had to wipe one more runny nose, I'm not sure what I would've done." She grinned. "I found Quen a job. You know Jonathan Campbell, right?"

Mrs. Lancaster nodded.

Caleb gestured across the road to a pasture filled with tall, waving grasses. "That's the beginning of his land, right there. His grandpappy passed down quite a spread."

"We're taking Quen to talk to him about doing his finances. Jonathan mentioned something about struggling to find time to do everything now that his father has passed. We thought Quen could help him."

"How marvelous." Mrs. Lancaster leaned forward eagerly. "I'm so happy you and Jonathan have met. What a perfect solution for both of you."

Manny's laugh turned into a cough. "They haven't actually met yet. We're taking Quen to his farm for the first time. Today seems to be a good day for getting things you don't expect." His humor came through loud and clear.

Quen frowned. What did he mean by that?

Manny fitted his hat back to his head. "We better get going. Got problems to solve." He slapped the reins on Bird's back, and the wagon jerked into motion. "Have a great day, y'all."

Jonathan jostled along behind the oldest mare in his barn while she pulled a seed drill through the freshly plowed field. Since the Percheron and the mule team had already broken the ground, the mare's job was easier. The rusty seat had long ago turned uncomfortable. He'd ask Ma to sew a cushion.

The seed hopper in front of him dropped corn kernels with an even distribution. He watched each kernel drop onto the soil with a feeling of quiet urgency. He simply had to have a solid crop this year. Everything depended on it. "Dear Lord, please bless our crops with rain and good sunshine this year."

"Jonathan." A voice called across the field.

He turned toward the house. Manny waved from his wagon, Abby tucked against his side. He squinted at the third person perched next to Abby. A memory tickled at his mind, but from this distance, he couldn't quite make her out. He pulled the brake on the hopper and jumped down, rubbing his smarting behind. Patting the mare, he left her. "Take a siesta, girl. I'll be back." He walked toward the visitors. "Hey, y'all. What are you doing in my neck of the woods?" Jonathan smiled, still trying to place the girl at Abby's side as they all climbed out of the wagon.

"Remember, I told you about Quen Martin, the accountant?" Manny grinned, mischief gleaming in his eyes.

"Yes." Jonathan glanced between the three.

"Here she is." Manny waved his hand in a sweeping gesture toward the girls.

Jonathan frowned. "This is Quinn?"

Quen stepped forward, Bree propped on her hip, extending a hand. "My given name is Quenby. Hello."

Jonathan took her hand in his grip, the movement automatic, his mind combing through his memory to place her. Her tall, lean body seemed so familiar. She had interesting eyes, not as brown as Manny's. More like caramel. He held her hand in his grasp a moment longer. He'd never met a woman who worked as an accountant. The term "bluestocking" floated through his mind.

He studied her. Was she pretty? He couldn't decide. "You've worked as an accountant before?" Doubt rang in his voice.

The girl flushed but lifted her chin.

Hmm. Prickly. His question must've struck a nerve.

Abby glanced at the field Jonathan planted. Several black birds had landed, drawing Robby's attention. "Uh-oh. You've got crows landing in your field. I hope they're not after the seed you just planted."

Quen followed her gaze. "In point of fact, those are ravens. You can tell by their larger size and the shaggy feathers at their neck. They're just as likely to eat any insects the plow turned up, being as they're omnivores."

Jonathan sucked in a breath and took a step back. Her! The girl from Solomon's store. The know-it-all. No way was he working with her.

Quen turned back to the group. "Fascinating fact—did you know they call a group of ravens an unkindness?" A strained smile stretched her face as she focused on him. "I'm sure I can help you. Not only am I well versed in the mechanics of an accounting ledger, but I also spent most of my life living in a small village in Nigeria where everyone farmed. I learned quite a lot following them around.

Perhaps I can share some of their valuable knowledge with you." Her words tumbled out.

"Um, I don't think ..." Jonathan struggled to voice his reluctance.

Manny stepped up and clapped his hand on his shoulder. "Jonathan can really use your help. All of it."

Quen leaned forward on the balls of her feet. "Excellent." She glanced toward the house. "Shall we get started? You may point me to your books, and I'll spend the morning going over them."

"Hang on." Jonathan glared at Manny. He grasped for a reason to turn the girl away. "I don't know how I could pay you." Forget what she might think of him and his inability to afford her help. He had to get rid of her.

"Hmm. I guess I have the onus to do my job well then, don't I? If I can't help you repair your financial problems, I don't deserve to be paid."

Could she not tell he didn't want her here? He drew a breath.

"Great! It's all settled." Manny reached for his daughter. "Come on, Jonathan. Let's introduce Quen to your family. You probably need to get back to planting your corn seed before those ravens eat everything."

Abby steered Quen away from the field, chatting as they stepped toward the farmhouse.

"Accept it, amigo. You need her help." Manny kept his voice low, but his eyes danced with merriment.

Jonathan bit back a snarl, then stomped along behind the cheery trio. He did need help, but from her?

"Criminy." *God, please help her make this right so she can get the heck out of here.*

His steps faltered. How was he supposed to explain this to Ma?

Chapter Seven

Jonathan trailed behind Manny, Abby, and *her*. How had this happened? A sensation of sweeping along like a log in a swollen river tumbled over him. He glared daggers at Manny's back. He couldn't believe his so-called friend had brought the mirror image of his school-day enemy to his home. She'd come back to haunt him.

They climbed the steps to Jonathan's porch. Manny held the front door open for the women. Jonathan brought up the rear, narrowed eyes shooting a message to Manny as he passed. If his thoughts had been audible, the girls would've blushed.

"Manny! Abby! What a nice surprise. Oh, you've brought the children." Ma bustled down the hall—hands clasped in excitement. "Belle," she called over her shoulder, "come see the babies." She turned back. Her curious gaze lit on Quen. "And who is this?" She extended a hand. They exchanged introductions.

Quen gasped as a small boy shot from a room behind her. She raised her elbows and twisted out of his way.

"Manny!" The youngster barreled into the cowboy, clasping him around the legs.

"Hey there, Bay." Manny chuckled, ruffling the boy's hair. "What kind of trouble are you up to today?"

"I'm not in trouble. Yet." The boy gave him an indignant look. He turned to play with the dangling foot of the toddler in Abby's arms. Robby kicked his leg with delight. "Can I take 'im fishing?"

Abby laughed. "Maybe when he's eight years old, like you. I think he's a little young for fishing."

Herschel came down the hall from the kitchen. He took a bite from a thick sandwich and raised the other hand in greeting. He mumbled around the bite of ham. "Hi, ev'er'ody."

Ma swatted his arm. "You weren't raised in a barn. Where are your manners?"

"Hey!" Bay brushed his hands through his hair. "You're dropping crumbs all over me."

Belle followed closely behind Herschel. "Move." She shoved him out of her way as she hurried to Manny's side. "I want to see the babies." She reached eager arms toward the girl. "Hi, Bree. Come to me."

The baby lunged forward so quickly Manny scrambled to keep her from pitching out of his arms. Her chubby hands reached for Belle.

Chaos crowded the hallway with noise and laughter. Jonathan glanced at Quen, anticipating judgmental scorn. She probably thought they were a bunch of hillbillies. Instead, wonder and amusement flooded her face. One hand covered her mouth, and her eyes crinkled at the corners. When her gaze connected with his, a bright smile plumped her cheeks, and she laughed. This girl confused him.

Ma shooed everyone toward the kitchen. "Let's go sit. There's still some coffee in the pot, or I can pour everyone a glass of water." She waited for Quen, then fell into step beside her. "I apologize for my hooligans. I swear, I raised them better."

Quen followed the mob, her face bright with fascination. "I experienced this camaraderie in Nigeria. Families who enjoy spending time with one another. I love it. Please don't apologize."

Jonathan, bringing up the rear, paused. He'd expected the mayhem surrounding them to cause annoyance.

Quen took a seat next to Abby. With everyone except Jonathan settled around the table, Ma shot him an enquiring glance. "So, Jonathan, tell us about your new friend."

Her tone suggested she expected a story.

His face heated. He couldn't very well say the annoying young woman was here to bail him out of financial ruin. And all he knew about her was her tendency to show off her big brain. He could say her favorite phrase to use was, "In point of fact."

"Er, this is Quen." He emphasized the "eh" sound of her name, sending a significant glance Manny's way. "She's new in town." He finished the introduction with the only personal fact he had.

"That's it?" Belle turned to Quen, dismissing her brother and his insufficient source of facts. "Where'd you move here from?"

While Quen launched into an explanation about their transfer from Nigeria to Galveston, Jonathan studied her more closely. She'd braided her hair and twirled the long strands into a complicated pile. Impossible to determine its length. Her nose was thin and straight. Good for poking into other people's business.

Every moment in her presence made him uncomfortable. "Let's get you to those books, shall we?" His words broke through the conversation in the room.

Four Campbell faces turned—identical surprise revealed in all of them. Abby buried hers in Robby's neck with something sounding suspiciously like laughter.

Jonathan moved through the doorway and into the hall. He paused in front of the study. He stood to the side, waiting for Quen to follow.

Quen took a breath. The quiet in the study pressed against her eardrums after the racket from the hallway and kitchen. Jonathan stepped aside with a wave, directing her toward the shelf. Manny followed and now leaned against the doorjamb, one ankle crossed over the other, thumbs tucked behind his suspenders, a grin she didn't understand quirking the corners of his mouth.

She cast a musing gaze over the men, then pursed her lips. Was she being used as some sort of joke? She shrugged. She'd agreed to do a job, so she'd hold up her end of the deal.

Turning to the shelf, Quen ran her fingers across the spines of journals with worn and tattered edges. She pulled one out at random and flipped open to the middle. Tightly written words filled the lines, no inch of space left unused. A date filled the corner at the top of the page.

"Your father wrote this?" She turned to Jonathan. He stood beside the desk, stiff as a branding iron.

"Yes. I've written only one. Pa died last fall."

"Oh dear." Quen's heart softened. "My condolences. I'm sure his passing left quite a void in your family. And put more pressure on you." She turned back to the shelf. "Which one is yours?" At his silence, she faced him again, eyebrows raised.

To her amazement, he flushed beet red. He coughed. "Um, I don't have a whole lot written yet. You won't get much out of my copy."

"*Au, contraire.*" She wagged a finger at him. "I need to see yours most of all."

He clenched his fists. Quen blinked. "Well," she rushed ahead, "I'll start with this one then." She moved to the desk. "May I sit here?"

Jonathan paused as if to refuse her, then gave a tight nod. "I need to get back to the field. Daylight's wastin'." He spun on his heel and marched from the room, brushing past Manny on his way out.

Manny shrugged, his grin unrepentant as he faced Quen. "One of us will be back later this afternoon to give you a ride home."

Quen shook her head. "That won't be necessary. I'll walk back to town. Many wildflowers I've never seen before are growing alongside the road. I'd like to investigate. Exploring is a pleasant pastime."

"Suit yourself. If you change your mind, send Bay to let us know. I'm gonna get Abby and the kids. Got work of my own to do." Manny left.

Quen settled in the creaky chair and sat motionless, letting the mood of the study seep into her soul. The space had the atmosphere of a room long occupied by a man. The desk was heavy, dark, scarred on the corners, rubbed smooth in places. Decorations were minimal. A painting of a horse hung opposite the desk. Had the beautiful animal been a favored pet on the farm, or was the likeness just a painting Jonathan's father liked? A plant perched on a stand in the corner near the window. Mrs. Campbell probably placed that there. Simple white cotton curtains hung from a rod, no frilly hems or eyelet lace to soften their lines.

She pulled the drawer open. Orderly sections contained writing utensils and paper. A few random tools shone dully in the light streaming from the window. Some she recognized. Others she didn't. The working room's organization and tidiness told her a lot about the man she'd never meet. Was Jonathan the same?

She stood and returned to the shelf, selecting the final book, the date *1863* written on page one. She settled herself in the chair to read.

The door swung open. Mrs. Campbell gave a start. "Oh. I didn't know ... I ..." She frowned. "What are you doing here?"

Obviously, Jonathan hadn't mentioned Quen's job to his mother. Did he intend for her to keep the financial situation a secret? She stood, discomfort clenching her gut. "Hello, Mrs. Campbell. Am I in your way?"

Mrs. Campbell frowned. "Well, no. But ... I'm sorry. I don't understand. Has Jonathan asked you to do something?"

Quen swallowed. What to tell her? "Abby mentioned something about Jonathan needing an accountant. I guess he told Manny he was so busy working the farm he didn't have time ..." Her voice trailed off.

"Oh, of course." Mrs. Campbell relaxed. "He did say something to me about the accounts. You're going to help with that mix-up about the corn? We certainly have a blessed abundance of seed this year."

Corn? What was that about? "Yes, ma'am. I'm lending a hand. In a conversation with Abby and Mrs. Lancaster, I mentioned I was bored, adjusting to life in San Antonio. They thought I'd enjoy having a job to do. Jonathan told me I could read through his farm journal to acclimate myself."

"You know Mrs. Lancaster?" Mrs. Campbell brightened. "Well, then. I'll leave you to work. May I bring you something to drink?"

Quen breathed a sigh of relief. "No, ma'am. I'm fine. I'll just read through this book, then I'll be out of your hair."

Bay's voice hollering at his sister from somewhere outside pulled Quen back to the present. She emerged from her mental historical dive, surprised to realize she wasn't counting bags of cornmeal at the mill or baling hay for storage in the barn. The story spelled out by Mr. Campbell's cramped handwriting sucked her in, immersing her in life on the family farm.

He, like his father before him, had built a successful business off their land, growing sufficient crops to feed their children, and producing enough extra to deposit savings each year. Failure would devastate Jonathan. She badly wanted to help him.

She tapped the paper in front of her. "Young Mr. Campbell, I may have found something to ease your struggle. I must see your journal to confirm my suspicion."

She searched the room for a ledger that seemed newer, not as thumbed through. Her gaze fell on a lower drawer, and she pulled it open. Aha! She lifted a journal from the hidden depths, squashing the niggling voice in her mind, warning her this was an invasion of Jonathan's privacy. The fact he'd left her here gave her permission to do whatever the job required.

She read, sending furtive glances toward the door. After a few moments, she frowned. Flipping back a page or two, she compared numbers. The chair creaked as she leaned back, staring into space. "Hmm."

Continuing to read, she turned a few more pages. She did not find what she looked for—a record of payments received. On two separate occasions, Jonathan's father recorded in his journal details of arrangements where he would be paid later. But she hadn't found the payments. Neither did they appear in Jonathan's. However, she found something else.

"Oh, my." Sympathy battled with excitement. The plan Jonathan recorded prior to ordering the corn seed detailed the need for twenty-nine bags. The bill from Mr. Nelson's store revealed the extent of the problem. Did he realize this happened? Elation surged through her veins. She could help him.

Closing the journal, Quen slid the book back into the drawer. "I've discovered your secret, my recalcitrant farmer." His reluctance to accept her assistance, to allow her access to this information, made sense to her now. He had probably been ashamed of this all his life. A bloom of empathy spread through her chest.

She would collect those payments. He may be too kind-hearted to ask for the money. Or maybe he was unaware the amounts were owed. Smiling with satisfaction, she pictured the conversation and his pleased gratitude. She would ask Mrs. Campbell where to find the two farms in question and would start today. She left the small study with a skip in her step.

As she walked down the hall in search of Jonathan's mother, a small voice whispered in her mind. *Talk to him first.* She paused, glancing toward the front door, uncertainty dimming her excitement. The urge to solve his problem overrode her caution. He'd be happy to see what she could do.

Chapter Eight

Quen walked along the road, contemplating what she'd uncovered in the journals. Jonathan needed cash, and fast. The two solutions she'd discovered already were easy fixes but provided an insufficient lifeline. She'd have to think of something else.

Wildflowers carpeted the fields. She'd mentioned her desire to learn their names to Mrs. Campbell. Her art supplies had arrived with the rest of their household goods, and Quen was eager to use her watercolors to paint the beauty in her new world. When Mrs. Campbell learned of her plans, she loaned a book titled *Favorite Field Flowers* that gave wonderful details of the various plants in the area. She even produced a basket for carrying home the spoils.

A zigzagging rail fence appeared on her right, providing a perimeter for a field. She slowed, studying the plants emerging in long straight rows. Deep green leaves unfurled, pushing up dark soil as they sought the light. The women in Nigeria had grown corn. These plants were identical.

A man approached, crossing the field. He had a hoe propped over his shoulder, and a wide-brimmed hat shaded his face. As he neared, a smile crossed Quen's face. This must be the outer edge of Caleb's farm. She waved to him.

"Good afternoon, Caleb." She called across the fence. "Working hard?"

He pushed the hat back. "Good afternoon, Miz Quen. I surely am. Where are you headed?"

"I'm paying a visit to Mr. Franklin." She paused, looking across the field. "May I ask you a question? How many bags of seed did you need to plant this field?"

Caleb scratched his head as he turned to survey the area. "I'd say this one took about five bags."

Only five? Quen flinched. Jonathan would have to plow up half of San Antonio to use ninety-two bags of seed. Solving his financial woes would be more challenging than she realized.

"Considering becoming a farmer?" Caleb's easy drawl carried a note of humor. His freckles seemed to dance on his face as he smiled.

"Unlikely." She forced a laugh. "Just learning more about my new community. Well, I'll be off. Have a nice day."

Mr. Franklin's farm came up next to Caleb's. She paused at the road, peering down the driveway to the house. Was anyone outside working? Ah. A man walked from the barn, carrying a bucket.

"Hello, sir. Excuse me." Quen waved.

He looked in her direction, then halted, a question on his face. "Yes, miss?" he called.

She approached, her basket hanging on her arm, and extended a hand.

"Good afternoon, sir. Are you Mr. Franklin?" She stood straight, using her best teacher's voice, perfected over years of instructing Nigerian children.

"Yes'm. What can I do for you?"

"I've just come from the Campbell farm, where I've been retained to perform financial tasks for the owner. I noted you entered into an arrangement last fall with the late Mr. Campbell, God rest his soul, to have two of your mares covered by his stud. In return, your payment to him was to be one of the resultant progenies. Unfortunately, I discovered no record of said payment. Can you enlighten me as to the progress of completing this deal?" Heat creeped up her neck. She forced herself to state the facts of the arrangement as unemotionally as possible, but the delicate subject matter was impossible to ignore.

The man blinked.

Quen shifted impatiently. "Did you ever pay the man, sir?"

"Oh." The farmer's glance slid away, and he stroked his beard. "Well, now. Two things happened. Firstly, the black mare slipped her *progeny* back in the summer, so there weren't no foal to give. Secondly, Campbell up 'n died, so there weren't no one to pay anyhow. I figgered we'd just let bygones be bygones."

Quen clasped her hands in front of her and eyed the man with a stern gaze. "In point of fact, the terms of the agreement were quite clear, Mr. Franklin. I offer my condolences for the loss of the hoped-for foal, but you failed to mention the second mare." She cleared her throat. Did her face flame as red as it felt? "May I assume she carried the offspring to its fulfillment?"

Mr. Franklin squinted. A smirk crossed his face. "Are ya asking if the mare dropped the foal?"

Quen pressed her lips together with impatience. "Yes, sir. Are you the proud owner of a new horse?"

He sighed, resigned. "That I am. A right bonny little filly she is too. But I don't have a second one to pay back Campbell."

Quen lifted her chin. "Perhaps we can agree on a suitable alternative. A reasonable solution is for you to pay half the value of the existing foal. In today's market, a good saddle horse sells for upward of $150."

Mr. Franklin's eyes widened, then his gaze turned crafty. "I don't have no way of knowing yet if this horse is gonna be a good 'un. Maybe she won't be worth that."

Quen hid a smile. Just as she expected. She pursed her lips, pretending to consider. "Quite right, sir. You make an excellent point. I believe $100 is fair. That would make your payment a mere $50. May I arrange to collect?" She reached into the basket and withdrew Mr. Campbell's journal. "I'd like to iron out the details today. We can agree on a date to meet in town."

Harrumphing, he dropped his bucket with a clatter. "I gotta fetch my spectacles. Never had nothing like this from Campbell in the past." He muttered as he stomped toward the house. "What's this world comin' to when your neighbor sends a girl to harass you about men's business?"

Quen followed him a few steps, then stopped to wait. The moment turned into minutes, but she never moved. Finally, the door banged open, and he returned, a bent pair of spectacles perched on his nose.

"Will you visit the bank tomorrow?" Quen paused with her pencil poised above the journal. "I can come back to your farm to collect, or I can meet you in town."

"In town. Tomorrow." He took the journal, squinted through the scratched glass of his spectacles, then scrawled his signature on the paper. "Here." He thrust the book back gracelessly.

Quen accepted it as if he'd granted her a tiara from Queen Victoria. "Thank you kindly, sir." She placed the journal back into the basket. She smiled. "My pleasu—"

A terrible screeching racket arose from behind the house.

"Pa! Come quick! A tomcat's gettin' after the baby geese." A child's voice cried out, shrill with panic.

Mr. Franklin charged around the house to the corral behind, Quen hot on his heels. A mother goose flapped her wings in the face of a large, scraggly cat, honking loud enough to wake the saints, intent on delivering violence to the marauder. The tom crouched in a corner formed by the wall of a pigsty and a stacked cord of firewood. A gosling dangled lifelessly in its mouth.

"Yah!" The farmer waved his hat toward the feline, running in his direction, adding his efforts to those of the goose. The animal turned, clawed its way to the top of the firewood, then bounded between the slats of the corral fence and disappeared into the field behind. The goose turned to her remaining brood and, spreading her wings protectively, led them away.

"Where's the dratted dog when ya need him?" he groused. "There went sure money." He glanced back at the payment agreement Quen had laid in the basket. She slipped a protective hand over the journal, arching an eyebrow.

"Look, Pa. This 'un is hurt." A gosling lay tilted over, one leg bent at an unnatural angle, blood on its wing.

The man sucked his teeth. "Give it here. I'll put it out of its misery."

Quen gasped. "You can't kill the poor thing."

"What do ya 'spect me to do?" Eyebrows raised, he stared. "Set up a nursery in my wife's kitchen and feed it by hand? No one here's got time for that."

Quen adopted a casual tone. "Well, if you're going to dispose of it, I could relieve you of the responsibility. My ... my little sister is bored and needs something to do. She could try her hand at the veterinarian sciences."

The man shrugged, eyeing her as if he thought she was crazy. "He'p yerself." With a baleful glance at her basket, he narrowed his eyes again. "Ye can knock five dollars off that bill."

Quen's lips pressed into a straight line, but she nodded. She'd add the five dollars back from her own purse. Hurrying to the small animal, she gathered it in her hands with gentle movements. Tucking the injured wing against the gosling's body, she slipped it into her pocket. "Don't you worry, dear sweet thing. I'll take care of you." She spoke softly, glancing around to see if the farmer had noticed. He was gone.

Quen let herself in, closing the front door with a quiet snick from the doorknob. The only sign of life was Prissy hammering out scales at the piano as if she was digging post holes. Her home was such a dismal contrast to the Campbells' noisy hall, the rowdy laughter.

She peeked into her pocket at the injured gosling. Good. Still asleep. Straightening, she strove for nonchalance as she headed toward her room.

"Quenby? Is that you?" Mother's voice called from the front room.

Quen clasped her hands behind her back, holding the basket Mrs. Campbell had given her. She stepped to the doorway. "Yes, Mother." Prissy sat at the keyboard, her eager face indicating how keen she was to be interrupted in her practice.

"Where have you been all day?" Mother's gaze traveled up and down her body. She frowned. "You're a mess. Why are your clothes so dirty?"

Quen leaned forward to inspect her skirt and shoes. Dust coated her toes, and strands of grass clung to her hem. "So sorry. I didn't realize. I've been exploring."

"Exploring? Where?" Mother's tone wasn't accusatory, but it wasn't a very far walk.

Quen chewed the inside of her mouth. What would meet Mother's rules of propriety and yet remain the truth? "You remember Abby? She introduced me to a family who lives out her direction. I visited Mrs. Campbell and her daughter, Belle, today."

Mother sniffed. "Is she a good Christian woman?"

Quen stifled the urge to roll her eyes. "I believe so. Mrs. Campbell seems very involved in the lives of her children. They're nice people."

Prissy leaned to her left. "What's in your hands?

She held the basket slightly away from her side. "This? Mrs. Campbell let me borrow it. I'm collecting flowers to add to my sketchbook."

A wiggle from her pocket bumped against her thigh. *Please keep your head down, little gosling.* Now was not the time to wake up and be curious.

Mother frowned. "You aren't traipsing through people's fields, are you? For heaven's sake."

"Merely walking down the road and picking flowers from the space in front of the fences."

Mother returned her attention to the needlework in her lap. "Go tidy yourself. Your father will be home for dinner soon."

With a sigh of relief, Quen turned to leave, holding the basket so it shielded her pocket. Her fingers brushed the journal containing the agreement signed by Mr. Franklin. Quen smiled as she continued toward her room, steps confident. Fifty dollars was a substantial amount for her to collect for Jonathan.

He'd be so pleased.

Chapter Nine

Bleary-eyed, Jonathan peered out the kitchen window where the sun lightened the sky from indigo to pale blue to pink. The morning rays stirred the rooster in the yard. Chores for the day waited. He drank the last of his coffee, then set the mug in the sink.

"His mercies are new every morning."

Repeating the familiar verse failed to calm him today.

What was the worst thing that could happen? She'd figure out he messed up. She already knew that. Another verse slipped into his mind. He was an earthen vessel, made of fragile clay. God's choice of building materials had been intentional, to allow divine strength to show up when human frailty failed. *My ego is involved. Dear Lord, help me lose myself and seek you.*

He'd watched Quen leave the house yesterday from his perch on the seed drill, peering under the lowered brim of his hat. His initial rush of relief gradually morphed into worry. What did she find after reading the journals? How many mistakes did he leave for her to discover? She probably thought he was a complete dullard.

She hadn't returned by the time he finished seeding the field. Were the books such a mess she'd given up already? He frowned. Did he want her there or not? The fear of being exposed battled the tiny flame of hope she could help. What if she told Abby and Manny about all the problems she'd uncovered? He shook his head, rejecting the worrisome thought. Manny would support him. They were like brothers. They'd always stuck up for each other.

He'd led the old mare to the barn for a nice evening meal and a good brush down. After removing her harness, he combed out the sweat marks on her chest, then picked clods of clay from her hooves, the tasks mindless. His attention had focused on the annoying girl. Highly unlikely she'd turn up anything helpful. He'd spent all their savings by ordering too much seed. What could she do about that? Nothing, that's what. If she returned the next day, would she rub his failings in his face? The thoughts circled, the train exhausting him.

He now faced the new day, tired before he started. The night's fitful sleep had not banished her from his thoughts. Sighing, Jonathan pushed the girl from his mind and headed to the barn. Regardless of what she thought, he had to do whatever possible to correct his financial mistake. Teddy and Ernest had made good progress on the field behind the creek. Perhaps they'd turned enough earth to make a second pass today, continuing to break up the incredibly durable root system of the prairie grass.

In the barn, the sight of empty stalls for the Percheron and the two mules told him the men were already at work with the plows. Guilt competed with worry. He should've been the first one out. Some girl was handling his books, a task he apparently couldn't manage, and now the hired help did his work for him.

He walked back outside, planning to head over and check.

Yikes! He took a step back. Her again.

Quen waited in the yard near the barn, wearing her hair in that same fancy pile as yesterday, a basket looped over her arm. She stood so stock-still and straight, he might've mistaken her for a fence post.

"Er," he stammered. "Can I help you?"

She smiled. "I'd say it's more like, can I help you? After all, that's why you hired me."

The leap of his hopeful heart conflicted with fear of what she would say next. If her next words told of how useless he was ... "I didn't hi—"

"I have a few ideas." She bulldozed right past his words. "They're still percolating, so I'm not ready to present them. But I'm confident we can turn your financial situation around."

A deep thud in his chest pulsed with anticipation. Confident? Maybe he hadn't left as many mistakes as he'd feared.

At that moment, a fuzzy yellow head, complete with two sparkling black eyes and a matching beak, popped up from the basket. A plaintive peep-peep-peep accompanied it.

"Easy now, Hans." She stroked a finger along the top of the fluffy head.

Jonathan squinted. "Do you have a duck?" He stepped closer to investigate and stuck a finger in the basket. He yanked back when the animal pecked at him.

"In point of fact, Hans is a gosling." The pleased tone of her voice affected him like fingernails on a chalkboard. "I rescued him from certain death."

Jonathan gritted his teeth. Could someone rescue him from her? Even if she came with all the solutions he needed, he couldn't take that know-it-all voice.

"I named him in honor of Hans Christian Andersen, a Dane who wrote a fairy tale called The Ugly Duckling. Poor little Hans has suffered some debilitating injuries. I've taken the matter upon myself to rehabilitate him. Of course, he may be of the female variety. I, er, have not checked that."

Jonathan snorted. "There's something you don't know?" He muttered the words, but apparently not low enough.

She blushed. "In point of fact, I do know how to check, but I'd rather not. The process is ... invasive of his or her privacy. I'm content to wait and let little Hans show me by his feather colors."

Jonathan cocked an eyebrow. He'd never been in a position to wonder or care what gender a goose was, and he wasn't compelled to change that now. "Why is it here with you?"

Affront stiffened her spine with the speed of a cracked whip. "I cannot very well leave him alone all day. He'll need food and drink. I must care for him."

Jonathan shrugged. "What are you going to do with a goose?"

"Why must he have a purpose? He deserves a life."

Jonathan struggled to contain an eye roll. "Maybe so, miss, but it's gonna eat. You'd better be able to make money from it, or it'll suck away your cash."

"I prefer to appreciate the beauty of things rather than be so mercenary about them. Does a creature only bring you joy by the value it brings? By what it does for you?" An injured look crossed her face.

How did she suck him into this discussion? He didn't want to be rude, but she would never succeed as a farmer. "Things on a farm either work or provide food. Do whatever you want with the goose." He turned before she could say anything else. "I've got to check the progress in the back pasture. Please excuse me."

She raised a hand to stop him, but he pretended not to notice. Teddy and Ernest waited for him in the fields. He'd already spent more time than he intended. He had a feeling he'd be here all day if he stopped again.

Quen bit back the words she wanted to say as Jonathan strode off. Drat the man. She didn't get to tell him about the money for the foal. She tapped her foot. The gosling peeped again. "Are you hungry, Hans?" She kneeled. Lifting the little bird carefully, she placed the downy body onto the ground. Thin strips of cotton held a small stick against the injured leg, acting as a splint. The gosling pecked with quick stabs of his black beak, plucking blades of grass.

Quen stared after Jonathan's receding back. Perhaps he would join the others at the house for lunch. She could time her return from the second farm to coincide with his arrival.

"Let's go, little chap. We have another visit to pay." She scooped the gosling into her cupped hands and returned him to the basket, settling him on a nest she'd made of old rags. She marched down the drive to the road, her strides long and purposeful.

As she walked, discomfort eroded the edges of her self-confidence. Jonathan's surprise when he'd discovered she wasn't a he had been obvious. "I should've addressed his attitude right then and there, Hans. But I'm not one hundred percent comfortable with confrontation. That's something you'll learn about me." No one with a lick of self-respect would shoulder her way into a relationship, even a business one, without being welcomed. "Hmph. At least I got through the front door. I'll bring him around."

She was determined to forge a path for herself that would allow her to live her life out from under the thumb of a man. That goal gave her the strength to soldier on. She could balance Jonathan's books and would give a valiant effort to help him turn his financial situation around. Her chin raised a notch. "He doesn't have to like me, Hans. My desire to help him and my ability to find solutions to his problems don't depend on that. He simply has to acknowledge I'm there for his good and allow me to help."

A sorry farm appeared as Quen approached the owner of the second unfinished entry in Mr. Campbell's journal. She paused at the gate, gazing with uncertainty at the house that stood mere feet away. "Heavens," she murmured. "This doesn't appear promising at all, Hans."

Fence rails lay haphazardly on the ground. They'd tumbled from the zig-zagged pattern where they'd originally been stacked. The small area in front of the house had no decorative plants or flowers, and repeated footsteps had long ago pounded the sparse wilted grass into hard-packed clay. Missing chinking exposed gaps between the logs of the cabin, large enough to allow entrance to any variety of small creatures. The contrast between this farm and Jonathan's couldn't be more glaring. The fence between them was like the boundary to a foreign country.

However, dried corn cobs filled every inch of space in the corn bin, positioned behind the house but visible from where she stood. He may be a horrible housekeeper, but he apparently knew how to grow crops. On land leased to him by Mr. Campbell. Quen swallowed her nerves, then straightened her shoulders.

She took a step toward the house. A dark shape rose slowly from the shadows, a low growl rumbling from the depths. Quen halted immediately. A tall brindle dog, wide of chest with a large, flat head, stalked a few steps in her direction, then halted, the ruff on his neck rising. His upper lip quivered as he snarled again, revealing long white teeth.

Quen pulled the basket against her midriff, splaying her hand across the top to prevent the gosling from escaping. She glanced around, seeking help. The yard was empty if one discounted the monster. Quen remained where she was. The dog didn't evoke the same overwhelming terror that had swamped her when confronted by a leopard once in Nigeria, but she wasn't eager to challenge him.

He quieted, lips lying smooth against his mouth, but his ruff did not flatten. He stared. She stared back. The pounding of her heart provided a backdrop for thoughts that scurried as she glanced around the yard. What to do?

A man walked around the house, halting when he spotted her. "Who're you?" He continued toward her, swiping his hat toward the dog as he passed. "Hyaw," he snarled at the brindle. The animal flinched away from the hat, then turned and slowly stalked back to his spot under the porch.

The farmer stopped when he neared Quen. "What do you want?"

She drew a deep breath, then cleared her throat. "Good afternoon, sir. Are you Mr. Garner?" At the man's nod, she continued. "My name is Quenby Martin. I'm here on behalf of Mr. Campbell."

The man spit. "Heard he died."

"Yes, sir. The senior Mr. Campbell did. I'm here on behalf of his son, Jonathan."

"What wrong with him he can't take care of his own business?" The farmer sneered.

Quen swallowed her defense of Jonathan, pasting on a smile. "Nothing's wrong, sir. He is extremely busy getting his crops in. I have free time on my hands, so I volunteered."

"Volunteered what?"

Oh, dear. This wasn't nearly as easy as yesterday. She swallowed, nerves drying her mouth, then the image of Auntie Aduka haggling at the markets in Nigeria came to mind. She'd learned from the best negotiator how to stand her ground and wear the opposition down. Besides, if she returned empty-handed, what use would Jonathan have for her?

She lifted her chin. "There is an entry in Mr. Campbell's farm journals detailing an agreement he made with you regarding the farthest corner of his property. The corner that abuts up next to yours."

The man scowled. "And?"

Quen's growing irritation fueled her courage. "And the journal states you leased his acreage to grow extra crops, for which you were to pay a one-fifth portion back to Mr. Campbell. I did not find a record of said payment. Therefore, I am here to make arrangements to collect."

"Seems like the person I should pay is Mr. Campbell. And since he isn't here any longer, the arrangement is null."

"Au contraire." A tight smile pinched Quen's mouth. "Your debt is considered an asset of the decedent's estate. Mr. Campbell's passing does not nullify the promissory note. The arrangement has merely transferred to his heirs. Your agreement with Mr. Campbell is alive and well, even if he is not."

"And if I disagree?" The man propped his hands on his waist, delivering a belligerent stare.

Quen tensed. "Why, sir, you cannot disagree with a contract. The deed is done."

"Maybe my crops failed. A fifth of nothing is nothing."

Quen raised her eyebrows, then sent a pointed glance toward the corn bin. "I believe you managed quite well with your crops, sir."

The man had the grace to flush. Whether from anger or embarrassment was unclear.

"I don't like you." The farmer stood with his feet wide apart, his arms held akimbo. His gaze flicked to the road behind her.

Quen ignored the temptation to glance over her shoulder. She shrugged at his words. Would the movement hide her trembles? "Your feelings about me have absolutely no bearing on the matter, sir. You made an agreement. If you are a man of honor, you'll abide by the terms."

"Hallo." A friendly voice called from behind Quen.

She turned. Her stiff shoulders relaxed at the sight of Caleb, sitting bareback astride a mule, his hat pushed away from his wide, smiling, freckled face.

"What a nice surprise to see you, Miz Martin."

Quen blinked at Caleb's slow, Southern drawl. He sounded ... different.

His smile grew wider if possible. "Good day t' ya, Mistah Garner. Mighty fine mornin', ain't it?"

Quen frowned at the sound of his uneducated, simple speech. What was he up to?

"Miz Martin, I'se happy you've had the chance to meet mo' neighbors. Mistah Garner here, why, he's a right handy friend to have. Always willin' to lend a hand. And he's a good farmer too." Caleb's wide smile blinded. "You're gonna have to tell the rest of us how you do so good in the fields, Mistah Garner."

"Seems yer kind would know all about farmin'." Garner's look was insolent.

Quen flinched at the barb, but stayed silent, unsure what game Caleb played.

"True 'nuf. We got a lot of experience, for sure." Caleb let the rude implication roll right off his back. "Mistah Garner, this here child is so kind. Why, she volunteered to he'p out at the Campbell place from the goodness of her heart. Seein' y'all know each other makes me happy." He paused, then raised his eyebrows, the very picture of innocence. "What're y'all doing? Anything I can help with? I woke myself this fine morn with a generous feeling in my spirit. God must've known I'd be passin' by and got me all ready to offer my assistance."

Quen swallowed. "In point of fact, I am here on business for young Mr. Campbell. I thought I'd save Mr. Garner the trouble of making a trip to send his portion of the corn crop from the last harvest."

Caleb slapped his hand against his thigh with a chuckle. "See there, Mistah Garner. That's exactly what I'm talking about. Kindness oozing from her very skin." He tilted his head toward the corncrib. "God sure blessed you last year with your harvests. I'm sure your heart is happy to send that payment to the Campbells. Life dealt them a bad hand, taking Mistah Campbell so soon, God rest his soul."

Quen glanced at Mr. Garner, drawing a confident smile. "Well, let's finish up this business, shall we, so you can get on with your day. May I save you a trip to the bank by picking up the payment from you here?"

"I've got the funds." Mr. Garner's words resembled a growl. "Don't place much faith in banks. Wait here."

Quen let out a slow sigh of relief as he walked inside his house. She turned to face Caleb, who still sat on his mule, waiting on the road.

"Caleb, what is this act?" She spoke in a hushed tone. "I don't understand."

"Miz Quenby, I learned a long time ago some White men don't take too kindly to what they call 'uppity Black folks.' Life just rolls along a little easier if I don't challenge people's preconceived notions 'bout me. He sees an uneducated, simple man. I do my part to keep the peace. If I don't threaten him, he's uninspired to threaten back."

Quen gasped in dismay. "But Caleb ... that's so unfair. You have every right to—"

"Ah, there he is." Caleb smiled so widely, Quen could almost count his teeth. "You're a fine gentleman, Mistah Garner."

The farmer stalked to where Quen stood and thrust a handful of crumpled bills in her face. "Here. Count 'em if ya want to."

Quen steeled herself to not back down from the hand invading her personal space. She reached for it, pleased her fingers didn't shake. She tallied the bills quickly, then flashed a smile. "Thank you, sir. I'll prepare a receipt for you, then be on my way."

She slipped the wad of money into her pocket, then set the basket on the ground. She pulled the journal out and wrote a receipt. As she handed the man the paper, a weakened "hee-haw" came from the pasture to her left. She gasped at the pitiful creature that met her gaze.

A scrawny donkey stood in the corral, ears perked forward, nostrils flaring to sniff. The hooves of the poor animal curled up almost long enough to create a backward C. Despite the painful stance, its eyes shone a liquid brown, and the expression on the long white face seemed curious.

"Oh, my stars. Mr. Garner, your animal needs attention."

The farmer scowled. "That donkey is past her prime. She offers no value to me. Just waiting on her to die."

Quen clenched her fist. "Mr. Garner! That's—"

"Well, shoot, Mistah Garner." Caleb interrupted, his voice smooth as butter. "I can take care of this for you. No sense in this little burro makin' a problem. Why don't I just lead her off, and you don't worry your head about her no more?"

The farmer's gaze turned wily. "She's worth something. Can feed her to the pigs at the very least."

Quen's haggling lessons took over before she could reveal emotions. "I'd say we do the greater favor here, Mr. Garner." She sighed dramatically. "However, I do see your point." She pulled the wad of money from her pocket and peeled off a dollar. Wordlessly, she held the bill out, daring him with her eyes to bargain for more.

Triumphant, he snatched the cash from her, then turned. He snapped his fingers at the dog as he left. It gave Quen one last warning snarl before rising and trotting after the man.

Quen narrowed her eyes at Mr. Garner's departing form. "Anyone with eyes in their head can clearly see you've not spent so much as a corn cob feeding this poor creature." Though highly indignant, she kept her voice low. She turned to Caleb. "Jonathan's farm is closest. How will we get her there? She can scarcely walk."

Caleb raised his eyebrows, pressing his lips to hold back his humor. "Miz Quen, are you sure Jonathan wants this poor beast? We can bring her back to life, but it'll take some doing before she's ready to contribute to her room and board."

Quen jerked as if she'd been slapped. "How could he turn her away? She is in need."

Caleb chuckled softly, sliding from his mule's back. He headed toward the donkey. "Farmers aren't a sentimental bunch. You'll be hard pressed to find one who'll stir himself to improve the situation of something that won't give a payback." A sardonic tone crept into his voice. "No sense in ownin' a thing if it can't contribute." He stopped at the fence. "Don't be crushed if he turns you away."

Caleb dragged the gate open. He approached the donkey with care, but she seemed eager for a human touch, nudging her nose against the palm he held out. He chuckled again, then eased his hand up her face and scratched behind her ears. Pulling a rope belt from his waistband, he tied it to the donkey's halter and tugged her forward. "Come on, lil' sis. We'll go nice and slow."

The animal minced forward, lurching on the grossly malformed hooves.

Quen wrung her hands. "Oh, poor thing." She reached for the rope. "Give her to me. I'll walk beside her."

Caleb faced her. "Miz Quen, I can't ride while you walk. It won't be right."

Quen drew back. "I can't ride bareback, especially in a skirt."

Caleb peered at her, contemplating. "I cannot ride while you walk. I guess we'll all just carry ourselves."

The trio progressed to the road where the mule patiently waited. He stretched his nose toward the smaller animal.

Quen checked on her gosling. Tucked in among the pieces of cloth, his eyes remained closed as he napped. "I understand how Noah must've felt." She smiled, pleased to have alleviated yet another animal's suffering. "What should we call her, Caleb? She gains a new lease on life today."

Caleb shrugged. "Don't suppose the name matters to the donkey."

"How about Phoenix? With your help on these awful hooves, our girl will rise from the ashes of her old life and fly into her new one."

"Rise she may, but you still gotta find her a place to live."

Quen patted the donkey on the withers as the animal hobbled painfully down the road. "Jonathan won't mind." Certainty rang in her voice. "Leave that to me."

Chapter Ten

After lunch, Jonathan hurried from the kitchen. Ma spent the time at the table talking to Herschel about leaving for university in the fall. She seemed as eager to keep the young man from the war as he was. His brother described a lengthy list of things he needed. All well and good except for one minor fact—no money in the bank. Worry choked his breath. He had to get out of there before they asked about funds.

Could he hide in the barn? He sighed. Avoiding his family was ridiculous. He would have to return to the house at some point. Think, think. How to put them off? With a last glance toward the kitchen, he tiptoed out the front door and slipped away.

He drew a deep breath, filling his lungs with clean spring air. The sun had risen hours ago. Now noise and movement filled the barnyard. Chickens clucked, responding to a crowing rooster. They scratched the ground, stabbing their beaks at seeds. Cows ripped bites of grass from the pasture where Belle had turned them out after milking, and the old mare whinnied a greeting when he approached the corral. The familiar noises soothed.

What if they lost everything because of him? Concern twisted Jonathan's gut as if he'd eaten a bellyful of green peaches. He loved this land, their house, the creation of nature that occurred each year.

With a sigh, he shook fear from his mind. God had always provided. He straightened. He'd place his faith in God and figure something out. If this door closed, another would open.

He would focus on getting that new pasture seeded, using up as much of the blasted corn seed as he could. Then they'd plant cotton.

Muffled sounds of conversation drifted from the road. Jonathan peered down the drive. Over the years, trees and grapevines had grown along the fence line at the front of the property, providing a nice wind break, reducing dust levels from passing wagons, but they also blocked the view of any passersby. Who was out there? And what was taking so long?

Caleb appeared, leading his mule by the reins. Jonathan frowned, studying the animal's feet. Had he thrown a shoe? He didn't limp.

A second person came around the tree line. Jonathan sucked in his breath.

Her.

He'd escaped an uncomfortable conversation in the house, only to walk straight into another one. He squinted as she came down the drive toward him. What pitiful creature did she drag with her? He hid his shock at the animal's condition.

Caleb gave a friendly wave. "Afternoon, Jonathan. How's your planting coming along?"

Jonathan focused on Caleb, ignoring Quen. He approached and shook the man's hand. "Making progress. Got the big field seeded, and the boys are plowing the back pasture now. Turning new sod. Gonna expand our efforts this year." Jonathan kept the woman in his peripheral vision, hoping beyond hope he wouldn't have to speak with her. She had that dratted basket on her arm again, undoubtedly still toting around the baby duck.

Caleb raised his eyebrows. "That's biting off a pretty big chaw. Sure you can handle that load with only Ernest and Teddy to help you?"

Could he? Doubt whispered. Maybe. He might have everyone who lived under his roof working in the fields this summer, hoeing, pinching off pests, then picking at harvesttime. The job would take all hands. But they would make it work. They had no choice.

The old mare nickered from the corral. Caleb's mule huffed a reply to her, ears pricked forward. An awful racket blared from the flea-bitten bag of bones standing next to the girl as the donkey hee-hawed its response. Flinching, Jonathan took a step back.

"Where'd you get that?" He frowned, inspecting the raggedy animal.

The girl stiffened.

Jonathan shook his head. She flared up quicker'n anybody he knew.

"*That* is Phoenix. I rescued her."

He snorted. "I've never seen anything less Phoenix-like."

Caleb coughed into his hand. "Miz Quen brought this here donkey away from her previous home. I'm gonna trim those hooves."

Jonathan glanced back and forth between them. Suspicion bloomed at the sight of humor peeking from the creases around Caleb's eyes. "Why are you bringing it here?"

A pink hue flooded the girl's cheeks. She glanced at Caleb as if seeking reinforcements. "Well," she waved a hand toward the coyote bait, "your farm is closest. And she will need much follow-up care. Since I rescued her, the responsibility should fall on me. Thankfully, my job will bring me here often. As you can see, she is in great pain."

Jonathan hitched his thumb over his shoulder toward the house. "I got a rifle that'll take care of that."

He cut an amused wink at Caleb when she gasped. Caleb shook his head in response, but his lips quirked.

"Young Mr. Campbell, I cannot entertain the idea of you—"

"Young Mr. Campbell?" Jonathan guffawed. "Do you hear yourself? Are you this hoity-toity with everyone, or just me?"

If she stiffened any further, she'd snap in two.

"In point of fact, I've been speaking with Mr. Garner."

Her answer put his hackles up. What business did she have with his slovenly neighbor?

"In point of fact—" He mimicked her annoying phrase but tensed as the obvious answer popped into his mind. "What were you doing at Garner's farm?" His voice grew deceptively calm.

She flushed, undoubtedly in response to his mockery. He pressed his lips into a thin line. He was normally a nice person. Why did she pull this reaction from him?

She lifted her chin. "My job, of course. I did what you hired me to do." She pulled her hand from a skirt pocket and thrust a wad of cash at him. "And I was successful. I collected the delinquent payment due your father's estate from the lease of land he agreed to last spring." She shook the bills at him.

Heat crawled up Jonathan's neck. He snatched the money to get her hand out of his face. "You told my neighbor I needed money? Criminy, woman. The whole town will gossip about us." He shot a glance at Caleb. Did he know?

Sparks snapped in her gaze, and the pink on her cheeks blazed brighter. A flash of attraction startled him, took his mind off her words. Then she opened her mouth.

"I did no such thing. I merely reminded him of his obligation, which he gladly paid."

Her gaze turned evasive as she stated her last few words. Something she said was untrue. Tamping the unwelcome and extremely unexpected sensation of physical awareness as deep down as he could, Jonathan turned to Caleb.

"Were you there? Is that what happened?"

Caleb tilted his head from side to side, the movement thoughtful. "More or less. Miz Quen did remind him of the contract, and he did pay her."

Jonathan stared at the woman, his jaw jutting sideways. "Hmm."

Quen broke first, glancing away. She scuffed her foot on the ground, then ran her hand through the stiff, bristly mane standing up from the donkey's neck.

"She noticed this poor creature's suffering, and Mr. Garner allowed as how he hadn't the time nor the inclination to care for her." Caleb filled the awkward silence. "So, we did him the favor of taking her off his hands."

"And now you're doing me the favor of dumping her at my farm?" Jonathan propped his hands on his hips.

"She won't remain here." Quen's answer shot back. "She needs a place to stay while she gathers her strength."

He quietly burned at the careless attitude of his neighbor. Who could leave a living creature to wither away in such poor health? Animals were beasts of burden, but the responsibility to care for them lay with their owners. He snuck a glance at Quen's face. Her tendency to save creatures in tough spots was endearing, though he'd never voice that aloud.

"Don't worry, she won't be in your way. I'll be here every day in my capacity as your accountant, so I will administer her care."

Every day? Jonathan suppressed a groan. A new thought shot into his brain like a tiny arrow. "What did you do yesterday when you left? Whose farm did you visit to find the duck?"

"The *gosling* was at Mr. Franklin's farm."

He frowned in confusion, bewilderment overriding annoyance at being corrected. "Why were you at Franklin's farm?"

"He arranged with senior Mr. Campbell to have your stallion service two of his mares."

Her cheeks went pink yet again at the mention of the services provided by the stallion. Jonathan snorted. No, she'd never make it as a farmer. "What arrangement?"

"They were in a journal from two years ago. Horses have a gestation period of eleven months, then foals require six to nine months to be fully weaned."

"Yeah, I know that." Jonathan ignored the realization he didn't know about the agreement. "You rustled up money from him too?"

Quen raised an eyebrow and peered down her nose. "A thank you would be nice, Mr. Campbell. I just bought you some time." Sudden awareness of what she'd revealed flooded her face, and she glanced at Caleb. When she met Jonathan's gaze with a cringe, an apology softened her eyes.

He shrugged his shoulders. Why not tell the man? Everyone else in town would know his secret before she was done. "I guess you've figured out I'm in a bit of a financial bind?"

Caleb nodded. "Yessir, that became clear." He grinned suddenly, tilting his head toward Quen. "If I were you, I'd feel a mite better about my situation, knowin' this one had my back. She stood her ground in the face of that ornery old Mister Garner. And his mean dog too."

Jonathan glanced at her. He'd not considered her as a fierce opponent, but according to Caleb, she had hidden strength. He admired confidence. However, he wasn't ready to yield that point. Her decision to track down the funds without consulting him first incensed him. "Do all accountants act like you? Seems like this is something we should've discussed." A thought occurred to him. "How did you know I hadn't already collected that money?"

She avoided his gaze, picking at the basket looped over her arm.

He ground his teeth. "You found my journal, didn't you?" Surely, if she'd read his notes, she'd found evidence of his difficulty. His chin dipped and his ears burned. The idea of seeming less in her eyes rankled. "Did you snoop through the entire house or just the office?" The harshness of his tone hung in the air, and he winced. *Father, please help me control my emotions.* He didn't like who he was around this woman.

Caleb cleared his throat. "Do you mind if I take this lil' donkey into the barn and use your tools on her hooves? You two can move this conversation inside and work things out."

Shame made Jonathan's armpits prickle with sweat. He glanced at Quen. She seemed as uncomfortable as he was and refused to meet his gaze. He stepped aside and bowed slightly, waving a hand toward the house. "After you."

Caleb chuckled as he led the suffering donkey away. "Let's go, Miz Phoenix. In an hour or two, you're gonna agree this is the best day of your life."

Quen hesitated, leaning with what looked like longing toward the pair. She drew a deep breath and turned toward the house.

He led the way to the study. Seating himself in the chair behind the desk, he reached down, pulled open the drawer, and removed his journal. Tossing the slim book onto the desk, he steepled his fingers and peered at her. She gazed back, unrepentant. He gave her a dry look and tried to temper his tone. "Did you find everything you searched for?"

Quen swallowed. His *hoity-toity* comment stung. She couldn't help her actions. When she was uncomfortable, her intelligence became a shield. Her language, her tone of voice—they were her defense mechanisms. Hitching her chin, she brazened through. She'd made a mistake in judgment by snooping through his things, and he had every right to call her out. She placed the basket with the sleeping gosling on the desk.

"I did find everything I expected. In point of fact, I found a little more." Drat. She said it again. She forced her shoulders to relax, tried to smile pleasantly. Her lips felt as if she stretched them into a rictus.

She hesitated. He was upset. Could she risk alienating him further? She screwed her courage to the sticking point. She was too far in to back down now.

"I apologize for being so persnickety. I'm aware of the trait, and I'm working on controlling my reactions when I'm in situations that make me uncomfortable." She drew a breath. It was now or never. "I know you have trouble writing." She blurted the words. "Possibly reading too."

He stilled, eyes widening.

"You needn't worry." She rushed to reassure. "I've seen this before. I can help you."

Jonathan's face flushed brick red, and he dropped his gaze. "I don't know what you mean."

He was a proud man. Would he allow her to see his vulnerability? She must make him understand she didn't mean to hurt him. Her tone businesslike, she forged ahead. "Certainly, you do. I saw the notes written in your journal. You transposed the numbers when Mr. Nelson took your order, didn't you?" She lowered her voice and leaned forward. "Let me help."

He clenched his jaw, a muscle twitching beneath his ear as he stared at the desk. "How?" Bitterness rang in his voice. "You think you can do better than Mr. Wainwright, all those years ago in school?" He focused his gaze over her shoulder. "I tried to be as smart as the others. When the fire burned Manny, I spent hours with him after school, pretending to help him stay caught up while his wounds healed, but really, I struggled to keep up with the rest of our classmates." He sighed. "I can't do it."

Quen's heart throbbed at the pain in his voice. This was no time for self-indulgence, however. Drawing on her teaching experience, she used her most stern teacher's voice. "Nonsense. You're obviously an intelligent man. We all have different strengths and weaknesses. One must ask for help when one has the need."

He glared. "What if one prefers others to mind their business?"

Quen's nostrils flared. But years of repressing her feelings in front of her aloof parents had taught her to control her emotions. She could deal with a cranky farmer. She straightened.

"Your friends seemed to think you could use my help. I've already secured funds for you that would've gone unclaimed had I not read your journals. And I have ideas to bring in additional income I'd love to discuss with you and your mother." She gazed at him, patience settling in her soul as she waited for his response. "Admit it. I can help. Allow me to continue. I know I can improve your situation."

Jonathan shook his head. He opened his mouth, only to be interrupted when Ma swept into the room.

"There you are. Good afternoon, Quen." She turned to Jonathan. "Herschel and I have a list of things he needs before leaving for Baylor this fall. We're going to town. We'll probably have to send off for some items, so we have no time to lose. Should we stop at the bank?" Mrs. Campbell smiled at Quen. "Did you find the farms you asked about?"

"Yes, ma'am. Your directions were very helpful." Quen smiled back. Perfect timing. Mrs. Campbell may've just saved her job. She snuck a peek at Jonathan.

Resignation settled on his face like a shadow. He glared narrow-eyed at Quen. "No need to stop at the bank. I have some cash here." He reached into his pocket and withdrew the folded notes Quen had thrust at him earlier. "I hope this is enough."

Quen repressed the urge to bounce in her chair, to clap, to cheer. Ha! She'd proven herself. He wouldn't sack her.

As Mrs. Campbell left the study, Quen strove to wipe any trace of triumph from her face. "So, do we have a deal?"

At that moment, Hans stuck his black beak over the edge of the basket and peeped.

Jonathan shook his head in defeat. "All right. You can stay. But stop bringing animals to my farm."

A lusty hee-haw screeched from the barn. Caleb must've begun his farrier work. Jonathan sent a look of disgust toward the window.

Quen leaned forward. "If I learned anything in my time as a missionary's daughter, I learned to quote the Bible. We are to care for the least of these. It's biblical, Jonathan." Quen winced at the asperity she detected in her voice. Had he noticed?

He stared with a contemplative glance. "Well said, Miss Martin. I have but one request."

Quen softened at his words of praise.

"How about you care for them somewhere else?"

Chapter Eleven

No one witnessed Quen's departure. She pulled the front door closed as she stepped past the threshold, peeking over her shoulder at the front room window. Mother and Prissy still sat, framed by the glass panes, heads bent over their latest sewing project, thick as thieves. She hurried to the street.

Quen frowned as she peered both ways. She hadn't seen her father that morning. Where did he go each day? Probably somewhere with other loud-spoken men who enjoyed using the Bible to tell others what to do. *Verily I say unto you,* she cared not where he went. She could quote with the best of them.

His attention usually came with instructions on how she could be a better Christian. Not that he appeared to be so great at emulating Jesus himself. Perhaps he had at one time, but his actions provided little reflection of the Christ he'd forced her to read about as a child. Quen shook her head. Sometimes, Bible stories seemed like nonsense. Made-up fairy tales.

She adjusted the basket on her arm, peeking at the gosling. Trailing a fingertip along the downy head where black-tipped feathers had sprung up next to the golden-yellow fluff, she spoke to him. "Ready for an adventure,

Hans? We're off to meet Mr. Franklin at the bank. Then we'll go see Jonathan and his family. I'll introduce you to Phoenix." The bird nibbled at her finger with his black beak, his fuzzy head jabbing at her like a woodpecker. Quen laughed. "You can't eat me, silly goose." She bent and pulled a handful of grass from the edge of her neighbor's yard, then dropped the blades into the basket. "Here. Help yourself."

Quen walked toward the center of town. The farther she moved from her home, the higher her spirits rose. Anticipation bubbled inside as she pictured Jonathan's family. Mrs. Campbell was so kind, and Belle and Bay's arguing made her laugh. Herschel stayed to himself, but he welcomed her every time she interacted with him.

Her thoughts turned to Jonathan. Hmm. His reactions toward her hadn't improved much since the day they met. His refusal to open up frustrated her. He didn't fool her by trying to hide his reading difficulty. While he wasn't actually rude to her, he was definitely cool.

However, her eyes brightened. Cool or not, he pulled at her. She ticked through his appealing attributes. He behaved with respect toward his mother. Showed kindness to his siblings. Displayed devotion to the care of their family farm.

Her imaginings took a more physical path. Tall. Lean. A friendly smile with straight, white teeth. His hands, with long, work-roughened fingers, caught her attention the first day she met him. And his ice-blue eyes almost shocked with their crispness when contrasted against his tanned skin. Her heart fluttered, and her steps slowed.

Jonathan was a farmer. She had never envisioned a future as a farmer's wife. She dreamed of an academic, a well-read man, one who had attended college. These feelings of attraction for Jonathan were pointless. She cocked her head. Could a man draw a woman even when there was no future there? She chewed the inside of her cheek. This was all new to her. "What am I doing, Hans?" Giving herself a little shake, she focused on the task at hand and picked up her pace.

Quen slowed when the sidewalk grew crowded with busy customers. A familiar black top hat caught her eye. She raised a hand to wave at Mrs. Lancaster, then slowly lowered her arm.

She frowned. The widow stood in front of a store that hadn't opened yet, where the foot traffic was much lighter. She talked with Caleb, which wasn't unusual. But Mrs. Lancaster's expression was serious, intent. Should she interrupt their conversation or pretend she hadn't seen them? Their friendship hadn't reached that level of intimacy. She walked on.

At the bank, Quen paused. Mr. Franklin was nowhere in sight. He wouldn't dare leave her standing there. Surely, he knew she'd come to his farm to collect if he didn't show. She pulled a face at the thought. "Come on, Hans. Let's see if he arrived before us."

Tugging on the heavy bank door, she entered. She took a moment for her eyes to adjust to the subdued lighting. No sign of the farmer. A man at the teller's counter turned and caught her attention. She sucked in a breath. The man from the saloon.

Brown pants tucked inside gleaming, knee-high black boots clung to his body, revealing firm, muscled legs. His white shirt gapped open at the throat, and a black vest draped over his wide chest. "Oh, my."

Her gaze returned to his face. Once again, he caught her inspection, one amused eyebrow cocked. A lazy smile stretched his lips, and he turned to face her fully, as if he gave permission to let her gaze roam. Flustered, Quen glanced away. What on earth must he think of her? She stepped back to the door and retreated outside.

She crossed through the flow of foot traffic on the wide sidewalk and stood next to a white wooden column in front of the bank vestibule where she searched the passing faces for Mr. Franklin.

A deep voice sounded low and intimate near her ear. "Hello there, miss. I don't believe I've had the good fortune of making your acquaintance."

With a jump, Quen turned. The man from inside stood at her elbow, the same lazy smile deepening the creases around his eyes. A languid hand reached up and tipped his hat. "I'm Samuel Jenkins. To whom do I have the pleasure of speaking?"

Quen leaned away, bumping her head against the column at her back. On her right side, the edge of the sidewalk loomed, its three-foot-high drop precipitously close. His body blocked her exit to the left. He had her pinned. She'd never been trapped by a handsome man before. By any man, for that matter. Was this what other girls longed for? Should she feel flattered?

He studied her face. Everything about him seemed coated in syrup, a torpid deliberateness that disregarded the world about him. His gaze smoldered.

She stiffened with alarm, suddenly out of her league. Pulling her basket to her middle, she created a barrier between them. "Sir, please step away. You are entirely too close." Her gaze darted around the sidewalk. Did anyone watch with a censuring eye? Would someone run home to tell on her? Father would ban her from leaving the house again.

The man chuckled, his warm breath puffing against her cheek. "Sir? No one calls me sir. Call me Samuel."

Quen stared. His gaze traced her lips. Her heart pounded.

"Miss ..." He paused, eyebrows lifting in a question. He moved his hand to position his palm against the column beside her shoulder.

Quen's nerve broke. She slipped under his arm, bolting into the flow of traffic. As she turned to leave, she stumbled into Mrs. Lancaster. "Oh!" Her shoulders went limp. "Mrs. Lancaster. How lovely to see you."

"And you also, dear." Mrs. Lancaster tucked Quen's trembling hand around her arm, clasping her fingers in a comforting grip. "Do you have business at the bank today?" Her tone was light.

The stare the widow focused on the impertinent young man was anything but. "Mr. Jenkins." She nodded her head toward him in a chilly greeting. "Please, don't let us keep you." Missouri hovered close at the widow's shoulder.

Samuel's regard hardened as he took in the two women. Missouri's face tensed, chin jutting. Quen glanced between the three. What was happening? A fresh voice joined the group. "There ya are. Let's get this matter done and over with." Mr. Franklin's grumbling broke the gathering tension. "Still can't believe Campbell hired a woman to do his finances."

Samuel trained his lazy gaze on Quen. "Campbell's got money troubles?" His smile seemed less welcoming than before, more predatory.

Quen gasped. She used her best quelling stare. "Whatever gave you that ludicrous idea? He is expanding his farming exploits this season and has little time to spare. I am here to relieve him of a burden, nothing more."

Samuel stroked his clean-shaven chin. "Expanding, eh?" His scrutiny turned insolent, traveling over Missouri's face again. "He's gonna need some darkies. I can assist him with that."

The hand Mrs. Lancaster placed over Quen's tightened enough to make her jerk in surprise. Her gaze jumped between the widow and Samuel. "Darkies? Is that a type of farm animal?"

Samuel laughed, white teeth flashing as he turned back to face Quen. "More or less, Miss—"

Mrs. Lancaster made a sound in her throat, her nostrils flared in anger. "Good day, Mr. Jenkins." She turned, sending her skirts whirling. "Come ladies. Let's not keep Mr. Franklin waiting." She stood aside, tipping her chin toward the young woman at her side. "Missouri? Will you get the door, please?"

The moment Missouri stepped forward, Mrs. Lancaster placed her body between the girl and the young man in a distinctly protective gesture. Quen glanced over her shoulder as they moved toward the doorway. Samuel's hard stare lightened when her gaze met his, and that lazy grin broke through once again, heavy lids half-closing over his brown eyes. He swept his hat from his head and bowed. Her heart gave a beat of excitement.

"I still don't know your name." He called after her as they stepped away. The dark hair hanging in his eyes did little to disguise the blaze that followed her as Mrs. Lancaster tugged her inside. The door closed, cutting off the sound of his chuckle.

Mrs. Lancaster released her, and Quen placed her hand against her throat. "Mercy. Whatever was that all about?"

Mrs. Lancaster waved Mr. Franklin toward the teller. "Never you mind, Quenby. You'd do well to stay clear of that man. He's trouble."

Quen pressed a palm against the butterflies in her stomach. What kind of trouble? The memory of his warm stare heated her cheeks. "I don't understand. What did he mean about the darkies?"

Missouri leaned forward, her voice scarcely audible over the conversation surrounding them. "He meant people like me, Miss Quen. Black folks."

Quen gasped. "You mean, he wants Jonathan to buy ... is he talking about ... enslaved people?"

Mrs. Lancaster's mouth pinched as if she'd tasted a lemon. "Precisely."

Quen's gaze darted to Missouri, then back to Mrs. Lancaster. Uncertainty tripped her words. "But ..." She stumbled over the statement, fearing to offend. "But you have Missouri?"

The widow stared over her shoulder. "That is a conversation for another time and place, my dear. Ah, here comes Mr. Franklin now." A strained smile crossed her face.

Hardly able to drag her attention away from the conversation, Quen turned to the farmer. He thrust his hand toward her, bills folded in his fingers. "Here. Does that satisfy ya? Are we done?"

Quen fumbled in the basket and pulled out her prepared receipt, evading a nip from Hans. She tucked the money into her pocket. "Quite done, Mr. Franklin. Thank you kindly."

With a pained harrumph, the man turned and left, jamming his hat onto his head as he stomped away.

The three women stepped outside. Quen darted a surreptitious glance around the sidewalk. Had Mr. Jenkins left? He was nowhere to be found. The atmosphere between her and Mrs. Lancaster swelled with unspoken words. Scrambling for a new topic of conversation, she turned to Missouri. "How are the biscotti coming along?"

The young woman relaxed, smiling with pride. "I think I did a right good job with the last batch."

Quen glanced between the two. "Perhaps I could stop in for a sample on my way to Jonathan's farm."

Mrs. Lancaster tipped her head in response, a beat slower than usual. "Of course." A glance flicked to Missouri, then back. She smiled. "You've yet to meet Mortimer."

Did they share a secret? "That reminds me." Quen talked over the awkwardness that had popped up. "I now have a donkey, as well."

"You continue to surprise me." Mrs. Lancaster's laugh wasn't quite as strained as her voice had been a moment ago. "We'll take our refreshment on the back porch. Mortimer comes to the fence when he sees me."

The talk of donkeys brought Caleb to mind. Might she work up the courage to ask Mrs. Lancaster about the conversation she'd witnessed?

Mrs. Lancaster led the way to her buggy.

Quen leaned back in the wicker chair, gazing across the cultivated flower gardens of Mrs. Lancaster's backyard. "Missouri, that was amazing. You're quite good at this, you know."

Missouri's grin lit her face. "Thank you, Miss Quen. I enjoy learnin' new things." She stood, gathering plates and discarded napkins. She pulled the door open, preparing to carry the dishes into the house.

"Wait. I'll help you." Quen pushed away from the table, and one leg of her chair bumped against Hans' basket, tipping it over. The gosling tumbled out and flapped his little wings. His leg had healed more quickly than Quen imagined, and he scampered away, evading her hands. He slipped through the open door and into the house in a flash.

"Hans, you little dickens. Come back here." Quen hurried after the gosling, chasing him into Mrs. Lancaster's parlor. She bent at the waist to scoop him up as soon as he was within reach, snatching him just as he passed a large wooden buffet. He struggled, and for a moment, Quen feared she would drop him. As she juggled his wriggling body, she tripped over the edge of a rug and staggered toward the buffet. She flinched as she stumbled, anticipating a painful bump to her hip. Instead, to her shock, the furniture rolled when she collided with it, exposing a hole underneath.

Quen balanced a hand against the wall, cradling the gosling against her chest. She stared in shock at the floor, her jaw dropping open in confusion.

"Oh, dear." She turned. Mrs. Lancaster stood in the doorway, stricken. "Please forgive me, ma'am." Quen's neck flushed with heat. Missouri had gone as still as Lot's wife, her hands covering her mouth, eyes wide. Mrs. Lancaster drew a deep breath, then forced a smile to her face.

Quen swallowed, blinking rapidly.

At that moment, Hans wriggled from her hand and dropped to the rug. Without a backward glance, he disappeared through the opening in the floor.

"Hans!" Quen reached for him, but she was too late. She glanced up at Mrs. Lancaster. "Where does this go? Can we get him?" Visons of snakes curled at the bottom of a dark chasm filled her mind. She frowned. Why was the buffet covering this hole? Wouldn't Mrs. Lancaster have hired a repairman if something had damaged her floor?

"My dear ..." The widow stretched out a hand, her gaze imploring. "Please. Come sit down."

A noise from within the hole drew Quen's attention, and she kneeled, fearing for the safety of the gosling. "Hans?" She squinted, peering into the darkness underneath the buffet. "Are you OK? Please come here."

"Quenby, dear ..." Mrs. Lancaster's strained voice penetrated Quen's concern, and she glanced over her shoulder. An unexplainable tension filled the room.

Peep, peep, peep.

Quen turned back, leaning farther over the hole. "Are you hurt, little goose? Come back to me so I can ..." She gasped and sat back on her heels, staring into space, thinking furiously. "Oh, my."

Quen faced Mrs. Lancaster and Missouri. Words failed her.

The older woman forced a trembling smile. "I see you've stumbled, quite literally, onto our little secret."

Chapter Twelve

Jonathan swept his hat from his head and wiped grit from his sweat-dampened face. Dirt rested in the creases of his pants and collected under his fingernails. But the same breeze kicking up dust from the freshly plowed pasture cooled the moisture on his brow. He rubbed his eyes for the millionth time. Felt like he had sandpaper under his lids. *But thank you for the cool wind, Lord.*

God seemed to answer his prayers. Preparing the new field had gone without a hitch. No broken tools, no injured animals. He'd drawn upon a verse in Joshua every day, sometimes multiple times a day, following the delivery of the pounds and pounds of seed. "I will not be afraid. I will not be discouraged, for you are with me wherever I go." He took a deep breath and whispered to the sky. "Forgive me for repeating the words, Lord. Sometimes, I gotta remind myself that surely you are my God, and I trust in you."

Teddy approached, walking beside his beloved Percheron. "You did good work today, Benny." The heavy draft horse's head drooped as he plodded along. Tackling and taming native prairie into a crop-producing field was backbreaking work. Ernest followed close behind, his mules damp with sweat as well. They walked together to the barn. The scrawny little donkey Quen had dumped on him hee-hawed her welcome as they approached.

"Whew. Glad that's done." Teddy sighed. "What's next, boss? Still planting cotton out here?"

"We're spreading ourselves pretty thin, Jon." Ernest frowned. "Will you be bringing on any new hands then? Happy I am that we're broadening our horizons, but my back is tired, and that's a fact."

I am with you wherever you go.

The lies Jonathan told suddenly carried the weight of a buffalo. He squeezed his eyes shut, said a prayer, then faced the men. He couldn't hold his secrets any longer. His lies and lack of trust showed disrespect, and these men had been nothing but honorable in their years of service to his father and his family. They deserved the truth. As did his mother and siblings. "Fellas, I have a confession. I didn't mean to order so much seed. I—" Words caught in his throat.

Do not be afraid.

"I have trouble reading and writing. Sometimes, letters and numbers mix up in my head. I thought I ordered twenty-nine bags of corn, not ninety-two." The words tumbled out in a rush, like a backed-up river flowing over a broken dam. "I had just enough money in the bank to pay Mr. Nelson."

He searched their faces. His chest tightened. Ernest, in his typical stoic manner, simply raised his eyebrows.

Teddy sucked in a breath. "Ninety-two instead of twenty-nine?" He paused, doing math in his head. "Boss, that's a heckuva lot of new ground to turn. I mean, I'm game, but can we actually handle that?"

"We could plow up every inch of this land before we used all that seed." Jonathan acknowledged Teddy's comment. "I know the solution isn't practical, but it's all I could think to do."

"*Ach, jüngling*. That's quite a burden to carry alone. Glad am I you've told us." Ernest clapped a hand on Jonathan's shoulder. "Now I understand many things I've noticed." He tilted his head. "I suppose pay will be late?"

Although his face burned, Jonathan breathed easily for the first time in days. "Yes. I'm sorry. We won't have cash until we see the harvest. I'll make things up to you, somehow. Not sure how, but I'll think of something."

Teddy shrugged. "Not like we're plannin' to go anywhere to spend that money. This is the busy season on a farm. Keep us fed and a roof over our heads, and we can wait till harvest." He paused. Rolling his shoulders back, he spoke. "I've been thinking about asking you this for a while. Maybe now is the time." Teddy drew a deep breath. "I'd like to discuss the option of sharecropping. Like what you did with Mr. Garner."

He hurried on, as though afraid Jonathan would stop him before he got the words out. "There's a nice spot in the back corner of your property, fed by an arm of the creek and clear of trees. If you agree to let me work the plot, we both win. I earn extra income from the crops I harvest, and you have another section of land broken in. I know it'd have to stay small because I'd spend most of my time working on your farm for you." He patted Benny's sweaty neck. "I think he's got enough strength left at day's end to go a while longer." He paused. "I'd use your seed, so I'd pay you more than the amount you arranged with Garner." Lips pressed together, he entreated with his eyes.

"It's not a bad plan, Jon." Ernest nodded slowly. "The land'll still be yours. And you'll reap the reward at the end."

"Just think about it." Teddy shrugged.

Light-headedness swamped Jonathan. They weren't angry. They wouldn't leave. Shaky laughter escaped in a puff. "Sure, I'll consider your plan, Teddy. I need to talk with Ma first, though." His gaze fell on Phoenix. Maybe Quen too.

Later, after they took care of the animals, Jonathan stood at the corral, one foot propped on the bottom rail, forearms resting against the top one. The scent of sauerkraut heating on the stove for dinner wafted from the house behind him. His stomach growled. The sharecropping idea bounced around his mind as he considered the pros and cons. He gazed at the brown rows of dirt which waited for the coming harvest. Could Teddy manage the extra time without sacrificing his effort on the farm? Jonathan would need every moment of every day to pull this off as it was.

A nudge pushed his fingers. Phoenix's long white nose snuffled at his hands, head tilted back as she reached for him, ears laying against her neck. Her warm brown eyes watched him.

"What?" He ruffled the bristly mane on her neck. "Getting around better now that Caleb fixed those hooves?" He peeked over his shoulder. Did anyone watch? "Phoenix." Snorting, he inspected her over the rails. "What a ridiculous name for such a scraggly critter. You're going to eat me out of house and home, aren't you, making up time for Garner's treatment? And how will you ever pay me back?"

Giving the donkey one last pat on her wide forehead, Jonathan stepped back. He followed the appetizing scent of sauerkraut into the kitchen. Time to face the music—and his mother.

Quen perched on the edge of a chair at Mrs. Lancaster's table, Hans safely back in his basket, palms pressed together, hands trapped between trembling knees. Shock was too mild a word to describe her feelings. More like how one must feel after surviving an earthquake. No. A meteor. When her gaze met the frightened eyes of the Black man in the cellar, she froze.

Mrs. Lancaster held herself stiffly, but the wringing of her hands gave her away. Missouri's ashy face held something approaching terror. Quen hardly registered their reactions, her mind working feverishly to piece the puzzle parts together.

"Quenby, dear. One hates to be wary or distrustful, but we must settle this matter before you leave my home." The widow's voice trembled almost as much as Quen's knees. "Lives are at stake, you see."

Comments and actions from the past few days coalesced. She stiffened as a realization swept her.

"Caleb is involved, isn't he?" She turned her gaze upon Mrs. Lancaster, finally zeroing in on the words spoken by her host. "Lives are at stake, you said. Yours. His. Missouri's. The life of that man hiding in your basement." She swallowed. Spoke with reservation. "And now mine."

"Dearest girl, I never intended to draw you into this. But now that you're here—"

"That day we saw you in front of Caleb's farm ..." Quen interrupted the widow. "Missouri had tears in her eyes. You tucked something into your glove. What did you plan?" Her gaze bounced from one tense face to the other, then over at the sideboard buffet, now restored to its rightful spot, covering the passage to the cellar. "Who is down there?"

Mrs. Lancaster's mouth firmed, and she laid a palm on the table. "Quenby, you are undoubtedly burning with questions, but I cannot satisfy your curiosity until I know where you stand. People have placed their trust in me. Not to sound dramatic, but I hold their very lives in my hands. Every detail I share carries the potential for disaster if heard by the wrong ears."

Awareness struck. "You're afraid I'll let your secret slip?"

Mrs. Lancaster met her gaze squarely. "It would be so easy. We are constantly on alert." She waved a hand toward the front door. "The society in which we live relies on free labor by unwilling participants to sustain it. One either places a higher value on maintaining that society ..." She cocked an eyebrow. "Or one believes in the unshakable truth that a human being owns him or herself. That one may choose one's own path in life." She paused, sending a probing gaze. "The desire for such a right I'm sure you're familiar with."

"Surely you don't think I believe in slavery?" Quen's words burst from her in a heartfelt declaration.

"No, dear girl. I do not. I pride myself on being an excellent judge of character. The very moment you sat in that chair after accepting my invitation to tea with your mother and sister, I believed in your goodness. But this is a hard secret to keep."

Quen subsided. "Then why do you doubt me?"

"Knowing a thing in my heart and hearing you speak that truth out loud are two different things. Quenby, you must understand. People have been murdered for the mere act of offering sustenance to an enslaved person attempting escape. This burden I have accidentally placed on your shoulders is no small thing to bear."

"But you bear it." She flung a hand toward Missouri. "And you. And I'm quite certain, so does Caleb. Not to mention those trying to escape a life of slavery."

"This is so. However, we made our own choices years ago. You did not. Your involvement was never meant to be."

Mrs. Lancaster's words rang a bell in Quen's memory. Excitement thrummed through her veins. The story of Esther filled her mind. *For if thou altogether holdest thy peace at this time ... deliverance may arise from another place ... whether thou art come to the kingdom for such a time as this?* She gripped the table's edge to steady herself.

"Or maybe it was." Quen stared at the widow. "I've been at a loss. I need an aspiration, a goal to accomplish. Why are each of us here, if not to serve some greater purpose?" She shook her head. "There must be more to the life of a woman than dressing up and attending teas."

Leaning forward, she earnestly clasped the widow's hand. "Let me help you."

Mrs. Lancaster covered Quen's hands with her free one. She glanced over her shoulder at Missouri, whose tense face had relaxed slightly. "Having you confirm my belief in you was not misplaced gratifies my heart. You cannot breathe a word of this to anyone." She squeezed Quen's fingers and peered at her as if she could read her very soul. "And I mean anyone."

The widow leaned back, her tension easing slightly. "Now. You must carry on today as if none of this has happened. I will speak to Caleb. We'll let you know when and how you can help. Quenby, dear girl, this is not a game. What we have committed our lives to is full of danger. Understand, you will be in harm's way."

Quen bit her lip. *For such a time as this.* She lifted her chin. "I'm not afraid."

The women stood. Missouri wrapped Quen in her embrace. "Thank you, my friend. May God rain favor on you for generations to come."

Quen leaned into Missouri, returning the hug. A small frown pinched her brow. The weight of the dilemma entrusted to her suddenly dragged like a chain around her neck. Could she keep this secret? She glanced at Mrs. Lancaster. She would learn from the best.

Chapter Thirteen

Jonathan glanced up from cleaning a headstall in the tack room. He winced at the sound of Phoenix's strident braying. Better than any guard dog, that one. Her noisy heehawing had a particularly annoying clamor this time, though. What could have her so riled?

"Hello?"

Jonathan put down the wagon rigging at Quen's inquiry. He sighed. Of course. Phoenix welcomed her rescuer. Quen moved through the open barn door.

Trapped. She blocked the only way out unless he planned to climb through a stall and sneak into the paddock. "Back here. In the tack room."

What could she want now? As she moved in, he scrutinized her. Muscles that had tensed at her arrival loosened. She'd come with only the basket on her arm. No new critters for him to feed.

She stepped farther into the barn. Pausing in the second doorway, her gaze took in the neatly hung bits of leather and braces in the small room. "Goodness. Is all this for the horses?"

Jonathan snorted. She couldn't know everything. "Horses and mules." He nodded toward a wooden yoke. "That's for oxen if we had any. When the last pair died, we didn't replace them. Horses work faster." He continued working, rubbing the leather in his hands with an oil-soaked rag. "What can I do for you, Miss Martin?"

He hid his grin at her pressed lips. Poker would never be her game. Her face showed every emotion. She didn't like being kept at arm's length with his politeness. She didn't answer right away but bent at the waist and slid the gosling—more like a goose every day—onto the ground. "Have you figured out if the goose is a he or a she yet?" Wry humor colored his words.

She narrowed her eyes at him. "I'm not entirely certain, although I believe him to be male. Time will tell." She tossed her head. "I didn't come here to discuss Hans."

Straightening, she clasped her hands in front of her. "I have some news for you, and also some ideas I'd like to discuss." Hans waddled to the open door and disappeared around the corner. "May we speak outside?" She was already moving to follow the wayward gosling.

Of course, Your Highness. Her wish was his command. Rolling his eyes, Jonathan put the rag down and trailed Quen, watching her move away. Why did she always walk so briskly, as if she had a list of important things to do? Her slim hips swayed with each step. The length of her skirt undoubtedly hid long, slender legs. Legs that might—

Appalled, he shook his head to rid himself of his wayward thoughts. Criminy! Where had that come from? He didn't find her attractive, for heaven's sake.

Squinting in the sunlight, he stopped several feet away, as if distance could prevent a recurrence of his imaginings. He propped his hands on his hips and waited.

With an annoyed tsk, Quen stepped closer, reaching into her pocket. "First, I have Mr. Franklin's payment for the stud service provided almost two years ago." She handed him a folded pile of bills.

Jonathan took the money, gratitude battling with an injured ego. *Pride goeth before destruction, and a haughty spirit before a fall.* "Thank you." He dipped his chin toward her, then slipped the bills into his breast pocket.

Her annoyance softened at his gratitude. "Second, I'd like to inspect your milking setup. In Nigeria, the women competed to come up with the most flavorful butters. If you have a sufficient supply of milk, perhaps Mrs. Campbell and I could experiment with some seasoning of our own, using the herbs and spices available in Texas."

"What are we going to do with fancy butter?" Jonathan frowned.

"Sell it, of course. We can start at the Menger Hotel, then inquire at the Veramendi Palace. We shall work our way through town."

Jonathan arched his eyebrows. How would Ma feel about that? The wad of cash sat like a lump in his pocket. He shrugged. Give Quen what she wanted. She'd already brought him a quarter of what he'd overspent. Belle might be excited to help.

"Follow me." He turned toward the cattle barn. Hans ruffled his feathers at him as he passed. "Settle down," Jonathan muttered.

Quen stopped beside the grain silo. "What's this?" She pointed to a brown pile on the ground.

"Cotton seed we pulled out of the bolls last year."

"Why is it lying here to rot?"

"We kept what we needed for planting this year. The rest is trash."

"Au contraire." Her voice was a mixture of excitement and scolding. "In point of fact, you may feed cotton seed to your cattle. It has a very high fat content and will greatly enrich their milk."

Jonathan's hackles raised. Gritting his teeth to keep from saying something rude, he shook his head. "Cotton seed causes abortion in cows."

Quen shrugged. "Then don't feed it to the ones who are carrying a calf. The women in Nigeria did this all the time. The difference in the butterfat content of your milk will amaze you." She turned to the pile. "Let's rake this into a thin layer to dry. You can start adding it to their feed tomorrow." She frowned. "Didn't I see on Mr. Nelson's receipt that you ordered cotton seed? Why would you pay for more when you had this here?"

Jonathan flushed at the implied criticism. He knew how to run a farm. She didn't. "That order was a last-minute decision. Cotton brings in good money, especially now with higher demands caused by the war, if I can find somewhere to sell the bales. I decided to plant more this year, but I figured this seed had gone bad. You'll find piles like this all over the countryside. Farmers consider them worthless."

Quen tapped one finger against her chin. He'd seen that move before. She was thinking. His nerves kicked in. Now what?

"Perhaps we could offer our services to the other farmers to remove their cotton seed piles. You'll go through this quickly once you start feeding it to the milkers. Second," she paused, cocking her head in question, "how do you plan to sell your cotton? When we were in Galveston, the Union Army had barricaded the port. No goods moved in or out of the harbor. Who will buy it from you?"

A grin tugged at his lips, and he gave a wicked chuckle. Quen's eyes widened, and her gaze focused on his mouth. Something twisted inside his gut at the look. Why did she suddenly look interested in a ... flirty sort of way? As heat climbed his neck, he coughed, then forged ahead with his answer. "I have a plan of my own for that. Still working out details. Or the war could end. Whichever comes first."

A look that might be admiration crossed Quen's face.

What was going on in that head of hers? He narrowed his eyes, waiting, but she said nothing more.

"Let's check your milking setup, shall we?" She whirled around and continued toward the cattle barn, followed by the devoted Hans.

Relieved to be freed from her scrutiny for the moment, he shook his head. He followed Quen and those slim hips again. Where had these sudden thoughts and feelings come from, and how could he make them go away?

Quen sat in Abby's kitchen, sipping a mug of coffee. "Mrs. Campbell can sell her butter to the restaurants in town if we concoct a way to make them extraordinary, like the women in Nigeria." She raised her voice so Abby could hear her from the bedroom. "They created different flavors by incorporating various spices. Do you have time to help me run through a practice batch?"

Abby returned to the kitchen after checking on the sleeping babies. "We should ask Manny's grandmother, Yaideli. She's better at all that than I am. When the twins wake up, we'll head over and ask. Manny should be here any moment for lunch. Eat with us?"

"Thanks. I'd love to."

The back door opened to reveal Manny toeing his boots off on the porch. "Speak of the devil." Abby greeted her husband with a quick kiss. "Perfect timing. Dinner is on the table. Quen is joining us today."

"Afternoon, Quen." Manny shot her a quick smile as he headed to the sink to wash his hands. He placed his hat on the counter. "What are y'all up to this afternoon?"

"Just visiting." Abby gestured to his chair, then sat in hers. "Sit down and eat, husband."

The next twenty minutes passed quickly as they ate and chatted about their plans for their farm.

Manny pushed away from the table. "Thank you for a delicious lunch, Mrs. Blair." He bent and pressed a quick kiss to her mouth. "Gotta get back to work." He paused just outside the doorway to pull his boots back on, then strode toward the barn.

Abby and Quen stood to clear the table. "He forgot his hat." Abby grabbed it and pushed the door open. "Manny, wait." She jogged the few steps to meet him.

Quen glanced through the open door, then froze, mesmerized by the tableau in front of her. Manny halfway faced the house, but his gaze fastened on Abby. She caught up to him and waved his hat at his head, saying something low that made him laugh. He reached for her, and his hands cupped her backside. Pulling her toward him, he flattened her hips against his thighs. His pelvis pressed possessively against her belly.

Abby looped her hands with careless ease around Manny's neck, the hat dangling, seemingly forgotten, from her fingers. The hunger on Manny's face as he stared at his wife stopped Quen's breath. Possessive, loving, caressing. Her heart resumed its pattern with a lurching thump. She eased back into the room before either of them noticed her presence.

She buried envy and longing deep down inside. If she could be certain her life with a husband would be like their life, and not like her parents', she'd be happy to marry. But what certainty could a person have?

A picture of Jonathan filled her mind. A small thrill of excitement quickened in her belly. Then reality closed in.

She wasn't a homesteader.

He didn't like books.

A picture of life with him, mucking stalls, performing backbreaking labor, sitting silently in front of a fire in the winter when the light failed early, scratched at her pleasant dream. What would they talk about? Her musings about a future husband had always revolved around an intelligent man, someone to challenge her. Regret tugged. Too bad Jonathan didn't seem to fit the bill.

When she peeked back outside, a safe space had appeared between the two lovers. Manny grinned rakishly at his wife, white teeth flashing in his brown face, then he jammed the hat onto his head.

"Many thanks, wife."

"My pleasure, husband." Abby's return smile held mysterious secrets.

Quen tossed her head. She had secrets of her own now. And a purpose that held meaning. It would be enough. Now, if Mrs. Lancaster and Caleb would just deal her in. Eager excitement fluttered in her stomach. *For such a time as this.*

Chapter Fourteen

Quen sat at the dining table in Yaideli's front room, fidgeting. Late-morning sun streamed through the window behind her, creating a square of light on the floor. The room offered a homey welcome with its bright yellow-and-blue decorations.

Abby had arranged a day of butter-making lessons with her Hispanic grandmother-in-law, and Quen was eager to absorb the older woman's knowledge. Yaideli stepped outside to collect milk from its cool storage spot in her well.

Mother could undoubtedly give this same lesson, but the fewer opportunities she had to ask about Quen's activities as a fledgling financial advisor, the better. So far, Quen always came home with a wildflower or two she'd picked along the way and immediately seated herself at her desk to sketch and then paint what she'd found. If Mother ever bothered to talk to Quen and discovered she was working, God forbid, she'd probably bring the entire enterprise crashing to a halt. She would confine her to activities with Prissy. And if that happened, the opportunity to help Mrs. Lancaster and Caleb would vanish. If Quen found herself in that position, she wouldn't lie to Mother. At least, she didn't think she would.

A knock sounded. Who else joined them? Abby hurried to the door with a welcoming smile. Quen's heartbeat jumped when Missouri entered, followed by a girl who appeared to be about sixteen. Quen's gaze met Missouri's. Her first test. Could she act normally around her secret abolitionist partner?

Abby ushered them to the table. "I invited Missouri to join us. She's always learning how to cook new things." She placed her hand on the other girl's shoulder. "This is Sarah, practically my sister. We traveled to San Antonio together on the same wagon train."

The girls shared a smile. The familiarity between them stabbed Quen with envy. She didn't have a friend like that in her life, at least, she hadn't in the past. Maybe that was changing. "Sarah is the oldest of three. She and her younger siblings, Frank and Coral, live with Pastor Green and his wife."

An excited grin spread across Sarah's face. "I've recently started a job at Mrs. Carter's boarding house. She's teaching me to help cook. I thought this would be a fun thing to know. She might want to use the butters with her meals."

Missouri moved toward the small room that served as the kitchen and peered through the doorway. "Where's Miss Yaideli?"

"She's fetching the milk from her well." Abby glanced into the cooking area.

"I'll see if she needs any help." Missouri disappeared. A door creaked open, then slammed shut.

Quen breathed a sigh of relief. No need to worry about awkward silences. When Missouri returned with Yaideli, the lesson would begin.

She studied Sarah. The girl had pale skin, a freckled nose, and strawberry-blonde hair in a tidy braid she'd wrapped around her head and pinned into place like a tiara.

Sarah returned the look with a quiet smile. "Abby said you've moved to San Antonio only recently?"

"Yes. We've been here a few weeks." She cocked her head. "You traveled here on the wagon train with Abby?"

The story Abby had shared with Quen involved eight other children, orphaned by cholera, forced to finish the journey to Texas alone. Sarah seemed too meek to withstand the rigors of a trip like that. She must have hidden strengths.

Abby spoke up from where she leaned against the doorframe to the kitchen. "She was our cook most of the way. She's pretty good at it. I thought she and Missouri should get to know each other."

Indistinct conversation announced the return of Missouri and Yaideli.

The older woman called the others to the kitchen. She and Missouri lugged a cup-towel-covered bucket. Yaideli thumped it onto the worktable next to her sink.

"Abby, did you wipe down the churn?"

"Yes, ma'am. It's right here and ready to go." Abby pushed the wooden barrel closer to the worktable.

Quen studied the churn. The one Mother used was similar.

Yaideli reached for a large flat spoon. "This milk has had time to separate. We're gonna scoop off the fat that rose to the top." She drew the utensil through the milk with a steady hand. Cream built up like the swell of a wave. She dropped the rich thickness into the barrel with a splat. After continuing until only small bits bobbed on the surface of the milk, she replaced the towel and pushed the bucket aside.

Quen peered into the barrel. A pint of cream covered the bottom of the churn. "How much butter will this produce?"

"Half a pound." Yaideli placed the dasher-staff into the barrel, then slid the lid over the pole, settling it against the lip. "We move this up and down, stirring the cream with the dasher. The liquid separates, creating a clump of butter. After that, we wash the buttermilk off the butter with water to prevent spoilage." She leaned back, one hand on her hip, one balancing the pole. "Who wants to go first?"

The four young ladies grinned at each other. Missouri raised her hand. "I'll go."

Forty-five minutes later, one bowl held buttermilk, and another held a large clump of washed butter.

Yaideli plopped the pale-yellow creaminess onto a piece of wax-coated fabric.

"Now we add the special flavors. Do you want savory *o dulce*?"

"Can we do both?" Quen asked.

"*Por supuesto*. For sweet, I add a splash of *vainilla* and a spoonful of honey." She divided the mound of butter into two sections, then placed one back into the bowl with the sweeteners. Sarah stirred the ingredients until the color was consistent and the texture smooth.

"Scrape that onto the waxed cloth," said Yaideli.

Quen ran her finger around the bowl and snuck a taste. "Mmm, this is delicious."

Yaideli pulled two wooden butter paddles from the cabinet and patted them against the sides of the yellow mound until she formed a square. She wrapped the finished butter in the waxed cloth and set it aside.

They repeated the process, adding thyme, rosemary, and garlic to the savory batch. Quen's mouth watered at the smell of the herbs.

Abby frowned. "Will you have enough cream to make this worth your while?"

"We're feeding cotton seed to the milkers to enrich the output of Jonathan's cows."

Abby clapped her hands. "I like it! I won't be able to help, but if Sarah comes and Belle pitches in, you could get quite a bit done in one day."

Quen nodded with satisfaction. "I need to talk with Jonathan and Mrs. Campbell, then we can start. Thank you, Yaideli, for teaching us."

"*Mucho gusto, niñas*. Come again any time."

In the front yard, Abby and Sarah climbed into Abby's buggy. "Missouri, I'll take Sarah back home."

Missouri mounted the small bay Quen had seen her ride before. "OK, Miss Abby. I'll be fine riding to Mrs. Lancaster's on my own. Besides, she wants me to stop at Caleb's farm on the way back. Y'all go on ahead."

"Quen, care to join us? I want to visit Frank and Coral. You could meet them." Abby waited.

"I think I'll walk with Missouri to Caleb's. I have a question about Phoenix's care." Quen shot a glance toward Missouri. Had that sounded like the lie it was?

"All right. We're off."

Sarah called over her shoulder as the buggy drove away. "Let me know when you're ready to start churning. I'll be there."

Quen and Missouri waved as the buggy rattled down the drive, leaving a plume of dust in its trail.

Quiet descended.

"Can you ride a horse, Miss Quen?"

Quen frowned. "Please, call me Quen. No need for formalities."

Resignation crossed the young woman's face. "It's better if I don't, Miss Quen. Never know when someone is listening."

Quen dropped her gaze to the ground, arguments forming in her mind. Then she sighed. She'd do nothing to put Missouri in danger. The tone of Sam Jenkins's voice at the bank as he'd uttered the word *darkie* at the bank passed through her mind. She shivered. No, it wouldn't do to draw his attention. Or anyone else's.

"So, Miss Quen. Can you ride?"

"I can. Not well. Is it proper if you ride in front? I'd be more comfortable if you had control."

Missouri smiled. She twisted at the waist and patted the bay's rump. "We can do that."

"OK, Miss Missouri." Quen mimicked her slow Southern drawl and stretched a hand up to grasp the young woman's. Missouri tugged, and Quen pulled herself to a seat, perching sideways behind the saddle. "Let's go."

On the road, the horse moved at a leisurely pace. Quen screwed up her courage and plunged into the questions that had plagued her since the afternoon in Mrs. Lancaster's house.

"How long have you and Mrs. Lancaster helped enslaved people escape?"

Missouri laughed. "You've been dyin' to ask about our secret since I walked through Yaideli's door, haven't you? I could see it on your face."

"More like since I discovered that man in Mrs. Lancaster's basement. Tell me, please."

"Mrs. Lancaster's had a spot in her heart for enslaved folks since she married her husband and discovered he owned people." She huffed. "Imagine believing one person has the right to own another person. As if we're nothing more than draft horses or cows."

Quen gasped. "Her husband owned slaves? How did she not know that?"

"They met in Philadelphia. He courted her there when he traveled. She discovered his property when she arrived at his family plantation in South Carolina as a new bride." Bitterness dripped from her voice.

Quen shook her head. "What a crushing disappointment for her. What did she do?"

"She made friends with a young Black man named Caleb who had a small family."

"Our Caleb?"

"Yes. The master trusted him, gave him quite a bit of freedom." Missouri spat as if the word *master* was a bug that'd flown into her mouth. "Caleb often traveled into town to run errands and such. Mrs. Lancaster accompanied him most times. He drove the carriage for her. They spent hours together, driving back and forth to town. Lots of chances to talk with no danger of a busybody to listen in." She chuckled. "I doubt they talked about makin' butter."

"Did she have ... feelings for Caleb?" Quen chose her words carefully.

"Not like what you're askin'. He was married, loved his wife and two daughters. She could see he was intelligent. Seeing him treated the way he was hurt her. She ached to help him, to help all of them, but didn't know how. Her husband wasn't a nice man, at least, not to his property."

"How do you know what Mrs. Lancaster thought or felt?" Quen leaned closer to Missouri's back.

"She told me the entire story much later, after I lived with her here. I wasn't even born when she first met Caleb."

"You lived on the plantation too?"

"Yes'm. My parents were owned by Mr. Lancaster. My mama worked in the kitchen. Black children had the run of the place until they were six. I mostly stayed under my mama's feet."

"Six? Surely, they didn't send children to the fields?" Outrage filled Quen's voice.

"No. They gave children small jobs, like shellin' peas or pickin' tomatoes from the garden near the house. Or dusting, sweeping, drying dishes that'd been washed. The foreman didn't send us to the fields until we were ten years old or so. Sooner if we were big and strong."

"Facing that every day must have been difficult."

Missouri sucked her teeth. "You don't know the half of it. The enslaved folks who worked in the fields lived in constant fear of the lash."

"Why did he whip them? What could they possibly do that was bad enough to deserve that?"

A mirthless chuckle lifted Missouri's shoulders. "Anything could bring the lash. A man could be five minutes late to his post in the cotton field. A pregnant woman might need to sit for a moment, to rest her back. A person picking cotton could break the stem holding a boll that hadn't bloomed yet. All depended on the mood of the foreman, the man who held the whip."

"Unbelievable." Quen murmured the word as she gazed unseeingly across the field they passed, pictures flowing through her mind. Memories of her own life at ten years old replaced the uncomfortable thoughts. She'd spent her days splashing in the cool river near their home, being coddled by her Nigerian aunties, learning to weave baskets from dried corn leaves. Always loved. Never terrified. She thought of Jonathan's farm. Gratitude filled her heart. He would never presume to own a human being.

"Mrs. Lancaster taught me my ABCs when I was four. Mr. Lancaster slapped her when he caught us one morning.

My mama told me later that night something died in the mistress that day. Said she was never the same."

"He slapped his own wife?" Quen stiffened in outrage. "I cannot imagine Mrs. Lancaster allowing that to stand. What did she do?"

Missouri's chuckle this time was heartfelt. "Well, first off, Mrs. Lancaster continued teaching me my ABCs, only we got sneakier. She'd scatter flour across the table in the kitchen, and I'd trace the letters with my finger. Once or twice, he came by and found us there, but she kept a ball of dough handy. She'd wipe her fingers through my tracings and plop the dough down on the table, get the rolling pin going. He demanded to know why she was in the kitchen working. That's what we were for, after all. She said she was sharing a family recipe with my mama, teaching her how to make something new."

Quen focused on the neat lines of black dirt in the field to their left, green seedlings poking through the top swell of each row. Birds sang, crickets chirped, a breeze stirred the leaves of the trees growing at the field's edge. The idyllic scene was peaceful. She tried to imagine a life where she poured sweat and tears into a project she would never reap, believing she had no future.

The idea repulsed her. An understanding of Missouri's willingness to risk punishment should Mr. Lancaster catch her memorizing her letters again grew. "You learned to read?"

Missouri nodded. "Mama watched over our shoulder, and I'd practice at home using a stick to trace letters in the dirt. She learned with me."

"Did Mr. Lancaster figure out your mother could read?"

Missouri nodded. "I heard my parents talking one night, after my sister and I had gone to bed. They discussed runnin' away. Mama told Papa she could write a letter that looked like Mrs. Lancaster gave us permission to be out. Sending a favored worker into town wasn't uncommon. But to be out after dark was risky. Any White man could stop a Black man to inquire about his business. The low Whites took pleasure in stopping Black folks, lordin' their power over them."

"Low Whites?"

Missouri snorted. "They weren't worth much, but in their eyes, they were better'n us, and they never let anyone forget it. Didn't matter if you were doing anything wrong or not. If they stopped you, you stopped." The hand resting on Missouri's thigh clenched into a fist. "And they weren't nice to young girls. Mama wanted us to be free. We'd heard stories that Black families lived like White folks in the North, where Mrs. Lancaster came from."

She drew a breath and stared straight ahead. After a moment, she continued. "So, Mama asked her about it once. After learning there was a place in this world where we could lead the lives we wanted, Mama couldn't get the thought out of her head."

"What would happen if anyone figured out your mother forged that letter?"

Missouri went silent for so long, Quen feared she'd offended her somehow. Finally, she answered, her voice cracking with emotion.

"They whipped her so hard she died. Mr. Lancaster sold my daddy and older sister in a fit of rage. Mrs. Lancaster demanded to keep me, saying I'd be her personal maid."

Horror congealed in Quen's throat. Nausea made her dizzy. She wrapped her arms around Missouri and hugged tightly. "I'm so sorry." The inadequate whisper couldn't convey the sorrow Quen experienced for the young woman.

Missouri breathed a long, shaky breath. "Not long after that, Mr. Lancaster took sick and died. Mrs. Lancaster freed all the enslaved folks living on the plantation and sold the land. She came to Texas because she'd heard the farmers out West didn't have slaves, leastwise not at the level of the tobacco and cotton plantations. She spent a lot of time tracking down Caleb. When she finally found him, she bought him from his owner. Now, we're tryin' to find my sister, Nora."

We? Quen straightened as sudden understanding dawned. "Missouri, is Caleb your father?"

Chapter Fifteen

Lantern light filled Jonathan's study, casting a warm glow over his desk as he studied his morning devotional. He traced a fingertip along the fine print in Pa's Bible. He knew the words by heart, which made reading easy. Pa had led the family in lessons most evenings. His slow, deep voice had etched many verses in Jonathan's mind.

Picking up where he'd left off the day before, Jonathan continued. A focus sharpened in his heart. He paused. Years ago, he'd learned to trust that still, small voice.

"Speak to me, Lord. I'm listening."

He read the verses more carefully. *That, if any obey not the word, they also may without the word be won by the conversation of the wives.*

"God, I don't understand. I don't have a wife, and I already believe in your Word. Why show me this verse?"

An image of Quen filled his mind. He frowned. "Um, where are we going with this?"

May be won.

Quen wouldn't leave his thoughts. He stared unseeingly across the study. Often, she seemed discontent. The brittle quality of her voice when she practically *flung* Bible quotes at him while making her case for Phoenix rang in his ears. In contrast, the moment in the hallway, surrounded by the Campbell clan, brought joy to her face.

Understanding appeared.

"She doesn't know you like I do. Is this what you're telling me?"

May be won by the conversation of wives.

Jonathan shook his head. "And I'm to play the part of the wife?" He squinted at the ceiling. Disgruntled, he read further.

But let it be the ornament of a meek and quiet spirit, which is in the sight of God of great price.

A quiet spirit. God could use him. But to serve Quen this way meant opening up to her, inviting her in. A relationship would develop. He sucked his teeth as a memory surfaced of watching Manny sweat his way through courtship with Abby.

"God, I'm not interested. Can't Abby do this for her? Wouldn't that make more sense?"

Silence filled his mind.

"You pulling my leg?" His spirit wasn't as quiet as he'd originally thought.

He gazed out the window of the study, where rays from the approaching sun lightened the horizon. Peace filled him, the same emotion that had comforted him when Pa died.

"Everyone should experience this, Father." He sighed. "Even her. Especially her."

More memories popped into his mind. Now that he allowed himself the permission to notice her, to actually see her, shame flooded him. He should've realized things sooner.

Why was she so eager to serve him and his family? Did she search for a sense of worth?

Why did she hide behind her big vocabulary when nerves attacked? Did she lack self-confidence?

She was very proper, followed all the rules. *Can't earn your way into heaven, girl.* Salvation was a gift.

He returned his gaze to the book and read to the end of the section.

But knowing that ye are thereunto called, that ye should inherit a blessing.

Give a blessing, get a blessing.

He bowed his head, closing his eyes. "Lord, I ask for your help. You know Quen prickles, and her quills irritate. Help me, Father, to see her through your eyes. Give me your words and your heart. Use me."

He straightened, determined. Helping Quen see God might help him too. He'd been far too worried lately. Time to give the financial situation over to God and trust in his guidance through this particular valley. Calm covered his shoulders like a blanket as he stood and headed outside.

The moment he stepped through the door onto the porch, a raucous noise greeted him.

Hee-haw.

His newly found calm evaporated like dewy mists before the sun. Jonathan glared toward the fence where Phoenix propped her long jaw across the top railing. She bellowed at him a second time when he met her gaze.

"Enough." He hissed through his teeth. He stomped to the fence but smiled despite himself once he arrived. Her long ears perked forward, and her ropey tail snapped back and forth like a dog's. Her nostrils flared and snuffled at the hand he slid down her nose. Whiskers pricked him, and lips as soft as velvet nibbled at his fingers. He scratched the wide place between her liquid eyes, chuckling.

"Mornin', glory. How're those feet today?"

She lowered her nose, butting his hand with her head, begging for more scratches. As he obliged her, thoughts from his morning study resurfaced.

Quen valued animals. One way to affirm her was to support her efforts instead of belittling her. "If I do this,

God, I don't want my farm to turn into Noah's ark." He snorted. Since when had bargaining with God worked?

Giving Phoenix a final pat, he turned toward the barn. Teddy's voice rumbled from inside. Ernest's lilting German accent answered. The men prepared to start the day.

"Teddy," Jonathan called as he passed through the doorway. "I have an answer about sharecropping. We'll discuss details over breakfast."

Between pancakes and coffee, Jonathan and Ma outlined which part of the property they agreed to lease. Ernest studied the map Jonathan sketched, nodding in approval.

"It's a *gut* deal, Teddy." Ernest encouraged the young man. "By the time you've saved enough, you'll have worked the land well. It'll be an easy move, should that day come."

Quen filled Jonathan's thoughts again. What changes might happen in her life if she grew to love God?

As if his thoughts conjured her, a knock sounded. Creaky hinges announced the opening of the door, and Quen's voice called from the front room. "Good morning. Anybody home?"

"We're in the kitchen," Belle called. "Come have breakfast."

"Stay here, Hans. Be a good boy." Her low voice floated down the hallway.

Jonathan resisted the urge to roll his eyes. He'd be supportive.

She walked into the kitchen, smiling at Belle and Bay. Her expression grew uncertain when her gaze touched on him. She quickly turned to greet Herschel, then said hello to the men, then gave Ma a quick hug as she passed by the stove.

His heart lurched. He made her feel unwanted. *Forgive me, Father.*

He scooted over on the bench, then set an empty plate in front of the vacant spot. "Sit here, Quen. I want you to see the plans we're making. Seems like something my accountant should know."

He kept his expression neutral, pretending not to notice her pleased gasp.

She stepped over the bench, tucking her skirt under her thigh, and leaned forward. A fresh scent drifted from her hair, which she wore in a new style. She'd braided the sides, then gathered them into a ponytail that hung down the back of her head. The rest draped loosely over her shoulders. The length fell almost to her waist.

Jonathan blinked. Since when did he notice hairstyles? He coughed.

She gazed up, her expression so eager it hurt him. Pleasing her took only this. Her lips curved slightly, the white gleam of her teeth peeking through as she placed her elbows on the table. "Show me."

Belle balanced a hand on Jonathan's shoulder and pressed between them, placing a platter of fresh pancakes on the table. The interruption seemed to break a spell. He shook his head. *What's going on, Lord?* He'd never noticed these things before today. He was here to help her get to know God. Nothing more.

Teddy jumped to answer. "Jonathan's gonna let me plant a share of his land. We're talking through the details of a sharecropping contract."

Quen's eyes widened. "That's wonderful. How will the arrangement work?"

He explained.

She peered at Jonathan. "This will use more corn seed. Excellent idea."

Enthusiasm turned her caramel eyes to amber. When she turned to face her plate, the length of dark hair she tossed over her shoulder sent a whiff of flowers past his nose.

He froze. *This is completely unnecessary, Father. I'll help her.* He didn't need to want her. He wasn't even sure he liked her.

Quen sipped from her mug, then turned back to him. He held himself stiffly. What womanly wile would attack him this time?

"How many acres do you have?"

"A little over five hundred. Grandpa claimed the maximum allowed when he came to Texas, then Pa snatched up the neighboring plot. We combined them."

Her gaze softened as wheels turned in her mind. Unsettled by the morning's revelations, he couldn't push himself to ask what she thought. Quickly, he changed the subject.

"Thought I'd drive you into town with the butters y'all made yesterday. We'll pick up Sarah, then you can visit the hotels and restaurants. I'll bring Cisco along so I can head home after dropping you off. You can bring the wagon back when you've unloaded the butters. How does that sound?"

Quen nodded, pleasure brightening her eyes. How easy to make her happy, simply by accepting her and valuing her help. *OK, Father. I get it. You don't have to clobber me over the head with this anymore.* He'd do better.

"I'll teach you to hitch the mare to the wagon. Time to learn how to be a farmer if you're going to work for me." He stepped over the bench and carried his plate to the sink. "Thanks for breakfast, Belle, Ma." He faced Teddy and Ernest. "I'll meet you at the new cotton field when I get back."

"On it, boss." Teddy saluted. He and Ernest headed out to hitch their animals to the plows.

Quen scrambled to join Jonathan. As they walked out the front door, Hans waddled over to her, nibbling the hem of her skirt. She reached down and stroked his head. "Come along, Hans. You can learn too."

Jonathan inspected the gosling with a jaundiced eye. Hans ruffled his feathers, his neck stretching like an evil snake. "What'd I ever do to you?" he muttered. He shot a cautious glance over his shoulder as they walked toward the barn. The rapidly growing gosling followed behind like a determined assassin.

A gust of wind drew Jonathan's gaze to the sky. The early morning rays were now clouded over.

"Oh dear." Quen eyed the scudding clouds with apprehension. "Are we going to get wet on the way to town?"

Jonathan shook his head. "The rain'll go as quickly as it comes, most likely. However, I'd like to get that cotton seed we spread out to dry raked up and stored in bags. Give me a hand?"

Pleasure flashed across her face once more. "Of course. What shall I do?"

Jonathan stepped into the tack room and plucked two empty feed sacks from the corner. He handed them to Quen, then grabbed a wide, flat shovel. "You hold. I'll scoop."

The wind picked up as he shoveled dried seeds from the ground. Quen angled the opening of the bag to catch them as he dumped them in. A long strand of her mahogany-colored hair blew across his face, slipping down his nose like a web of silk, tangling in his whiskers. Unbidden, a picture invaded his imagination so shocking his breath stilled.

In his mind's eye, Quen leaned over him, her hair a heavy, hanging drape, pooling beside his head. He reached up and buried his fingers into its slippery depths, pulling her face toward his. The curling lengths drifted across his bare chest, as soft as the downy fur of Belle's rabbit.

With a muffled curse, he stumbled back. Holy moly. Where had that come from?

Quen glanced up, startled. "Did I step on your toe?"

Jonathan forced a smile. "Your hair." He waved his hand in front of his face, pulling the strand away. "It ... got in my eye." He chuckled like a toad croaking on a summer night.

Quen straightened, her cheeks flaming. She touched the heavy length falling across her shoulder with a tentative hand. "I'm sorry." She glanced around as if searching for a hiding place she could disappear into.

Jonathan intervened. "Don't worry. Nothing I haven't experienced before." The image of Quen moving over him flashed through his mind again. "With Belle, I mean," he hurried to amend. "Working." He cleared his throat. For Pete's sake. This was growing worse by the second. *Shut up, you idiot.*

Quen smiled uncertainly. She patted the pockets of her skirt. "If I had something to pull it back with ..." Her voice trailed off.

Another long strand of silk blew toward Jonathan's face as a blast of chilly air buffeted them from the storm's front.

"Here, use this to tie it up." Desperation strangled his voice as Jonathan yanked his bandana from his back pocket and thrust the square of cloth toward her.

Quen took it, then tilted sideways, letting her hair tumble over her shoulder. She fumbled with the bandana, attempting to roll a rope. "I've done this a million times." She tsk'd.

"Hold on. I've helped Belle do this." Jonathan laid the shovel down, then stepped behind Quen. Denying the sensuous images in his mind, he forced himself to nonchalance. Grasping the ponytail she'd gathered, he pulled it away from her neck. "Hand me the bandana."

He twisted the thick length of hair once, then wrapped the cloth rope around it. He tucked the ends of the fabric into the knot, the way he'd seen Belle do many mornings.

As he pulled away, the gathered tail of silky strands slipped over his skin. He slowed as it cascaded across the back of his hand, then caught the ends between his fingertips. His heart beat with heavy thuds.

Quen glanced over her shoulder—her cheeks as pink as if she'd spent the afternoon in the sun. "All done?" She sounded out of breath, like she'd been running. His gaze met Quen's and held. He stared as if she was a snack, and he was starving.

"Jonathan." Bay's voice hollered from somewhere behind him. "Ma asked if Quen could help her grab the laundry off the line before the rain comes."

Jonathan jerked as if something stung him. Stepping back, he waved his hand toward her. "Go ahead. This is almost done." He focused on the remaining seed at his feet.

She turned without a word and hurried away, Hans waddling protectively at her feet.

Jonathan bent over and picked up the shovel. He paused, then stabbed the point into the ground, curling his fingers around the handle. "I'll be dipped," he murmured. "How is this going to work?"

Chapter Sixteen

Quen stared out Mrs. Campbell's kitchen window as rain drew lines down the glass. Her world tilted, as transitory as the paths forged by the water on the panes.

The straight edges of the barn in the distance wavered with each rolling drop, the water-distorted view hiding Jonathan.

Mrs. Campbell moved quietly behind her, folding the clothes they'd rushed to grab. Quen stirred but didn't turn. Her thoughts held her captive.

If Bay hadn't called ... was Jonathan about to kiss her? She traced her lips, pondering the look he gave her. His gaze had been intense.

A kiss? Surely not. She was mistaken.

Straightening, she blinked away her conjecture. She turned to Jonathan's mother. "May I help?"

Mrs. Campbell gestured toward the pile on the table. "I never refuse a helping hand."

Quen reached for the article on top and held aloft a pair of boy's dungarees with a hole starting in the knee of one leg. She smiled as she smoothed the length of rugged material. Bay was such a funny boy, making her laugh with his pointed remarks, always teasing his older siblings.

A kernel of need unfolded inside. She paused. A child of her own. The idea had been in her heart before but had never stayed. This one settled, sent down roots. She glanced over her shoulder, past the raindrops. So many unexpected possibilities had unfurled in the past few days. She didn't know where she stood.

Folding the pants, she laid them aside. She reached for the next item, plucking Jonathan's shirt from the pile. He'd worn it the day she brought payment from Mr. Garner. A smile tugged as she pictured him stuffing the bills into his breast pocket, mouth flattened with annoyance. She brought the shirt to her nose. Inhaled.

Mrs. Campbell chuckled, giving her a knowing look.

Quen looked away as heat crept up her neck. "I love the smell of laundry fresh off the line. It smells like sunshine." Not like Jonathan. What was she doing? She didn't recognize this stranger she'd become.

Jonathon was a farmer.

She'd be happy with his simple aspirations?

She wouldn't. The life she dreamed of would hold far more adventure, more excitement than what being the wife of a farmer could provide.

An idea spoke in her heart.

What does the LORD require of you but to do justice, and to love kindness, and to walk humbly with your God?

Quen frowned. The verse from Micah was one she and Prissy had committed to heart in Africa. Why did these words resurface from the quagmire of her memories? Learning them had held no more meaning for her than memorizing a poem.

The back door opened, bringing a gust of cool air and the smell of wet earth. Jonathan stomped his feet at the door before stepping inside, his gaze calm and friendly. He smiled. "Rain stopped. Ready to learn how to harness the horse to the wagon?"

Kind and humble.

Could those qualities be enough to make her happy for a lifetime?

Half an hour later, Quen sat quietly on the far end of the wagon bench as Sarah, seated between her and Jonathan, chatted on the trip through town. They'd stopped at Pastor Green's house to pick her up. Quen hung back, pretending to un-snag her hem from her boot, allowing Sarah to climb into the wagon first.

With just her and Jonathan in the wagon, talk had focused on instructions on how to steer the wagon, use the reins, set the brake. Now, Sarah took over the conversation.

"Fannie Belle spends half her day getting onto Frank. Coral is terrified she'll tire of us and dump us on the road. I've assured her she won't, but I can't convince her."

Jonathan chuckled. "What shenanigans does Frank pull that bothers her so?"

Sarah threw her hands in the air. "He leaves dirty clothes on the floor. Tramps mud in the house. You know, boy stuff."

Quen picked up tidbits about Sarah's siblings as the wagon rumbled along. But Jonathan's replies were far more interesting. He paid attention. Commented. He interacted this way with his men, his family. In fact, he treated everyone with this same calm regard. Everyone except her.

A conversation from her early teenage years came to mind. Her mother had been short with her all day. Finally, in a moment of frustration, Quen demanded an explanation. "I seem to be a continual disappointment. Can I do nothing correctly? Why are you never pleased with me, Mother?"

Mother pursed her lips. For a moment, Quen feared she would deflect the question with one of her usual platitudes. Instead, in a rare case of honest communication, Mother blurted, "Because you vex me."

"Vex you?" Quen furrowed her brow. "What do you mean?"

"You march straight ahead, ignoring my instruction. You are headstrong and impulsive. You're on a road to ruin."

Quen stiffened. "Perhaps you're wrong. What if being headstrong is precisely what I need to forge the path I want to take?"

Mother's face arranged itself into resigned lines. She paused, then her words came low, sorrowful. "Because you are exactly the same as I was at your age, and my attitude brought me nothing but heartache."

The words floored Quen. She rejected the supposition her obstinate ways would lead her to ruin. But more disturbing was the idea of sharing any similarity with her mother. Heaven forbid.

She pushed the memory aside, but that word stayed with her. Did she vex Jonathan? The emotion displayed on his face beside the barn wasn't annoyance. Well, not exactly. He didn't seem angry, more ... bothered.

"Don't you think, Quen?" Sarah's voice penetrated.

"I'm sorry. I missed that last thing you said." Quen shook her head. Focus.

"Let's start at the Menger Hotel. They're the largest. If they buy a lot of the butter, we may not need to make as many stops to sell everything. The fewer times, the better. I'm nervous. I feel like I'm auditioning for something."

"That's an excellent idea."

Jonathan steered the wagon toward the Menger and halted in front of their wide porch. They disembarked. Quen leaned against the side of the cart, stretching for a pail that held rectangular slabs of butter wrapped in square, waxed cloths. She turned, then jerked. Samuel Jenkins leaned against a wooden column, watching her with his lazy grin. Actually, if the direction of his gaze was accurate, he contemplated her backside. Speaking of feeling vexed ...

He pushed his hat up with a languid finger, a smile spreading across his face like honey melting off a hot biscuit. "Good morning, miss. We meet again." He stepped forward. "May I help?"

Quen clutched the pail to her midsection as if it would protect like medieval armor. "No thank you, sir. I'm quite capable."

Sarah joined her, a second pail hanging from her arm. She gazed with caution at Samuel. "Who's your friend, Quen?"

A light gleamed in Samuel's eyes. "Ah! The mystery lady is finally revealed. Quen, eh?" He turned his charm onto Sarah, who blushed, fidgeting under his warm regard. "Is there a last name to go with that?"

Sarah's high-pitched giggle revealed her nervousness. "You two don't know each other?"

Jonathan appeared at Quen's elbow. "Ready?" His utter lack of attention dismissed Samuel, but a tenseness replaced his earlier calm demeanor. His body appeared as coiled as a rattlesnake. Hmm. He didn't like Samuel either.

Samuel zeroed in on Sarah, a hunter seeking the weakest member of the herd. "What's in your buckets?" His handsome face carried a friendly expression. Anyone would have thought it rude to not answer. Sarah folded without a whimper of protest.

"Flavored butters. We're selling them for the Campbells."

A light of triumph glowed in Samuel's eyes as the indolent smile returned.

He'd use this information as a weapon. Quen frowned. But how?

"Ah." He turned his now-cool gaze to Jonathan. "Is this your attempt to fix that financial situation our mutual lady friend mentioned, Campbell?"

Quen's jaw dropped. She drew a breath to decry his insinuation, but the words died when Jonathan's smile hardened into a thin line. His hand clenched at his side. Impossible for her to explain Samuel's leap of logic. She'd let slip the smallest sliver of information in a moment of confrontation, and the irritating man connected dots she hadn't provided.

"How long will you be in town?" Samuel pressed Quen, walking down the steps, and approaching the wagon. "I'd be pleased to treat you to a refreshing lemonade after your busy morning of peddling."

Quen couldn't put a finger on what in that sentence offended her, but she'd rather pound sand than accept his offer.

"No, thank you. Good day, sir." Quen brushed past the aggravating man.

Samuel placed a light hand on her forearm, curling his fingers around her bicep.

Jonathan immediately stepped forward.

Samuel slid his hand away like it'd never touched her.

Quen swallowed at the expression on Jonathan's face. If looks made sounds, this one would snarl.

"Jenkins, the lady's not interested."

The flat expression on Jonathan's face told Quen all she needed to know about his feelings toward her at the moment. Nevertheless, he stepped up to defend her. *Do justice.*

Samuel smirked, a bully who got a rise from his victim. "Another time, perhaps." He stepped back, unruffled. With a nod, he turned and strolled away.

Quen turned to Jonathan. "About what he said—"

Jonathan slid a cold glance her way as he reached for the last pail. "I'll help you carry these in, then I need to get back."

"Jonathan—"

He strode to the carved mahogany door of the hotel and pulled it open, leaving her to follow. As hard and imposing as the door, he stepped aside to let them pass. He handed the bucket to Sarah as she entered. The look he gave Quen as he waited for her could've frozen steam erupting from a geyser. He turned away the moment she moved across the threshold.

Quen swallowed her impatience. Obviously, he was in no mood to listen to reason. She would talk to him at the farm.

Once inside, she glanced back. He yanked Cisco's reins from the tailgate of the wagon, then the ponderous door slowly closed, cutting him from view. A heavy sigh escaped. Her earlier consideration of the feasibility of becoming a farmer's wife seemed ludicrous now. Yes, she definitely vexed him.

Their first venture selling butter proved an unequivocal success. Quen climbed into the wagon after their last sales pitch with a sigh of relief. Just as Sarah hoped, the Menger Hotel purchased the lion's share. They sold the rest at various diners, ending at Mrs. Carter's boarding house. They promised to deliver follow-up orders the next week.

A vision of handing Jonathan a folded stack of bills eased some of Quen's nervousness about facing him and explaining Samuel's words. Perhaps the cash in her pocket would thaw his pique with her.

"Who was that man in front of the hotel?" Sarah interrupted Quen's worry. "I don't think you should be friends with him."

"He's not a friend. I've seen him a few times in town. I don't know him, but he's quite gregarious. He just stopped to talk."

Sarah furrowed her brows. "He grabbed your arm."

Warmth flooded Quen's face. "He didn't grab me."

Sarah huffed. "Jonathan didn't like it. Even I saw that."

Quen ignored her comment.

"Come to think of it, Jonathan reacted like a jealous boyfriend." Sarah pushed past Quen's silence. "Is there something between y'all?"

The heat on Quen's face radiated to the tops of her ears. "I'm sure I don't know what you're talking about."

Sarah twitched her mouth sideways. "Hmm. If you say so."

The old mare's back drew Quen's undivided attention. Thankfully, Sarah let the matter drop.

Quen drove the wagon during their errand, with Sarah giving a running commentary on how best to steer and handle the horse in the busy traffic. She dropped Sarah off, then drew a bracing breath. She could handle driving the wagon on her own. Tentative confidence strengthened Quen as she turned toward Jonathan's farm. She was at the edge of town when Caleb approached, riding his mule.

"Afternoon, Miz Quen." He tipped his hat toward her.

Quen's heartbeat sped up at the sight of him. Maybe he and Mrs. Lancaster had discussed how she could help with the underground railroad.

"Afternoon, Mr. Caleb." Quen fought to keep her voice even, excitement thrumming through her veins.

"What a happy coincidence to run into you." Caleb's voice drawled slow and thick, as comforting as a warm quilt on a frosty night. "Miz Lancaster sends along some information." A friendly fan of lines radiated from the corners of his eyes.

Quen's pulse jumped. Finally. "I'm going to Jonathan's now."

"I'll keep you company. We can talk on the way. What business did you have in town?"

Quen explained about the butter. The memory of Samuel's smug face stirred uneasy nerves in her stomach. His use of the word *darkie* popped into her mind. Would an association with him put Caleb and Mrs. Lancaster off? She'd keep that to herself. What if they believed she agreed with his mindset?

She drew a breath. "What have you and Mrs. Lancaster decided?"

Caleb's gaze grew serious. "I must emphasize the seriousness of this undertaking. This isn't an adventure for you to lighten the boredom of your days, Miz Quen. People have a lot of money invested in keepin' Black folks enslaved. They don't take kindly to interference in their efforts to maintain life as they know it."

Quen swallowed. "I understand."

"I doubt you do, but God willing, you will." Caleb pressed his lips together, his freckles standing out against his brown skin.

His words settled into her mind. The jingle of the harness filled the silence between them. The clomping hoofbeats of the old mare and the mule provided a syncopated backdrop to her thoughts. After a moment, Caleb continued.

"We're not organized like the railroad up North. We do our best to help folks on their way, but Texas is too spread out to have safe places lined up to give helping hands. Most enslaved folks do little more'n steal a horse—a gun, if they're lucky—then ride like the dickens for Mexico."

"How do you help?"

"We provide a package of vittles and a gun when there's one to be found. Change of clothes to make folks seem less like a slave and more like a person living their life. Miz Lancaster writes a letter of passage with made-up owner names they can flash if they get stopped." He glanced at Quen, seeming to take stock of her fortitude. "We have a hidey-hole where we stash stuff for the runners. Missouri and me take turns. Miz Lancaster doesn't do that part. Folks'd find it strange to see her hiking across a field."

"I could do that." Quen interrupted. "I walk back and forth nearly every day from home to Jonathan's. And I always have a basket on my arm to carry Hans. If anyone has taken any note of me at all, they've seen that already. Nothing would draw attention."

"Miz Lancaster said the same thing." Caleb agreed. He described the location of the tree growing against the fence line between Jonathan's and Mr. Franklin's farms. "Look for a grand old live oak with one large arm stretching out sideways, pointing toward the road. There's a hollow spot inside."

Caleb glanced around. The driveway to Jonathan's farm waited on Quen's right. Buzzing cicadas and twittering birds were their only company. He pulled a small bundle from his knapsack and handed it over.

Quen unrolled it. She uncovered sandwiches, a jar of water, a shirt and pair of overalls, a letter, and a pistol. The sight of gleaming black metal caused a lump in her stomach. She quickly tucked it back together and placed it in the basket at her feet.

"Is anything in your basket that would excuse you bein' at the tree in case someone comes along?"

"I carry a sketchbook. If anyone sees me, I'll act like I'm drawing. No one will suspect a thing."

"If anything seems off, if someone acts overly interested, wait till later. The runaway will be along under the cover of darkness tonight to pick this up. Miz Lancaster always has a back-up plan. We can tuck him away in her cellar."

Quen swallowed sudden nerves. She peered down the drive to Jonathan's farm. "I should take the mare back."

"I'll leave you be, then." He paused. "You're a good 'un. Thank you, Miz Quen." Caleb touched his fist to his heart. "Go with God."

Quen tilted her head as Caleb continued down the road. Go with God? Would he listen this time if she started praying again?

Chapter Seventeen

Jonathan headed home, rancor settling in. He stewed. What business did Quen have wagging her tongue about his private affairs to Samuel Jenkins? Why on earth was she socializing with him, anyway?

If only he'd seen it coming, the betrayal might not have stung as much.

By the time lunch break rolled around, his hostility rode his back like an itchy sweater. Jonathan hardly spoke three words to the others at the table. After his initial rebuff, they stopped trying to talk. Fine by him.

Lunch over, Teddy and Ernest pushed away from the table and carried dishes to the sink. Ma's chicken and dumplings, a long-time favorite, sat heavy in Jonathan's belly, kept company by injured pride. He followed the field hands through the back door, slapping his hat onto his head. They hurried away.

Phoenix brayed, the obnoxious noise grating on his nerves.

"Who appointed you watchdog of the farm?" Jonathan glanced down the driveway as he strode toward the barn.

Quen. There she was, wagon stopped on the road, talking to Caleb. Anger replaced his tender emotions from that morning, rising again like lava in a volcano, considering whether to erupt.

Dear Lord, help me lose this feeling. Did prayers work when the person praying was mad? Wasting energy this way was pointless.

She remained with Caleb, deep in conversation. Did they discuss Phoenix? What else could they have in common? Caleb handed her a bundle. She laid it in her lap and unrolled it. Jonathan frowned. What were they up to?

Caleb tipped his hat and turned his mule toward his farm. Quen steered the wagon to the barn.

Her treason burned the back of Jonathan's throat. Loyalty was important to him. She obviously didn't live by the same creed.

The attraction he'd finally acknowledged flooded his mind, refusing to be stuffed back into the bag from which it'd escaped. He rubbed the back of his neck. How could he still feel anything for her? Clearly, she harbored no fidelity toward him or his family.

She probably had another wad of cash to hand him after selling the butter. Relying on her help held as much appeal as mucking out the stalls in the barn, but he was in no position to turn her away. Herschel's tuition at Baylor was due soon. He wouldn't let his family down because he was upset with Quen.

She drove the wagon like a pro as she headed toward the barn. She was no slouch in the brains department, that was for sure. Jonathan waited for her to arrive.

A small, mean emotion crowed in triumph when she jerked at seeing him there. Good. Let her feel at odds for once. Immediately, shame seeped into his heart. Why did Quen discombobulate him so?

He stepped toward the wagon. "I'll turn the mare out to pasture. You're free to go." He forced himself to serve her.

He grasped the traces with one hand, patting the horse's neck with his other, using the action as an excuse to avoid Quen's gaze.

She climbed from the wagon. At her silence, he glanced over. Uncertainty rested in the crease between her brows. In an unnaturally cheery voice, she said, "We sold all the butter." Withdrawing the money from her basket, she stretched out her arm, bills fluttering in the breeze. "Here. Add this to your account book."

How he hated to accept. He took her offering and shoved her charity into his pocket. "You should probably be the one to write it. We know the mess I made doing it myself. And apparently, so does Samuel."

Quen huffed. "Things didn't happen the way Samuel implied. He took one sentence I uttered and extrapolated an entire scenario, all on his own."

Jonathan snorted. "I don't use fancy words like extrapolated. But until today, my personal affairs remained personal. Thanks to your loquaciousness—" he let his word of the day hang between them "—Samuel Jenkins knows things he has no business knowing."

She had the grace to flinch. "I merely answered his question as to why I was at the bank. He took that and ran with it. Jonathan, honestly. Have I not convinced you yet I'm on your side? I'm not loose-lipped. My mother taught me well about the dangers of being a gossip." She gazed at him earnestly. "I swear. I did not talk about you to that man."

She pleaded so prettily—his anger softened a notch. Was he foolish to let her sweet talk him out of his bad mood? His gaze lit on the bundle in her basket. "What's that?"

Quen stiffened. Her mouth worked, but no words emerged.

He cocked a sardonic eyebrow. Waited.

"Art supplies." The words blurted as if they came unexpectedly. "Mrs. Lancaster sent them. I've been sketching and doing some painting." She clamped her mouth shut.

He narrowed his eyes. She was incredibly horrible at lying. Anger notched right back up.

"Right." His curt reply dropped a brick wall between them. "I'll take this cash into the house, then I'll turn the mare out." He eyed the basket with a healthy dose of skepticism. "You can go ... paint."

He turned away before she could speak and stomped back to the house. He banged every door on his way to the study, then slammed the drawer shut after tossing the bills inside. How much had she given him? Was the headway they made even close to getting them back into the black? Annoyance itched at him like the rash from poison ivy. No way would he be able to focus. Anything he wrote now would be a jumble.

He stalked back to the wagon to unharness the old mare. After setting her loose in the pasture, he walked into the barn to hang up the leather traces. A moment later, he hurled himself back to the yard, ornery goose in full pursuit, neck stretched, beak snapping, wings held aloft like a banshee.

"Dagnabit!" He turned and wagged a stern finger at the goose. "You don't even live here. Quit chasing me."

Hans ruffled his feathers and shook his wings as he tucked them against his body. He seemed pleased and wandered to the grass to nibble.

Giving him a slit-eyed gaze, Jonathan turned and headed back to the field where the men worked. As he neared the back of the property, a flash of color caught his eye. He focused on the corner near the road. Quen stood at the live oak tree that grew along the fence line. She set down her basket.

"Hmph." His angry mutter fed the volcano bubbling inside. "Getting ready to use those painting supplies?" He paused. Was she actually doing what she'd said?

When she reached into the basket and withdrew the bundle, his eyebrows rose to his hairline. He moved closer to the fence, concealing himself among the trees growing along the boundary. She glanced down the road, the movement furtive. Quickly, she tucked what looked like a wad of clothes into the hollow space left from a broken branch. She stepped back, brushed her hands against her skirt, and grasped the basket. After climbing over the fence, she turned and walked down the road.

"What in tarnation?" Jonathan breathed the question, fists propped on his hips. Not his business to check up on her, but curiosity singed his morals. Whatever she was involved with took place on his land. He had every right to investigate. He waited, giving her plenty of time to move away, then hurried to the tree. Darting a glance over his shoulder, he pulled the bundle from the hollow space. Placing the unexpectedly heavy parcel on the ground, he unrolled a pair of pants and shirt, exposing the treasure hidden inside. Frowning, he held up a jar of water and a bandana tied around a packet of food.

"What are you doing?" Jonathan murmured.

He placed the jar back onto the piled-up man's shirt. The glass clunked against something hard. He set the jar aside, then carefully picked up the garment. A pistol fell with a thump onto the grass at his feet.

Jonathan froze. "Quenby Martin, what have you gotten yourself into?"

The image of Caleb handing her the bundle slipped through his mind. He drew a breath.

"No, no, no. Quen, you'll get yourself killed!"

The snap of a twig had him twisting around so quickly, he tumbled to his bottom. Phoenix stood behind him, her inquisitive nose stretching for a sniff of the bandana. Giving a shaky sigh, he pushed her away. "Pretty sure this is for someone else, girl. Someone with a far greater need than you. Sorry. You can't have it."

He wrapped the bundle back up, overwhelmed with worry someone would come along and catch him, asking questions he couldn't answer. He returned it to the hole in the tree. Phoenix moved closer and stretched her neck, snuffling.

"Leave it alone." He turned back to the field, deep in thought. Phoenix walked along beside him, head bobbing companionably with each step.

"I understand Caleb helping enslaved people escape. But costs add up. Where is he getting the money to buy clothing? And guns?"

Phoenix didn't answer.

Caleb's farm was smaller than Jonathan's. He basically grew enough crops to live on. He did odd jobs, like being a farrier, repairing machinery, helping build barns or houses. He also seemed to do a lot for Mrs. Lancaster.

A chill settled in his soul.

"Phoenix, our girl may be in over her head. She has no idea the lengths folks will travel to keep enslaved people under their thumbs. Creeps like Jenkins make their living hunting runaways." He shook his head, wondering again why she spoke to the scoundrel.

He halted. Phoenix stopped, waiting patiently by his side.

Did Jenkins know what Caleb and Quen were doing? Was the attention he paid Quen merely an attempt to weasel his way into their alliance? If Jenkins had made the leap about his financial straits from a single sentence uttered by Quen, how long before he figured out their schemes?

The chill snaked down his spine. He should confront Quen with his suspicions. Force her to tell him what was going on. Warn her about Samuel.

He continued walking along the fence line. Shortly, he came upon the field where the two men toiled. In the far corner, Teddy was building a small house. He'd staked his claim on the sharecropping portion of the farm. The man must work into the wee hours of the mornings to get so much accomplished this quickly.

Ernest gave Jonathan a wary look as he approached, the bad mood from breakfast clearly not forgotten.

Phoenix trotted to Teddy, stretching her lips back to show her teeth, braying happily. Jonathan latched onto the donkey as a conversation piece, forestalling any questions that might come his way.

"I've never seen such a noisy critter as this one." Jonathan forced a chuckle as he moved toward the plow.

The men traded glances but seemed relieved. Ernest laughed, reaching out a hand to scratch behind the donkey's ears.

"No one will be sneaking about so long as she's around, that's for sure."

Sneaking about. The vision brought on by Ernest's choice of words settled like heartburn. Samuel Jenkins was going to discover what she did. He had to stop her. He just had to figure out how.

Chapter Eighteen

Quen strolled along the wooden sidewalk in the morning sunlight, a list of assignments dictated by Mother resting in her pocket. She didn't mind being sent out as errand girl. Leaving her gloomy household behind and watching people bustle through the busy town all far outweighed the indignity of carrying out the duties of a housemaid.

Caleb exited Solomon's ahead of her and paused outside the door, tucking his purchases into a saddlebag.

Just as she lifted her hand to call out to him, Samuel Jenkins reined his horse to a stop at the hitching post in front of the store. She darted sideways to hide in a nearby doorway. A barrel bristling with broomsticks provided cover.

When the coast was clear, she'd speak with Caleb. Her imagination painted a picture of a hungry, grateful person reaching into the hole in the trunk and withdrawing his bundle of goods, hope surging, strengthened to continue his journey to the southern border of Texas. The urge to revel in that triumph twirled through her insides. She forced herself to wait.

Samuel climbed the steps, tugging leather gloves from his hands, a cruel sneer of handsome arrogance lifting the side of his mouth.

"Well, well. What have we come to when darkies can spend money in the same store as the genteel folk of San Antonio?"

Caleb stilled and looked up, his gaze meeting Samuel's evenly for only a moment before he lowered it to the floor.

Why couldn't Samuel accept Caleb as an equal?

Samuel stepped closer. Caleb had two choices—hold his ground or assume the meek caricature of the man he naturally was and step back.

He moved one step away.

Quen's heart broke.

"Can I he'p you with somethin', Mista Jenkins?" Caleb's voice had taken on that subservient drawl. The act he was forced to play sickened her.

"Yes. You can disappear. You don't belong here. Slaves have no rights."

Caleb tilted his head, still gazing at the space between Samuel's boots. "Yessir, that's true. But I's no longer a slave, Mista Jenkins. I's a free man. My mastah gave that to me. I have the paper to prove it."

Samuel slapped the gloves into his palm. The sharp snap hit Quen's ears like an explosion. He was goading himself into an act of violence. Would she stand here and watch it happen? Her pulse beat in her ears.

Come on. Do something.

She couldn't bring herself to move.

"If you were on a deserted road one evening, a man could be excused for believing you were a slave running from your rightful owner, bring you to the auction block, and send you back where you belong."

Caleb remained silent—his face impassive. Quen clenched her fists. She longed to defend him.

"Your little piece of paper wouldn't mean much then." Samuel cocked his head. "Come to think of it, lots of

Accepted

runaways I'm hired to track head through San Antonio in their feeble attempts to slip away down south. You wouldn't know anything about that, would you?"

Quen froze. What had Samuel learned?

"Answer me." Samuel's hand raised with a jerk.

Sheriff Moore stepped out of Solomon's, joining Caleb on the sidewalk. "Morning, gentlemen. Fine day, isn't it?"

Quen sagged against the wall.

Caleb wore a weak smile. "That it is, Sheriff."

The lawman shot a piercing glance toward Samuel. "Haven't seen you around lately, Jenkins. Everything well?" Sheriff Moore shifted so slightly it was nearly imperceptible. But his body was now a barrier between Samuel and Caleb. "Funny, things have seemed nice and quiet around here." He gazed placidly across the street as if searching for a troublemaker to arrest.

Quen's soul soared. Sheriff Moore recognized Samuel for the blackguard he was, and he was having none of it. Her pounding pulse slowed.

Samuel's eyes narrowed. "Glad you can spend your working hours relaxing, Sheriff." He sent a malicious glance toward Caleb. "Some of us have important things to do."

Sheriff Moore took a step in Samuel's direction. "Well, we'd hate to keep you from them." His smile gave Samuel no incentive to fight back. His friendly voice couldn't offend anyone.

Samuel slapped his gloves one more time, then brushed past the lawman and headed into the store.

A small bud of shame took root in Quen's heart. Would she have stepped forward had the sheriff not arrived? So much for being Esther.

Sheriff Moore tugged the brim of his hat toward Caleb. Wearing a satisfied smile, he strolled down the sidewalk, whistling a tuneless song through his teeth.

As he passed, Quen slipped from behind her camouflage of broomsticks and hurried to Caleb.

"Good morning."

Caleb smiled. This time, his face flooded with his usual good humor, as if those past few moments had never happened.

"Mornin', Miz Quen."

"May I walk with you for a moment?"

Caleb darted a glance inside the store, then turned away. "Of course."

The moment they were alone on the sidewalk, Quen spoke quietly from the side of her mouth.

"Did our friend find his present?"

Caleb's lips quirked. "He did. I'm sure he's well on his way, hope for the future guiding his steps."

Quen clasped her hands. "Perfect. When do we repeat this? Who's next?"

Caleb chuckled—eyes gleaming with pleasure. "We take 'em as they come, Miz Quen. Me or Miz Lancaster will send word when we need you again."

"I'll be waiting." Turning with a swish of her skirt, she headed back, spotting Samuel in the distance. He leaned against a wooden column in front of the store, watching her, motionless. She swallowed against the sudden onset of nerves, then crossed the road, giving the store a wide berth.

Jonathan, the field hands, and his brothers worked in the corral behind the barn. Today, they branded calves born that spring and castrated the young bulls. Ernest brought his horse to the farm, and Herschel saddled Cisco.

"Start with these two." Jonathan directed the ropers. Together, the two men sailed lariats through the air and snagged the back feet of each calf. The horses backed from the milling crowd of bawling calves, dragging the trussed animals.

Once the calves were away from the tromping herd, Jonathan waved Bay over, and together, they leaned against the animals' necks, pinning them to the ground. Spittle from the thrashing calves flew as sweat carved paths through the dust coating Jonathan's skin. Teddy pressed steaming branding irons against the hips of the terrified animals. He then castrated the bull calves while the cowboys held them down.

The work was hot and messy. Squeals of pain competed with the instructions Jonathan shouted. Quen would hate this. He was glad she wasn't here.

Where was she?

Jonathan snorted. On his mind again. His discovery at the tree had kept him awake long into the night. He chewed the matter like a dog with a bone. Finally, he prayed and placed her in God's hands. The message he'd sensed during his morning devotional, the one that told him he could show Quen how God loved, that he could be her example, reappeared fresh in his heart. Was this how Jonah felt when instructed to go to Nineveh and save the inhabitants? He sighed.

As the last bleeding, branded calf escaped through the corral gate, Jonathan stretched with a groan. He tugged his bandana from his neck and wiped his face.

"A good day's work, boys."

Tired grins were his reply. Teddy guzzled half the contents of his canteen in one gulp. Ernest led his horse through the gate and over to a trough. He splashed water against his head and neck while the animal drank. Herschel collected the branding irons. Bay clomped to the corral fence, dragging himself to the top row where he sat, hooking his boot heels over the rail.

Jonathan's heart lurched. Quen leaned against the fence. From her appalled face, she'd been there long enough to witness some of the goings-on.

She pressed a hand against her throat. "My word." She swallowed. "Is this completely necessary? Don't you have to treat their wounds?"

He walked to the fence and leaned his forearms against the top slat. Damp fabric clung to his back. He probably smelled to high heaven, but he was too tired to care.

"No treatment. The burn crusts over. And the incisions heal on their own." He hid a smile at her blush. "And yes, it's entirely necessary. Brands identify our cattle, particularly if rustlers get involved. And steers won't fight bulls."

The back door slammed.

Ma and Belle walked toward the lingering fire the men had used to heat branding irons, arms loaded.

All the men looked toward the house. Ernest smiled. Teddy pumped a fist in the air. "Whoo-eee! I was hoping we'd see that."

Bay climbed down from his perch on the fence and hurried to collect more firewood.

"What's this?" Quen met them and reached for a tray.

"It's a tradition." Jonathan joined her, taking the heavy cast-iron Dutch oven from Belle's hands. "After we finish the calves, we eat Ma's chorizo, but we cook outside over the fire, like we'd do on a cattle drive." Jonathan kneeled to stir glowing embers, then added the wood Bay brought. He scooped a hole into the ashes, then tucked large potatoes into the depression and covered them to bake.

Belle lifted the lid from the Dutch oven. Summer pudding, dotted with dark berries, filled the pot. A tantalizing smell teased Quen's nose. Was that vanilla? Or cinnamon?

Quen stepped back a pace. "I only came to bring proceeds from our latest butter sales. I should leave you to it. Mother will expect me."

"Nonsense, Quen." Ma interrupted her. "Surely you can stay and eat with us. You're part of the family now."

Warmth flooded Jonathan's chest at her words, and he darted a glance at Quen. Her gaze skittered away as quickly as a lizard rattling through leaves.

Shortly, everyone had a heaping plate of food. Lively conversation, punctuated with laughter, filled the warm evening air.

"How is construction on the house going, Teddy?" Quen asked.

Teddy preened. "Caleb's helping, so I'm almost finished with the walls. Won't be long before I can start living there."

The strident tones of a beaten triangle shrilled through the dusk.

Jonathan jumped up, alarm tightening his face. "That's coming from Caleb's place." The men joined him, peering across the road toward Caleb's farm.

"Fire!" Ernest pointed.

An orange glow lit the darkening sky.

"Get buckets." Herschel leaped to his feet. "I'll get saddle blankets."

Ma dashed to the tack room. "With me, girls. Grab empty feed bags." They stopped by the water trough to submerge the material, then yanked them out dripping and ran.

Jonathan's boots pounded as he bolted across the road. The clanging alarm had ceased. The rush of fire crackled, roared, filling the night. Caleb's barn burned. Flames consumed the hay stored in the loft with greedy hunger, roaring toward the animals penned inside.

"Dear God." Jonathan stalled as he took in the sight.

Caleb ran from his well with a dripping bucket, then flung water against the wall nearest him. The liquid sizzled, ineffective.

"Line up!" Jonathan shouted over the rush of wind feeding the fire.

Caleb headed back to the well.

"I'll get the animals." Teddy shouted. He ran to the other end and pulled open the barn doors.

The others formed a line. Sloshing buckets passed back and forth from the well to the barn. Wet bags slapped against flames shooting from the wall.

Jonathan shook his head. "We'll never put this out." The fire consumed everything.

A pounding rose above the roar of the flames.

"How many animals are inside?" Ernest hollered to Caleb.

Caleb dropped his bucket, giving up on putting the fire out. He ran to the doors at the other end to help Teddy. Panicked bellows rose from inside.

"Hurry!" Herschel ran inside and opened stall doors Teddy hadn't reached. A cow galloped out, followed by a calf. Jonathan passed Herschel to open the next stall.

Ol' Blue bucked, frantic. Caleb pushed past Jonathan and dragged the gate open. The mule wouldn't come. Jonathan tugged the stall door out of the way. The older man reached for the animal's halter. The mule tossed his head, knocking Caleb off balance. Stumbling, he cracked his forehead against the post and crumpled to the ground.

Jonathan gripped Caleb under the arms. Dragged him toward the door. "Grab his feet!" Ernest hurried to do his bidding.

The mule's panicked bucking thumped against the wall. Despite the open door in front of him, he wouldn't leave. Terrified brays filled the air.

Jonathan straightened—thankful they got Caleb out alive. He turned toward the barn to survey the damage. A flash of color from Quen's skirt caught his eye. She vanished inside.

His heart stopped.

"Quen! No!"

Chapter Nineteen

Quen rushed through smoke. The mule tossed his head. Ears were flattened against his neck, and the whites of his eyes flashed with terror. Heat hit her like a brick wall. She pushed past it. Stepped into the stall. The animal was beyond sense. Could not respond to her calming voice. The sight of the fire drove him wild. Sparks popped from the burning loft. One landed on his shoulder. Hair singed immediately. Quen slapped her palm against the burn.

The mule wouldn't follow her. She couldn't leave him there to die. Frantic, she undid the buttons at her waist and yanked her skirt down. Her white pantaloons glowed through the smoke. She wrapped the skirt loosely around the mule's head. Unable to see the horror around him, he followed the tug on his halter. Another spark fell on his back. He reared. The unexpected movement yanked Quen's arm. She struggled to maintain her grip. As he came down, he bumped her. She stumbled to her knees. The mule rushed past. With blind luck, he thundered through the doorway.

Quen's shoulder slammed against a wooden post. She hissed with pain. A huge splinter of wood pierced her arm. Black smoke swirled around her. She coughed. Labored to regain her footing. Tears streamed from her stinging eyes.

A painful grip clasped her wrist. Jonathan pulled her up. He scooped her like a bag of potatoes and tossed her over his shoulder. All the breath left her body.

She couldn't think straight. Her head tilted toward the floor as he fought to keep his footing. She propped her hands against his hip. Each step bounced her midriff against his shoulder. She struggled to maintain balance.

"Be still." Jonathan barked as he jogged toward the doors.

After agonizing seconds, the air cleared of smoke. Her view blurred. Quen coughed again. Had flames directly scorched the back of her throat?

"Down," she gasped. Her legs bounced in an undignified manner as he ran from the barn. She clutched the shirt bunched at his waist, desperate to right herself.

Jonathan didn't slow.

She pounded his thigh. "Jon … a … thon!" His steps punctuated the word. "I can't … breathe. Put me … down."

Finally, thankfully, he slowed, then leaned over to place her feet on the ground. The hand gripping her knee slid down her pantaloon-clad calf. His touch activated every nerve in her skin. He didn't release her wrist. Instead, he yanked her close as he straightened.

"What in the world did you think you were doing?" His nose almost touched hers as he shouted. He gripped her shoulders with both hands. "You *didn't* think."

She cupped a hand around the elbow of her injured arm, holding the limb motionless. Soot added streaks to his dirty face. Blue eyes blazed at her.

Her gaze dropped to his mouth. His jaw jutted forward, and his lips pressed into an angry line. Her heart flipped painfully in her chest. With a sigh, she stopped fighting the attraction he held for her and allowed herself to enjoy the picture of masculinity currently on parade.

He gave her a shake. "You could've died." His words snarled.

"Well ..." Her voice lacked strength, a mere wisp of air, more croak than words. "I didn't." She swayed toward him. How furious was he?

The hands on her shoulders tightened. His gaze dropped to her mouth, became intense. A strand of her hair lifted in the wind and strayed across his face. She leaned farther. Close enough so his breath passed over her parted lips.

A beam inside the barn crashed to the ground. Quen startled and stepped back. She darted a glance around the dark yard, lit only by the glow from the flames. Belle and Mrs. Campbell tended Caleb, who still lay on the ground. The men and boys rounded up escaped animals. No one paid them any attention.

She laughed shakily. "I'm bleeding." She twisted her arm to gaze at her bicep.

He gripped her wrist, turning her so the gleam of the moon highlighted the wound. A frown creased his face. "When did this happen?"

"When Ol' Blue knocked me against the wall."

He turned toward his mother, then slid a hand to her back, fingertips brushing with the gossamer touch of a butterfly. "Ma'll fix you up." With a strained chuckle, he glanced at her legs. "And I'll go find your skirt."

Quen sat leaning against an oak tree, cradling her arm. Mrs. Campbell had dressed the wound with a folded pad she tied in place using torn strips of cotton. Everyone had vigorously rebuffed her efforts to help, and instead sent her to sit out of the way like a naughty child.

The men worked, pulling down scorched walls that leaned precariously. Burned posts pierced the night sky like broken teeth. Caleb insisted on helping, but they rejected his help as firmly as they'd dismissed Quen. They doused the glowing heat with buckets of water, then stirred through the sloshy mess with hoes and shovels, searching for embers that could flare up again in the night.

Quen was past the hour when she should've been home, but she was beyond caring. Mother would focus on the wound to her arm—hopefully—and perhaps the probing questions she feared about why she'd been at Jonathan's would be forgotten. Her white shirtwaist was filthy with soot, her skirt rent by the throes of a panicked mule. The reek of wet ashes and charred wood permeated everything. Her hair hung in straggled tangles around her face.

Quen sat motionless, watching the men work, thoughts tumbling. She stood at a fork in the road, with a new path appearing, seemingly from nowhere. Options floated up, were discarded, floated up again. What direction did she want to go?

Mrs. Campbell and Belle returned to the farm, reappearing with thick sandwiches and a fresh pitcher of lemonade. Everyone ate with sudden, ravenous hunger. Bay staggered over to where Quen leaned against the tree and lay down with a sigh. He was sound asleep within moments. One by one, the others joined them, dropping to the ground, shoulders slumping.

Ernest clapped a weary hand on Caleb's shoulder. "A blessing none of your livestock perished in the fire."

Caleb nodded, saying nothing. He gazed at the ruined barn. A spark flashed in his eyes, but then he drew a breath, let it out, and something inside him seemed to settle. "Yes. God is good."

Quen stared. How could he be so sure? Caleb had suffered at the hands of others, far more than she. Yet, this faith ...

Jonathan scrubbed at his face with both hands. He slapped them onto his thighs with decision. "Let's take your animals to our farm. They'll board with us while you rebuild. We'll help."

Caleb smiled. "I 'preciate your friendship, Jonathan. I'll take you up on your offer to shelter my animals. But it'll be a while before I can build a new barn. It'll take some doing to scrape up funds for lumber."

Teddy spoke up. "You can use some of what I purchased for my house. I was 'bout to start a second room, but I can wait."

Ernest nodded. "And I can split some planks from trees I cut down. No cost for that."

Caleb held up his hands. "I can't take that—"

Jonathan stood. "Yes, you can. And you will. You do for us all the time. It's time for us to return the favor."

Obstinance flooded the older man's face.

"Keep track of the cost if you want. You can pay us back later. That's unimportant." Jonathan yawned. "What is important is getting these animals to our place, getting Quen home, washing the stink of today off, and going to bed. In that order."

He stretched a hand down to Herschel and hauled him up. "Do you have it in you to carry Bay home?"

Caleb stood as well. "He can ride Ol' Blue."

Quen stood. "I think I know who did this."

Everyone stalled, turning to face her. Apparently, the possibility someone intentionally set the fire hadn't crossed everyone's mind. It crossed hers. She met Caleb's frowning gaze. Clearly, it crossed his too.

Jonathan squinted. "You think someone started this fire?"

Mrs. Campbell gasped. "Who would do such a thing?"

Quen paused. This might start a plethora of questions Caleb wouldn't want to answer. But she couldn't stand by for the second time and watch Caleb be hurt.

"Samuel Jenkins." Her teeth worried her bottom lip.

Belle shuddered. "He gives me the creeps."

Jonathan stared at Quen. "What's your connection with him?"

Caleb raised a calming hand. "Now, now. We don't know nothing 'bout that. No sense in bandying words that might come back to haunt us."

Quen shrugged. "I may be wrong." She gazed directly at Jonathan. "And I have no connection with him, any more than you do."

Jonathan huffed. "And yet, you think he, of all people, set this fire?"

Quen met Caleb's gaze. "I overheard him talking to Caleb in town. I ... I didn't hear exactly what he said, but the words seemed unfriendly." The shame in her heart sprouted a new leaf at the lie. It was a small fudge of the truth. "The sheriff stepped in and hushed him up. It appeared to make him angry."

Jonathan turned to Caleb. "Is that weasel bothering you?"

Caleb shook his head, the gesture dismissive. "No more'n normal. Small-minded men take ever' opportunity to make themselves feel big. It was nothing."

Jonathan glanced back and forth between the two of them. He narrowed his eyes. "Hmm."

Herschel interrupted. "Can we talk about this later? I'm about to fall asleep on my feet."

Jonathan grasped Ol' Blue's halter. "Yes. Let's get all these animals to the farm."

Mrs. Campbell raised a hand. "If we truly believe someone intentionally started this fire, I don't like the idea of leaving Caleb here alone, wounded. He should come with us."

"Miz Campbell, that's not necessary." Caleb dismissed her concern.

Jonathan gave the ruined heap a considering stare. "Actually, that's smart. Sometimes, taking a knock on the head makes you sick in the night. You shouldn't be alone." He turned as if he expected no argument and walked toward the road with Ol' Blue, one hand holding a nodding Bay in place.

Quen hung back, waiting until she could walk beside Caleb. They moved forward with no conversation for several steps. Clearing her throat, Quen checked the others. They were too far ahead to overhear. "That confrontation with Samuel was not nothing."

Caleb patted the cow lumbering beside him. "You may be right, Miz Quen. It doesn't bear thinking about, though. I can't do anything."

"How do you stand the unfairness?" She hissed the words to him, unable to hold them in. "How do you not live your life in a state of rage every single moment of every single day?"

Caleb smiled sadly. "That was my life as a young man. Before. I couldn't reconcile the horrible reality of my life as a slave with the goodness of God."

"Before what?"

"Before I truly gave my broken heart to the Lord. I lived every day in a state of humiliation. My pride as a man made it impossible for me to swallow the degradations heaped upon me. I fought that treatment like a wild mustang bucks against his first saddle. And it almost killed me."

"How did you ever accept that?" Quen shook her head in disbelief.

"Two things happened. First, I became very ill. They let me stay in my cabin, in bed, but called no doctor. Finally, Mr. Lancaster relented and agreed to pay for medical attention. Not because he felt Christian charity toward me, a fellow human being. No. He was unwilling to incur the loss which the death of an animal would bring him. He could sell me for $1000. He wouldn't squander that. I realized at that moment my worth as a man was nothing, except in the eyes of God."

Quen couldn't think of a thing to say to that.

"The second thing was this. God, my ever-present help, sent me a message. All the enslaved people on the plantation sat through a Bible reading each week, led by the master as he blessed us with his Sunday morning kindness." His voice was dry. "He read to us this verse: Be joyful in hope, patient in affliction, and faithful in prayer. I believe he wanted us to focus on the instruction to be patient. Lord knows we had affliction. But I grabbed the word hope. And hope came."

"From where?" The words squeezed past the emotion constricting Quen's throat.

"From God. But he used many vessels to deliver it. One was a man, purchased to help in the cotton fields, who had a Bible. He could read. He committed the Good Book to memory and shared it with us. I learned about the Israelites who escaped bondage in Egypt. They went four hundred years without hearing from God."

Caleb stared ahead—his gaze focused on the darkness. "I learned about the torment Jesus endured to accept the burden of the cross. His trials were so much more than mine. He didn't have to do it. Could've backed out. Could've called upon legions of angels to strike down those who crucified him. But he didn't. He bore his suffering. On my behalf." He paused. Glanced at Quen. "On yours."

Quen swallowed tears. "Those are just words in a book. How—?"

Caleb spoke. "He used a person, a real, living person who made me believe in the goodness of mankind. Who gave me the ability to see a future."

"Mrs. Lancaster?"

Caleb nodded. "This world is full of evil things, bad people. Enough to make you want to curl up and die. But now and again, one comes along who hears the Word of God, who listens to what Jesus said. And that person hands you the rope that pulls you from the pit. The rope Jesus created when he died."

A calm smile lit his features. "I know God is for me. And if God is for me, don't matter who comes against me. I could choose to live my life in anger, consumed by hatred. Or I could choose to live my life in love. God is stronger. He will prevail. All I need do is trust him. And wait." He paused. "I choose God."

Quen trembled, balancing on the edge of a precipice. Could she possibly have that kind of faith? She blinked through tears swimming in her eyes. If Caleb was this unshakable after all he'd been through, surely, she could trust God with her puny problems.

She reached through the moonlight and grasped Caleb's hand. His palm was wide, scratchy with callouses. But his grip was warm and comforting as he squeezed back. Caleb had learned to let go of his anger. She could too.

They walked the rest of the way in silence.

Chapter Twenty

Back at Jonathan's, Quen dipped a washcloth into tepid water and scrubbed her face, the bandage on her arm making the task difficult. She tidied her hair with Belle's brush. Her absence and late arrival would be difficult to explain to Mother.

Mother had always easily believed the worst about her. With Jonathan delivering her to her door at such a late hour, what would she think?

One look at her clothes, and Quen snorted a quiet laugh. Soot blackened everything. The odor of wet, burned wood permeated her very skin. She had a substantial alibi.

She walked outside and paused, peering toward the barn. The full moon cast a glow over everything in the yard. Jonathan stood in front of the water trough, the windmill wheel creaking slowly above him, his shirt dangling from a nearby fence post. He splashed himself with water and scrubbed his skin with his hands, rubbing away sweat and ashes. He bent and dunked his head into the water, then straightened with a shake of his hair. The broad expanse of his back gleamed, water tracing trickles that shone in the moonlight. Her gaze followed his spine to where it disappeared into his waistband. "Oh, my."

She acted the part of a voyeur but couldn't drag her gaze away. The memory of the embrace she'd witnessed between Abby and Manny the day at their farm popped into her mind. She swallowed. Hard. Blinking, she gave herself a little shake.

Jonathan plucked his shirt from the post and turned toward the house. When his gaze met hers, he pulled up short. His steps faltered.

He cleared his throat. "I'm gonna grab a clean shirt. This one almost stands up by itself." He rubbed his empty hand against his pant leg, then gestured vaguely toward the door. "'Scuse me."

Quen pulled her gaze from his bare chest and stepped aside with a jerk. "Pardon me." Heat flamed across her face.

"Back in a sec, then I'll take you home." He tossed the words over his shoulder as he went inside.

Quen waited. Which room was his? She'd only seen the hall, study, and kitchen. Curiosity nibbled. Was his room tidy? Did he have a small bed for one, or one large enough for two? A pulse leaped in her throat.

Taking a deep breath, Quen whispered, "God, I'm willing to give this relationship with you another try, but you must make it happen. It seems like I'm talking to a made-up person right now. Whatever faith I had as a child withered away."

A Bible verse about a Roman soldier asking Jesus for help surfaced. "I'm asking the same thing he did. I believe— at least, I *want* to believe—but help me in my unbelief." She stared at the starry sky. "If I trust you with my life, I can ask for help, right? You say in the Bible we can request wisdom and you'll give it. I'm asking. If he's the man for me, please make it clear. And if he's not, please close that door so my feelings won't be hurt."

A creak from the back door alerted Quen to Jonathan's presence. The tops of her ears burned. Did he overhear her praying about her future love life? She squeezed her eyes shut, mortified.

"Let's hook up the wagon." Jonathan approached. "Your mother must be worried."

When he said nothing else, she relaxed.

He tucked his shirttails into the back of his waistband. The position of his arms stretched his shirt taut across his chest. Quen studied him through lowered lashes. A pulse beat in the hollow of her throat again.

She would enjoy the time she spent with him. Wait for the door to either crash closed or open so wide she couldn't miss it. She followed him to the barn.

Jonathan quickly hitched the old mare. Quen climbed onto the wooden bench seat, smoothing her skirt across her lap, a ridiculous vanity considering the state it was in. The wagon lurched into motion with a jerk.

They rode in silence. Quen searched for something to say that would give her a reason to turn and look at him. She leaned her arm against the backboard.

"If Samuel started that fire, can we do anything to bring justice for Caleb?"

Thoughtfulness softened Jonathan's face. "I believe Sheriff Moore is a good man. If we tell him what we suspect, I bet he'll keep a close eye on Jenkins."

Quen chewed the inside of her cheek. "If only we could prove it was Samuel." She leaned toward Jonathan and touched his forearm. "We can go back to Caleb's and investigate. Perhaps Samuel left evidence."

Jonathan's gaze focused on the spot where her fingertips touched. He raised his chin and stared into her eyes.

Quen swallowed—her mouth dry. She slid her hand away, fussing instead with the collar of her blouse.

"Perhaps." His deep voice was warm. His Adam's apple bobbed. Gazing forward again, he coughed. "I'll go tomorrow and see if anything catches my eye."

"Will the sheriff do anything?"

"We'd need some pretty strong proof." He shrugged. "San Antonio doesn't have anything near the plantations back east. Most farmers grow what they need for their families, plus a little more to sell. Like us. Not too many people in these parts see the need to own a slave. This whole business with the war just isn't a problem for most." He paused. "However, the wealthy plantation owners carry a lot of weight in town. People listen to them. Some around here have a different attitude toward Black folks than you and I."

As the wagon rattled down Commerce Street—an empty wasteland at this hour of the night—a figure caught her eye. Something about the way the man moved, or maybe the tilt of his hat, seemed familiar. The man strode to the edge of the wooden sidewalk in front of the saloon and paused. The tilt of his cowboy hat covered his face. She frowned. Was that Samuel? A frisson of fear snaked through her. She shook her head. So, what if it was? She wasn't doing anything wrong. And Samuel couldn't know she'd mentioned his name back at Caleb's farm. Unwilling to bring his name up again, she forced the thought of him from her mind.

"But people like Caleb, don't they?" Her teeth worried her bottom lip.

"Sure. He does a lot for townspeople. However, I've heard a comment or two. Not from folks I'd generally pay a lot of attention to. But the squeaky wheel gets the grease. If somebody got it in their head to cause him trouble, I don't know as too many people would go outta their way to stick up for him."

Quen stiffened. "In point of fact, you know ..." She ticked her fingers as she mentally counted. "... ten people. It falls on us to be on his side."

Jonathan chuckled. "You get persnickety when you get riled up."

His laughter disarmed her. Caleb's problem and the specter of Samuel slipped into the back corner of her mind. She tilted her nose up, glancing down its length.

"I don't know what you're talking about."

He laughed louder. "In point of fact, I'm sure you know exactly what I mean." His eyes crinkled with affection. Her laughter joined his.

They neared Quen's street, and she directed him to turn. As they drew closer to her house, her merriment faded. She faced him again. "Jonathan, when we first met, I thought you didn't like me."

A blush strong enough to glow in the moonlight washed over his cheeks.

Jonathan shifted uncomfortably. What could he say to that?

"If I'm gonna be honest, I didn't." Jonathan ducked his head. "I'd spent most of my life hiding my struggles with reading, and you were about to march right in and expose all my secrets."

"What about now?" Her voice was almost too quiet to hear.

He pulled on the reins, stopping the wagon in front of Quen's home. His stomach flip-flopped.

A conversation he'd had with Manny back when Abby first came to San Antonio suddenly popped up in his memory.

He'd encouraged Manny to be open to the possibility of a courtship, even though he risked rejection. Interesting to see if he could take his own advice.

He climbed down from the wagon and walked to her side, holding a hand to help her descend.

Quen grasped his hand in hers as she stepped down, then gave him a little yank once she stood before him. "Well?"

His cheeks puffed as he blew out a sigh. "Now, I think about you. A lot. More than I want to."

He was pretty sure she glared at him.

"What does that mean?" She crossed her arms.

Yep. Persnickety. He smiled.

Risk it. Say it. Be honest.

He stared over her shoulder and drew a bracing breath. "It means I think of you with an affection that could easily become stronger, but I'm not sure you'd ever return the feeling. It means I'm afraid you're so much more educated, I'd bore you within a year of being together. It means I don't know if the life I want, the life I love, would be enough for you." He glanced at her face.

Her mouth fell open.

A huff of frustration left him. His hands cupped her jaw, fingers sliding back to thread into her hair. He leaned toward her, then paused. Did she want his kiss? "And you? Do you have affection for me?" The words passed from his lips onto hers, she was so close.

She nodded. Her gaze dropped to his mouth.

He pressed his lips against hers.

The world around him receded, his heart pounding against his chest. Could she hear it?

He leaned back just enough to break contact, still cradling her head in his hands. "Oh, boy." His forehead pressed against hers.

"What do we do now?" Her words were little more than warm breath against his mouth.

The moment suspended in time. What, indeed?

The sound of a lock turning behind him jolted Jonathan back to reality. They stood in front of Quen's house at an ungodly late hour. Her parents must be frantic. And furious. The last thing they needed to see was him kissing her. He dropped his hands and stepped back.

"Now we tell your mother where you've been and hope to high heaven they don't run me off at the business end of a rifle." He whispered from the side of his mouth as he held out his elbow to escort her to the house.

The door opened. "Quenby? Is that you?" A querulous voice wavered through the nighttime air.

Quen straightened, lifted her chin. "Yes, Mother. I've had quite an exciting day. You'll want to hear all about it."

Jonathan stopped at the steps. An invitation to come any farther did not seem to be forthcoming.

"Well, I'll certainly be hearing something, young lady." The words dropped like acid.

To her credit, worry pinched the woman's face. The hour was too late for a responsible, respectable young woman to be out with a man. Mrs. Martin had every right to be upset.

Jonathan withdrew his arm and tipped his hat. "Good evening, Mrs. Martin. I'm Jonathan Campbell. My mother is Elaine Campbell, who I believe you know. We have a farm outside of town. Miss Martin was with my family this evening when a fire started at a neighbor's. We all pitched in to put it out. I apologize for the extremely late hour. It was unavoidable."

Mrs. Martin seemed to take in their appearances for the first time. Her eyes widened. "A fire? Was anyone hurt?"

"The neighbor took a knock to his noggin, but he'll be all right. Miss Martin suffered a wound on her arm when she bumped against some rough wood. My mother dressed the cut as well as she could in a dark barnyard, but you can do a much better job now that you have her home."

Mr. Martin joined his wife at the door. Prissy pushed past them and flew down the steps. "Quen! You're hurt?" She reached for Quen's hands.

Jonathan met Quen's gaze calmly. Her lips pressed together as if to hide a smile. The drama of Quen's injury had taken the spotlight off the dubiousness of their behavior that evening.

"It's nothing." She allowed her sister to pull her away.

Mr. Martin turned to Jonathan. "Campbell, you say?" He gave Jonathan a searching glance, doubt clouding his face.

"Yes, sir."

The older man frowned. "And why was my daughter at your—"

"Oh, Prissy! Careful! It's tender." Quen pulled her arm close, protecting it. Her gaze met Jonathan's over Prissy's head.

All eyes turned to Quen again. Jonathan stepped back. "Well, sir, the hour's late and I know you'll want to see to Que—Miss Martin. I'll head home now."

Mr. Martin seemed undecided on whom to focus. In the end, he turned and followed his family through the front door.

The snick of the bolt dismissed Jonathan. He turned back to the wagon with a jaunty kick to his step.

"Well." He rubbed his chin, his pulse quickening at the memory of the kiss they'd shared. "I didn't see that coming." He suppressed the urge to pound on his chest like a gorilla as he climbed back onto the seat and slapped the reins.

"What do we do now is a very good question." He glanced up at the carpet of stars filling the night sky. "God,

I know you have plans. I have no idea what to do next, so I'll leave this up to you. I'm just along for the ride."

He turned the wagon around. As he drove onto Commerce Street, the shadowed face of a cowboy leaning against a column in front of the saloon flared into bright relief as the man struck a match and lit a cigarette. Samuel Jenkins watched him, his face impassive as gray smoke swirled lazily around his head.

"Why do I keep running into him? Seems he's everywhere I go lately," Jonathan muttered. He met Samuel's gaze and stared back unblinkingly. Had Jenkins seen him take Quen home? Did he now know where she lived? A prickle of uneasiness trickled through Jonathan's veins. He set his jaw with determination. Family meant everything to him, and what Ma had said was true. Quen was now family. If Jenkins thought he could intimidate her, he had another think coming.

Chapter Twenty-One

Quen packed her art supplies into Mrs. Campbell's basket, preparing to slip from the house. If anyone ever asked to see the results of all these supposed sketching field trips, she would be hard pressed to explain why her notebook was practically blank.

Last night, Prissy had heated water for a bath and helped Quen wash the heavy length of her hair while the injured arm hung over the edge of the tub. Mother placed a clean bandage over the wicked slash. Her concern constituted the most maternal attention Quen had received for longer than she could remember.

She paused as she left her room. The half-lies she'd told over the past few weeks festered uncomfortably, bubbling like acid in her upset stomach. Now that she'd reopened lines of communication between herself and God, lessons she'd learned as a child bombarded her.

Honor your father and mother.

What if they don't deserve it?

She flinched at the recollection of her mother smoothing the white cotton pad gently across her arm. *God, are you trying to tell me something?* She gave a light snort. Mother holding her first daughter in high esteem? Quen'd need more than a five-minute effort at nursing to convince her of that. Mother did what any parent would do. Her duty.

Quen tugged at the short sleeve of the light-weight cotton shirt she'd donned. The hemmed edge almost covered her bandage. Slipping the basket handle over her other arm, she turned to leave. She reached for the door when footsteps sounded behind her.

"Quenby ..." Mother's strident tones halted her mid step.

Sighing, Quen turned and faced her.

Mother twisted a handkerchief in her hands. She cleared her throat, seeming at a loss for words.

Quen frowned at this unusual indecision.

"What are you doing today?" Mother's strained smile didn't match the concerned tone she'd adopted.

Quen stood, motionless. Did her mother actually care what her plans were?

"I see you have your basket." Mother waved the handkerchief toward her. "Are you planning to sketch again?"

Quen couldn't stop a rush of hope. It was beyond her to crush this tiny olive branch, to ignore this forced attempt at friendship.

"I'm not sure. I'm returning to the Campbell's farm to see if there is anything to be done for Caleb."

"Caleb?"

"The farmer whose barn was burned last night." Quen paused. "He's Black." Mother couldn't possibly have a problem with that. She took her to Nigeria, for heaven's sake. But social expectations carried a lot of weight, particularly in the Martin household.

Mother's hand fiddled with a broach at her throat. "He's Black?"

Quen stood, defiant, saying nothing.

"Oh dear. Is someone here treating him badly?" She curled one hand against her stomach and held the handkerchief to her brow. "For people to behave this way is simply un-Christian. Is there anything we can send to help him?"

Surprise rooted her to the spot. "I ... I'm not sure. I'll find out today and let you know."

Mother smiled, the expression coming more naturally. "Do that, Quenby. And ..." she paused, giving her an entreating glance, "... please be careful, dear. I worry about you gallivanting around alone all day."

Quen stared. "I will." On impulse, she stepped forward and pressed a kiss against her parent's cheek. "Thank you for your help last night." With Mother's pleased gasp whispering in her ears, she turned quickly and pulled open the door.

Quen strode toward Commerce Street, her attention focused inward. Questions about her future with Jonathan competed with bafflement over the scene in the hallway. Despite telling herself for years she didn't need her mother's love, the smallest offer reduced her to the child she'd been in Nigeria, desiring parental esteem.

She climbed to the steps to the sidewalk. As she walked by the bakery, Missouri stepped out.

"Good morning, Quen." Missouri touched her arm, then pulled her hand away from the bandage with a gasp. "You're hurt."

"Just a cut."

"What happened?" Missouri stroked the edge of the cotton pad with a gentle finger.

"Have you not heard?" Quen glanced around to see if any eavesdroppers lurked nearby. "Caleb's barn burned last night."

Missouri's mouth dropped open. "What? No one told us." She swallowed thickly. "Was he harmed?"

Quen gripped Missouri's trembling fingers with a comforting grasp. "He's all right." She recounted the events of the night before.

Missouri frowned. "Did the house burn too?"

"No." Quen shot another cautionary glance down the sidewalk. "But I think the fire was no accident. In fact, I think Samuel Jenkins set it."

Frustrated tears sparkled in Missouri's eyes, and she pressed her lips together in an angry line. Her gaze moved to a point over Quen's shoulder, and she sucked in a breath.

Quen looked behind herself and froze.

Samuel stepped onto the first stair leading to the sidewalk. He balanced one hand on the banister. The other pushed his hat to his brow. "Mornin', Miss Quen." His handsome face beamed, and he smiled with what seemed genuine consideration. He shot a derisive glare at Missouri but said nothing.

His charm held no attraction for Quen. She nodded coolly.

He frowned slightly at her reaction, then lowered his gaze to stare at her arm. Seconds ticked by. He lifted his chin and gave her a direct look. Stepping closer, he placed a hand carefully under her arm, holding it so her bandage showed. "You have an injury." An eyebrow rose.

She pinched her mouth in a replica of a smile. "How astute of you to notice." Quen tugged her arm. He didn't let go.

His eyes narrowed at the sarcastic tone. Regret flashed on his face. Had he harbored hope for a relationship? "You should be more careful, Miss Quen. Especially as much time as you spend out in the country, writing in your book, all by your lonesome." His tone frosted the air between them. His fingers spasmed in a painful grip. "This is a dangerous place. Anything could happen."

Quen's jaw dropped. Was that a threat? And how did he know where she spent her time?

"Quen can take care of herself." Missouri's words dropped from a curled lip.

Samuel turned, eyes blazing with derision. "Did you just speak to me?"

Missouri took a step back.

Quen eyed him with disbelief. "For heaven's sake, Mr. Jenkins. You assume quite the airs, do you not? Missouri is a living, breathing human being, and she may certainly speak to anyone she pleases."

Samuel shook his head as if Quen had confirmed something. His hand fell away, and he sighed, his focus dropping to the boot resting on the stairs. "So, it's true. You're an abolitionist." He met her gaze once again.

Quen said nothing.

He straightened. His face twisted in pain as if he'd made an unpleasant decision which hurt him to acknowledge. Quen could almost see the mental brush of his palms as he washed his hands of her. Was the pain on account of her? She shuddered.

His eyes narrowed at her reaction. He glanced at Missouri. "You'll learn soon enough, Miss Quen, we do things differently in the south. We live a different lifestyle, have different needs. Here, we know the proper order of things, and everyone plays their natural part. And animals stay in the barn."

Quen drew a furious breath and glared.

Samuel seemed not to notice. Or perhaps not to care. "Sometimes animals get loose. I'm real good at catching them. Taking them to a new place to live. Sometimes a whole new plantation on which to serve." He gave Quen a dead-eyed stare and spoke with the emotion of a snake coiled on a rock. "If you have any animals hankering to get loose, you'd best see to it they don't. You might never see 'em again."

"Of all the nerve—" Quen stammered in reply.

"Hey, ladies." Abby's happy voice interrupted the tense tableau on the sidewalk. "What fun to run into you today. Morning, Samuel."

The hateful man moved away—his face pinched like he'd stepped in a cow patty. Giving one last narrow-eyed gaze at Quen, he turned to Abby. He bent in a narrow bow and stepped back into the street. "Good morning, Mrs. Blair." He tugged his hat in her direction. "If you'll excuse me ..." He turned and sauntered away.

Abby gave the women a considering stare. "Pardon my interruption, but you two look like you've swallowed toads." She glanced over her shoulder at the departing man. "What's going on?"

Quen forced her gaze to stay trained on Abby. The weight of this deception, as necessary as it was, sat heavily on her conscience. The sudden realization of the gravity of her lies was almost more than she could bear. She couldn't afford for Abby to see her and Missouri trade silent glances. To think they teamed up to deceive her. Or didn't trust her. Her smile felt like a sorry imitation of the real thing.

"It's nothing, really. Samuel Jenkins has been rather forward in his attentions toward me, and he makes me uncomfortable. Perhaps today he finally got the message I'm not interested." She chuckled, but the sound was thin. "What are you doing in town this morning? Where are the babies?"

Abby's piercing gaze bounced between the two of them, but she smiled easily. "Yaideli is at the house, watching them. She always seems to sense when I'm at my wit's end and can use a baby break. I don't have an urgent need for anything in town, but I'm taking some time to myself. I'm going to stroll up and down every aisle in Solomon's store and enjoy listening to adult conversations." She dropped her gaze to Quen's arm, then frowned. "You're hurt."

Quen waved the bandaged arm with a careless gesture. "There was an incident at Caleb's barn last night. I was at Jonathan's when the barn caught fire, so I ran with them to help put it out." She explained how she'd received the injury. "It's not serious. I'm far more concerned about Caleb."

Abby covered a gasp with a shaking hand. "Oh, Lord, no! Manny and I will help when they rebuild. I'm sure Manny's father, Gabe, will as well. Does Caleb have plans yet?"

"I was walking to the farm to find out when I ran into Missouri." Quen turned to the younger woman. "Are you doing errands for Mrs. Lancaster? Can you come along with me to check on Caleb?" She darted a glance around the street, searching for Samuel. "If not, I can walk you home."

Abby studied Missouri, a tiny frown creasing her brow. She transferred her measured gaze to Quen, resuming her pleasant smile. "How considerate of you."

Quen glanced sharply at her friend, but the bland look on Abby's face hinted at no suspicious thoughts. Eager to be gone before she blurted a confession, Quen reached for Missouri. "Ready?" She waved at Abby. "Enjoy your quiet time. I'd like to share an afternoon treat at the Menger again the next time you're free. Let's make plans. But now we should find out if Caleb needs anything. We'll see you later."

Abby waggled her fingers nonchalantly as they left.

Quen's heart sank. She hadn't been fooled. "Oh, Missouri, that was awful. All of it. First Samuel and his disgusting threats, then having to lie to Abby." She shook her head. "I hate keeping secrets."

Missouri gave her a warning glance. "You promised."

"I know. It's far more important to hide your operation than to worry if Abby gets her feelings hurt."

They walked along the sidewalk, both immersed in their thoughts.

"May I share something with you?" Quen's confusion about the events with Jonathan the night before needed airing.

Missouri nodded, giving her full attention.

Quen chewed on her lip. "Discussing this seems almost disloyal, but I've never had a confidant before. I need to talk about this with someone."

"You can trust me." Missouri met her gaze directly.

Quen drew a deep breath. "Jonathan kissed me last night."

Missouri's eyebrows shot to her hairline. "What? Did you want him to?"

Heat climbed Quen's neck. She nodded.

Missouri's worry morphed into a smile. "When did you two start courting?"

Quen shrugged. "I wouldn't say we're courting. I'm not exactly sure when everything changed. All I know is I've been thinking about him more and more. I never believed I would be content to be a farmer's wife, but after spending time with his family and seeing how he loves the land, I understand the pull."

"Wife?" Missouri exclaimed. "He proposed?"

Quen's ears turned hot. "No. But he said some things that sounded like he's thought about the possibility." She gripped Missouri's hand. "I've never experienced this before. I don't know what to do next."

"Let's tell Mrs. Lancaster. She'll be thrilled." Missouri tugged Quen's hand and pulled her along.

Moments later, the two spilled into the sitting room, eager to tell Quen's news.

"Mrs. Lancaster, Quen needs advice."

Tears shimmered on the widow's lashes, and she held an opened letter in a shaking hand.

Missouri's smile faltered. She rushed to Mrs. Lancaster's side and kneeled. "What's wrong?"

Mrs. Lancaster placed her palm on Missouri's cheek. "Oh, child." She breathed the words through her tremulous smile. "We've found her. We've found your sister."

Chapter Twenty-Two

Quen helped Missouri to a seat at the table. Her skin turned ashen at the widow's teary declaration.

"You're sure this person is Nora?" Missouri's intertwined fingers tucked under her chin with anticipation.

Mrs. Lancaster waved the letter in the air, as joyful as if she held an announcement that she'd won a gold coin at the county fair. "My investigator says so. He's experienced and thorough. If he says he found her, then she's found."

"Where is she?" Quen asked.

"On a small plantation near Cibolo Creek, about fifty miles away. In the buggy, the trip takes two days. Detective Durant tells me a boarding house sits halfway between. I'll get a room for the night."

Missouri frowned. "Why are you saying I, instead of we?"

Mrs. Lancaster placed a hand on her knee. "Dear child, I'll not risk taking you over Natchez way. The farther you stay from anything resembling a plantation, the better. You remain here. I'll only be gone four days."

"I'm coming with you." Missouri's jaw jutted with a stubborn thrust.

Quen cleared her throat. "She may be safer if she accompanies you."

Mrs. Lancaster turned to her. "Whatever do you mean?"

The two women recounted their experience with Samuel and the fire.

Mrs. Lancaster's mouth pinched. "That scoundrel."

Quen studied Missouri's face. "Why don't you stay with Caleb?"

Mrs. Lancaster pursed her lips. She thought for a moment. "If he remains at the Campbell's, we would impose to add Missouri's care to their generous offer. However, if Caleb returns home, the two of them are now conveniently positioned to receive someone's bad treatment. If Mr. Jenkins is emboldened to threaten Missouri, what's to stop him from taking them both, especially if Caleb is wounded and weakened? He gets two birds with one stone. No, I will not leave you alone here, and I absolutely will not take you East. But we cannot trust this to someone outside of the family. This task is too important to hand off."

For such a time as this.

"I'll go." Quen forced herself to sound nonchalant.

Missouri gaped. "Are you sure?"

Mrs. Lancaster eyed her with calm consideration. "That might work. The road between here and there is well traveled, and there will be little to cause trouble. You should reach the boarding house long before nightfall." She paused. "I hesitate to send anyone else along because sharing this news opens us to questions I don't want to answer. But perhaps we can find a man to ride with you."

Quen shook her head. "I can't travel with a man I don't know. I'll be fine."

Mrs. Lancaster hesitated, a hand rubbing at her temple. "I'm uncertain about this, Quenby."

"You were going to make the trip. Why is it OK for you, but not me?" Quen sat quietly, giving her time to think.

Mrs. Lancaster relaxed, and her hand dropped to her lap. "You're a capable young woman. I believe you can do this."

Quen bit back a smile. A few days out from under Mother's purview, and she got to help.

"Let's make plans. Now I know she's so close, I want to snatch her from the jaws of danger. She's within arm's reach." Mrs. Lancaster studied the letter again. "I need to visit the bank. You should have no trouble convincing the owner to sell Nora. Mr. Durant says he's in financial straits. The Union blockade of ports in the Gulf has hurt cotton farmers. Plus, he is apparently in poor health, and needs money to pay doctors. Your visit should be nothing more than the work of an afternoon where you offer my price, sign a paper, and come back home."

An eager thrill coursed through Quen's veins. How exciting. Now to come up with a cover story to tell Mother.

"Meet me here tomorrow morning, and I'll have everything you need." Mrs. Lancaster stood and embraced her. "Thank you, dear girl. This is quite a sacrifice you're making."

She saw a sacrifice. Quen saw an adventure.

Where was Quen? Jonathan's attention made more trips to the road in front of the house than a cardinal flying out to find materials for its nest.

Questions bombarded him the moment his eyes had opened that morning. Did her parents berate her about coming home so late? Had anyone seen him kiss her? And as for that kiss, what did Quen think? Did she regret it? Yearn for another one? He'd puttered around the barn like a lovesick calf, finding little odd jobs so he would see her when she arrived, but he'd run out of things to do. Time to give up and head back to the fields.

He pulled the door to the tack room closed. Phoenix's lusty bray announced a visitor.

"I bet that's Quen." The obnoxious noise was now a harbinger of good news. His heart thumped. He headed to the open door of the barn, then paused, sending a cautious glance first to the left, then right. Where had that darned goose gone?

Hans was by the corral, wings lifted as if he planned to hug Quen, who stood at the fence petting the donkey. Her little fan club greeted her as if days had passed, not hours, since she'd been there. He snorted. They had the same reactions as he. Could he waddle over and throw his arms around her too?

He walked to where she stood. She turned at the sound of his approach.

"Good morning." More words piled up behind his teeth, but he kept them to himself.

You're a sight for sore eyes.

Did you sleep well?

Have you thought of me today?

She smiled at him, eyes bright and cheeks flushed. "Good morning." She peered past him to the barn. "How is Caleb?"

"Moving slow, but Teddy and Ernest took him to his farm to check the damage in the light of day. They'll make a schedule to rebuild."

"I ran into Abby this morning. She said Manny and his father will help when the time comes."

"Good."

They gazed at each other, an awkward silence filling the air.

"Did your mother—"

"What time did you get—"

They laughed, delighted with each other.

Jonathan reached out a hand and hooked a strand of her hair with his finger, moving the silky length from her face. "You look nice."

Quen blushed, her eyes shining. "Thank you."

"Did your parents nag you last night?"

"Not really. Their attention was on my arm. My mother spoke to me this morning as I left the house, which was unusual." Quen twitched her mouth sideways. "I'm not sure what to do with that."

"Your relationship with her isn't good?"

"Hmm, I'd say cool is a better description." Quen shrugged. "I'm used to her treatment. But, enough of that. I'm here to balance the books with our latest butter income and check with Belle about the delivery for next week."

Jonathan nodded. "Come by again tomorrow and help with the next batch. Ma would love to have you stay for dinner."

A shutter closed over Quen's face. "Um, I'll have to check. I'm not sure if I'll be free."

Jonathan squinted. "What else are you doing?"

She wouldn't meet his eyes, instead fussing with her bandage. "Mrs. Lancaster mentioned needing my help. But I don't know when."

Jonathan had watched his younger siblings lie to Ma enough times to know when someone was deceiving. Hurt swam through his gut. Doubt chilled his growing affection like a bucket of cold spring water. "I see."

Quen's worried gaze caught his for a moment. A forced smile crossed her face, and she cleared her throat. "I'll go inside and get the account caught up."

Jonathan hitched his chin in her direction and shoved his hands into his pockets. "Sure. Go ahead." He watched her walk away, followed by the devoted goose. Phoenix's nose bumped his arm through the rails of the fence.

Absentmindedly, he scratched behind her ears. *Lord, what is Quen thinking?* Was he wasting his time?

His previous suspicions about her involvement with Mrs. Lancaster rose in his mind. Quen seemed as straight as an arrow. Lying was not part of her makeup. But he'd seen how protective she could be. What was she mixed up with to cause her to act this way?

Forcing himself to squash his hurt feelings, he studied the problem as objectively as he could. He'd seen with his own eyes the package she'd put in the tree for Caleb, something he was almost certain rendered aid to an escaping slave. But what was the connection between her and Jenkins? The ratbag was a known bounty hunter. Caleb's very presence as a free man would be a burr under Jenkins's saddle. She accused him of setting fire to Caleb's barn. Had the man gotten wind of her words?

All those ingredients mixed together to create a volatile and secretive situation. And somehow, Quen was smack dab in the middle of the mess.

"OK, Miss Quen. Poke your nose into that business too. You're good at that. But I'm keeping my eye on you. For your own protection."

Jonathan headed out to the fields. Quen would undoubtedly take advantage of his absence to slip away this afternoon, avoiding another uncomfortable conversation at lunchtime. He'd figure out an excuse that would allow him to accidentally run into her tomorrow, see what was going on. She wouldn't be able to hide her secrets for very long.

The next morning, Quen entered the front room. "Mother, you remember my friend Abby?"

Her mom laid her book down, transferring her attention to Quen. "Of course."

"Sometimes when the babies get sick, Abby gets overwhelmed with chores and such, and she needs help. I would like to be the friend who could volunteer for things like that. Don't you think it would be nice if I spent some time with Abby if the babies are ill? Mrs. Lancaster mentioned the possibility, said volunteering would be a very Christlike thing for me to do."

Mother tilted her head. "I agree."

Quen swallowed hard. She didn't feel very Christlike at the moment. She'd crafted those words carefully, so she wasn't actually telling a lie. OK, only a little bit of lying. *It's for a good reason, God.* "I hoped you would say that. I'll be gone for a few days, four at the most." She turned to leave before Mother could ask questions.

"All right, dear. Be as careful as you can not to get sick yourself."

"I'm not worried, Mother. I'm going to go pack."

Quen hurried to her room and grabbed a carpetbag stuffed with items she'd need on her journey. Mrs. Lancaster told her to sleep at the boarding house on the way there and back. But an irrational fear kept her awake most of the night. What if she arrived at the plantation near Cibolo Creek with Mrs. Lancaster's money in hand, and the owner demanded more? What would she do if there wasn't enough?

She'd decided in the wee hours of the morning to take supplies and sleep on the side of the road. Stories of cowboys on cattle drives had filled hers and Prissy's ears all the way from Galveston to San Antonio when they'd first come. If cowboys could camp out, she could too. She'd save the cash. If she didn't need the extra, she and Nora could treat themselves to a nice dinner there on the way home.

She lugged the heavy valise down the hall, the weight banging against her shins. She straightened, doing her best to act as though nothing more than a nightgown and a change of clothes were enclosed as she passed the doorway to the front room.

"I'm heading out, Mother." She called without stopping. "I'll see you in a few days."

"Have a good time, dear." Mother didn't rise from her seat on the sofa.

Quen sighed with relief. A few houses down, she paused, set the bag on the ground, and rolled her shoulders. Taking a deep breath, she grasped the handles with both hands and struggled on down the road. Good thing Mrs. Lancaster lived nearby.

Once at the widow's house, Quen placed her bag into the back seat of the waiting buggy already hitched to a pair of bay horses. Mrs. Lancaster and Missouri joined her outside.

"I've sewn money into the hem of this traveling jacket." Mrs. Lancaster handed her a lightweight wrap. "If anyone stops you, nothing of value will be readily noticeable." The widow pressed more bills into her hands. "This should cover the cost of the inn."

Quen accepted both. She slid the loose bills into her skirt pocket, then laid the jacket across the seat.

"Here is a letter for the plantation owner, giving permission for you to purchase Nora on my behalf, although he probably won't care two shakes one way or the other. I've also included Detective Durant's directions to Cibolo Creek. Everything sounds straightforward. Do you have questions?"

"No, ma'am. I'm ready. God willing, I'll be back in a few days with Nora by my side."

Mrs. Lancaster leaned forward and gave her a fierce hug. Missouri followed suit. Quen climbed into the buggy, shook the reins, and headed down the drive.

Quen held her breath until she passed out of the city limits. When no one shouted or waved her down, she relaxed. She'd made it. Now she could enjoy the trip.

The sun traveled across the sky as the hours passed. She watched the boarding house come up in the distance and sighed with regret as it receded behind her. Hunger pains growled, announcing the time had come for sustenance. However, she was determined to travel as far as she could and not spend a penny she didn't have to. Finally, she gave in to the demands her body made and searched for a place to stop for the night.

A small grove of trees offered privacy, and the ground appeared relatively level. This would make a fine place to bed down. "What do you think, girls?" She turned the horses off the road. "This should suit us well."

Quen climbed down and stretched her legs. Concentrating on how the buckles and straps fit together, she unharnessed the mares and hobbled them. They immediately began grazing. Finally, she returned to the buggy for her meal.

Climbing up to the seat, she reached into her carpetbag. With a tug, she pulled a small picnic basket from inside. She turned and gazed at the grassy area. Where should she sit? And perhaps she needed a fire? She peered into her carpetbag. No magical fire-making implement revealed itself. How did one start a fire, anyway?

She straightened with a sniff. "We don't need to heat anything." She spoke to the mares, who ignored her. "And the seat on the buggy makes a nice sideboard on which to spread my dinner." Setting the basket on the bench beside her, she opened the lid. Inside, fried pies, wrapped in a cloth napkin, waited at the top. "I'm saving you for dessert." Next to them were a pair of fluffy scones and a small glass jar of clotted cream. She smoothed a red-checked napkin across her lap. Spooning cream onto the scone, she took a bite. "Hmm." She closed her eyes, enjoying the blissful flavors.

A coyote yapped in the distance. Quen's eyes flew open. She peered through the tree trunks. Did anything move? She eyed the length of the buggy seat. Perhaps the boards would suffice as a bed. Up, off the ground. Out of reach of any animals that might come nosing around in the night.

The sound of approaching hooves drew the attention of her mares. The animals lifted their heads and whinnied. Quen's gaze darted to the copse of trees for a less conspicuous place to wait. She should've concealed the buggy behind them. No time to hide now.

Standing, she peeked under the seat. Did she have anything she could use as a weapon? Pounding hooves drew nearer. Visions of highwaymen flooded her imagination. Why didn't she stay at the inn? Whoever approached could certainly overpower her should they care to. Clutching her spoon in both hands, she whirled to face her visitor. A drip of clotted cream slid down onto her fingers.

"Quenby Martin!" Jonathan's angry voice rattled her eardrums. "I don't know what in tarnation you're up to, but you're not doing it alone."

Chapter Twenty-Three

Jonathan hauled on Cisco's reins, pulling him to a stop beside the buggy. He bit back a self-satisfied smile. Good. He'd startled her. Paybacks were the devil. He dismounted. The gelding's head drooped, sides heaving after the long gallop.

"What are you doing here?" Quen smoothed her hair.

The fancy fixings she'd pulled from her picnic basket spread across the seat. "What are *you* doing? You're in Mrs. Lancaster's buggy, alone, hours from town."

She gave him a haughty stare. "I'm taking a trip."

He scoffed, crossing his arms across his chest. "And you brought *that* for provisions?" He nodded toward the food spread out on the seat. Stepping forward, he inspected the items, raising his eyebrows. "Didn't you forget the butter dish? Where are the salt and pepper shakers?"

Quen shot him a cross glance, and a flush brightened her cheeks. "Please pardon my ignorance. In point of fact, this is my first camp-out."

"Camp-out?" Jonathan couldn't stop a harsh snort. "This is your idea of a camp-out meal?"

She huffed.

He'd better cut this off at the pass before her tail feathers get any more in a snit. He turned to peer down the road in the direction she'd been driving. "Where are you headed? And how is Mrs. L involved?"

His abrupt change of topic derailed her. Tugging her lip with her teeth, she dropped her focus to somewhere in the vicinity of the buttons on his chest. "She isn't. She merely loaned me her buggy."

"Balderdash." Enough with the lies. He leaned closer, wagging a finger in her face. "Let me tell you what I think."

Her startled gaze jumped to meet his.

"First, your face gives you away when you fib. Second, you're up to your ears in something involving Mrs. L, Caleb, Missouri, and probably Jenkins. Third, you're helping enslaved people escape." Satisfaction flooded him at the sound of her gasp. He knew it. "Mrs. L would never have sent such a greenhorn on an overnight trip unless she had no other choice. It's not safe. So, what the devil is going on?"

Her chin tucked into her neck. "Greenhorn?"

He shook his head. He dressed her down, and she chose to be offended by the name he used? Her outrage didn't put him off. "Spill it, Quenby Martin. If I figured this out, others may've too. If you're doing something dangerous— or illegal—I need to know."

"You're not in charge of me."

The affront on her face almost made him laugh. He should've known better.

"All right. I'll rephrase that. As your friend, I'm concerned you may be doing something that has put you in danger. Can you explain to me why you are all this way out here, alone?"

Her mouth opened and closed.

He tilted his head and cocked an eyebrow, waiting.

"I ..." Her gaze jumped around like a cricket evading a bird's beak.

"I'm not leaving, so you might as well trust me."

She pressed her lips together.

Stubborn little minx. He'd bide his time.

A clatter of hooves interrupted the stand-off. Jonathan stepped back from Quen and faced the approaching riders. He frowned. With their scruffy beards and dusty clothes, the three men couldn't appear more disreputable if they tried. Coiled whips hung from each saddle.

"Howdy, folks." The rider in front tipped his hat. "We're looking for a few runners. Have you seen any slaves sneaking around?"

Jonathan ignored Quen's gasp and kept his gaze trained on the man who appeared to be the leader.

"Sorry, friend. We haven't seen anyone at all for the past few hours. Running or otherwise."

The man sucked his teeth. His face conveyed his skepticism, but he said nothing.

A second man nudged his horse forward. "You'll hold 'em for us if you find 'em, right? It's against the law to aid a slave attempting to escape."

Jonathan gritted his teeth. "I'm aware."

The leader narrowed his eyes at Jonathan's tone. He transferred his attention to Quen, and his gaze turned predatory. "Strange place to stop for the night seeing's there's an inn back a way. Everything OK?"

The scruff of Jonathan's neck rose. "We're doin' just fine. Thanks for asking." He stepped closer to Quen. "Don't let us keep you."

The man snorted, then glanced at his companions and shrugged. "Let's go." They kicked their horses into motion.

Jonathan's gaze followed them as they left, then he turned his attention back to Quen, who'd sat as motionless as a mouse evading the sharp eyes of a hawk. "You see what you're up against? Now, you were about to answer my question ..."

"I can't say anything!" Her tortured gaze met his. "I promised."

Making progress. "Was that before or after Caleb's barn burned to the ground?"

"Well ..." She chewed her bottom lip.

"Let me help you." His voice lowered.

She took a deep breath, then the plan tumbled from her like melting snow spilling from a spring waterfall.

As she described the operation they ran, right under the noses of the citizens of San Antonio, Jonathan struggled to keep his expression neutral. When she explained her purpose for the trip, he frowned.

"You're going to Cibolo Creek to buy Caleb's daughter? Does this man know you're coming?"

Quen's brows drew together. "That wasn't entirely clear. I don't think so."

Jonathan closed his eyes. So many things could go wrong with this plan. *Dear Lord, please go before us and prepare the way.* "Very well." He glanced at her basket, his tone lightly mocking as he continued. "No one brings dishes and napkins on a camp-out."

Her chin went up in the air. "Do you mean to tell me you ate with your fingers the entirety of your cattle drive?"

He sighed with exaggerated patience. "Of course not. But we didn't bring dishes that break." He peered into her carpetbag and frowned. "What else is in there?" She stiffened with the same snap to her spine he'd seen a dozen times before. Whatever she said, he couldn't laugh.

"If you must know, I have bedding, a change of clothes—"

"A bedroll?" He smiled to soften the surprise that rang in his voice.

"Certainly not." She scoffed. "I have my quilt, a small pillow, and a washcloth for my fa—" She smacked the hand he stretched toward the carpetbag.

He couldn't help it. Laughter burst from him as he shook his head.

Quen's frown lowered like a gathering storm. "I fail to see what is so humorous about bedding."

Ma could make lemon bars from the sour expression on her face. "Is there also a mattress under the seats of that buggy?"

The hurt on her face hit like a punch in the gut.

"I'll show you how this is done." He forced a factual, instructive tone to his voice. "First, we'll lay wood for a campfire. The flames'll keep wild animals away during the night, and we'll be able to make coffee in the morning."

"Coffee?" Quen glanced into her carpetbag.

"You didn't bring coffee?"

The hurt look deepened. "I have tea leaves." She snatched up the tea tin and wagged it in his face. "And a teapot with which to heat water. And a sturdy earthenware mug my father uses from which to sip it."

Tea? Wait till he told Manny. He hurried on. "Tea is fine. Did you water the horses?"

Quen pressed her lips together. That gathering storm on her face now threatened a rain of tears.

He waved his hands to calm the brewing emotion. "I'll take 'em to the creek."

Her shoulders slumped. "I should've stopped at the boarding house like Mrs. Lancaster said."

No kidding. "You know, accepting direction from someone doesn't mean you're not capable." The thought of all that could've happened out there sharpened his voice.

"I felt very strongly I should keep the boarding house money, just in case I didn't have enough to buy Nora's freedom."

For Pete's sake. "Mrs. Lancaster sent extra money, and you didn't use it? Quen, that was foolish. Don't you think she planned for that?"

Quen climbed down from the buggy, her body rigid and jaw set. "I did what I thought was best. I didn't realize I was being stupid."

"You're not stupid." Jonathan reached for her hand.

She yanked her fingers from his grasp. "I'm obviously not good at your kind of life. I don't know what I'm doing."

"What do you mean? Look at how you've helped my family with our finances."

She rejected his words. "You've only been here five minutes and you've pointed out nineteen different things I've done wrong. My skills are better used in other ways. There's no place for me here." She might as well nip those daydreams of belonging, of fitting in with Jonathan's family, before they took root. Her heart gave a whimper, but she ignored it with ruthless disdain.

"Quenby Martin, you'll be the death of me." Jonathan raked a hand through his hair, leaving the sandy-blond strands standing in spikes. "You're suitable for anything you set your mind to. Why do you think I followed you?"

Her heart leaped. Was he saying he wanted her to get used to this life? A life with him? She shook her head. She wouldn't open herself to this possibility again. "Be reasonable, Jonathan. No man in his right mind would consider me wifely material. My strengths lie elsewhere."

Jonathan propped his hands on his hips. "You open your mouth and start talking, and I want to take you by the shoulders and shake you."

The need on his face surprised Quen.

He moved a step closer. "Either that—" His voice lowered. "Or take you by the shoulders and kiss you."

The distance between them shrank by another step. His gaze fastened on her lips.

Why *didn't* she bring the butter dish? Think of anything other than his mouth.

He was near enough to touch. He reached for her fingers. Turned her palm up. His fingertips traced the outline of hers. She drew a shaky breath and resisted the urge to wipe her damp hands against her skirt.

He'd laughed at her.

Unable to accept his approbation, she stared at his throat.

A pulse pounded there. The sight mesmerized her.

A sudden image of herself, placing her lips on that fluttering spot, sent a wave of dizziness through her head.

"I wonder." He murmured, the timbre of his voice deep. "Is that mouth, so skilled at instructing me what to do and think every minute of every day, equally skilled at driving me crazy?"

"I ... I don't know what you mean." But she was afraid she did. The vision of Abby curling her body against Manny's, sharing his passionate kiss, filled her mind.

"Don't you?" His words were a sigh. He flattened her hand against his chest. A steady thump pounded beneath her fingers. Did she do that to him?

He slid his palm down her arm and curled his fingers around her elbow. His mouth hovered close as he tilted his head toward her.

Ensnared like a moth in a web, she couldn't take her gaze from his. Her chin lifted, placing her lips a hair's breadth from his. "Maybe I do."

The whispered breath that left her mouth had the effect of a lightning strike on dry timberland.

With a muttered curse, he slid his hands into her hair at the base of her skull, threading his fingers into its length, then his lips touched hers.

The ground tilted.

He pulled away, rubbed his thumb across her lower lip. "I probably shouldn't have done that." The low sound of his voice sent a shiver through her.

She stepped back. His reaction bolstered her flagging confidence. "Why did you?"

He shrugged, grinned. "Maybe I'm a glutton for punishment."

A surprised laugh burst from her lips. The tension of the moment dissipated.

Jonathan turned. "I'm taking the horses for water. I'll bring wood for the fire." He paused. "What else is packed in that picnic basket? My saddlebags have hardtack and beef jerky. I bet whatever you brought is better. Is there enough to share?"

Her heart leaped. "Of course. Do you prefer sliced cucumbers in vinegar, or stuffed mushrooms?"

His bark of laughter accompanied the sound of his receding footsteps. This time, though, the laughter didn't sting.

The cheerful, crackling fire did an excellent job of holding yapping coyotes at bay. Quen yawned. "I believe I'm ready to turn in." She gave Jonathan and his bedroll a stern glare over the fire. "You stay on your side of the fire, good sir. I'll not have you sneaking over in the night to avail yourself of my superior quilt. Or my little pillow."

"I wouldn't dream of it."

His gaze rivaled the heat from the flames, unabashed admiration glowing in the firelight. Quen's cheeks grew warm under his regard. "Very well. I'll see you in the morning." She curled up inside her cover and closed her eyes. She'd never fall asleep with him staring at her.

She awakened to the sound of chirping birds. The sun inched its way above the horizon, shooting rays of orange and pink into the indigo bowl curving above them and sending the stars to bed. Jonathan hitched the mares to the buggy. She watched him for a moment, admiring his long legs, his broad shoulders. His hands worked efficiently. This was a man confident in his own abilities. He knew what he wanted from life.

She wanted to be that sure about her future. *Will you please guide me, God? Will you show me the path I am to take?*

He turned and caught her staring. "Mornin', glory." He smiled. "I took the liberty of helping myself to that teapot. Your mug is steeping next to the fire. We can split the last of those fried pies." He checked the mares' traces. "We need to get on the road. I'd like to get this over with. I don't know how much money Mrs. L sent with you, but carrying it makes me nervous."

Soon, the buggy rolled down the road, Cisco tied at the back. Quen showed Jonathan the directions Mrs. Lancaster shared with her.

The morning dragged on, anticipation building inside Quen as steadily as the heat of the day.

Nearing noon, Jonathan nodded at a house drawing up on the right. "This is the place." He slowed the buggy and turned down a long, winding drive. He frowned.

Quen tensed. "What's wrong?"

Jonathan waved his hand toward the empty fields. "Where is everyone? I don't understand."

He pulled the buggy to a stop in front of the large white house. As he climbed down, the door opened, and a well-dressed man stepped outside. He carried a satchel in one hand and tugged a bowler onto his head with the other. He faltered, surprise on his face.

"May I help you?" The man stepped toward the porch stairs, pressing them back a step as he advanced without slowing.

"I hoped to purchase ..." Jonathan stumbled over the words.

Quen stepped in. "I was told there's a young woman here by the name of Nora. I want to bring her home with me, to work at my house in San Antonio. We want to buy her."

The older man frowned. "Have you not heard?"

Jonathan and Quen traded glances. Dread curled in her stomach. "Heard what? Please enlighten us."

"Mr. Smith, the owner, died two days ago. They sent all slaves to auction. I don't know who this Nora is, but you won't find her here."

Chapter Twenty-Four

The man turned back to face the door. His announcement about Nora's whereabouts shot a cannonball through Quen's plans. He inserted a key, then twisted it. Tumblers clicked, a death knell to Quen's hopes. The man couldn't leave before she got answers.

What would she tell Caleb and Missouri? Oh, to have come so close.

Jonathan's voice broke through her whirling thoughts. "When did the ... people go to the auction block?"

"What people?" The man scowled. "Do you mean the slaves?"

"Nora." Quen's voice cracked. She had a name.

He waved a dismissive hand, shooing them away.

"Sir!" Quen hurried to block his steps. "When did they leave?"

"Yesterday." He brushed past. "Now, if you don't mind, I have papers to file. There'll be kinfolk coming from every corner of the state." He stomped toward the barn, his tirade trailing behind. "Why don't people leave wills?"

She ran, placing herself in front of him again. "Please. One more question."

He stopped, his chest deflating. "Yes?" His toneless voice invited her to leave him be.

"This auction—where is it?"

He pointed to the road. "Keep heading east. This leads to Natchez. A barn stands at the intersection of the road coming up from Corpus. They hold auctions there. Now," he gave her a theatrical bow, "may I be excused?"

Quen stepped out of his path, holding her palms up. "By all means."

She hurried back to where Jonathan studied the map sketched by the investigator.

"Do you know the place he described?" Her chest tightened.

He placed his arm around her shoulders and squeezed. The strength in his embrace calmed her. "I know the place."

She closed her eyes. Deep breath in, slow exhale. *God, please let her still be there.*

Jonathan released her and turned to the buggy. "Relax. Everything'll be OK."

Within moments, the mares trotted down the road, Cisco following behind, snorting at the dust kicked up in the dry afternoon.

Urgency pounded through Quen's veins. "What if she's been sold already?"

"No point worrying." Jonathan placed his hand over hers. "She'll be there, or she won't. If she isn't, we'll find her again." He laced his fingers through hers and pulled the buggy to a stop. "Let's pray."

Startled, Quen fell silent. Did he mean for her to say it?

He bowed his head, fingers still threaded with hers.

"Father God, we place Nora in your hands and ask for her protection. We believe in your goodness and mercy, and we turn this situation over to you. You brought all the Israelites from bondage in Egypt. You can deliver one woman. Teach us to trust you and accept your guidance. In Jesus's name, amen."

His confidence steadied her. *Yes, God. All of that.* Would turning to God ever become her default reaction to a problem?

"Now," he slapped the reins again. "We won't fret about it one more minute. Whatever happens, happens." As the buggy picked up speed, he glanced at the picnic basket under her seat. "Is there anything left to eat?"

Quen straightened on the bench. A building grew larger as they approached. The auction block was little more than a barn. Weather-beaten planks stood gray against a lowering sky.

Jonathan steered the buggy into the yard and tilted his chin toward the building, the movement abrupt. "Looks like they're inside."

Wagons sprawled across the area in front of the stage, and horses shifted as if uneasy, taut reins binding them to the trees. Sweltering air hung leaden. Somewhere in the distance, a metal chime tinkled, the sound incongruous with the setting. Quen studied the scene where human beings sold others like chattel, foreboding settling in her stomach.

A wooden platform stood out front. The auctioneer forced enslaved people to pose, by his actions declaring them to be nothing more than property. A sour smell of sweat hovered in the air.

Beside her, Jonathan shook his head. The murmur of his voice carried to her ears. "Father God, please send your presence here. Let your goodness replace this evil. We need you. Please help us find Nora."

Men stood in groups, talking. A few sat on wagon benches during the lull between the next sale, waiting with the patience of a copperhead, curled, eager to strike. Several Black men stood beside horses hitched to carts.

Caleb's life flashed in Quen's mind.

He was free, he owned property, and he was self-sufficient.

What did these Black men think? How could a person wake each morning, knowing he was helpless to control a single aspect of his life?

"I hope these people know Jesus." Jonathan's heartfelt mutter tugged at her. "Surely, leaning on God for strength and comfort is the only thing that gets them through each day."

A hot gust of wind blew through, whipping up a dust devil from the ground. Jonathan peered at the sky. "It's gonna rain." He murmured the words. Quen glanced at him. He wasn't talking to her, more voicing his thoughts. "We need a good, strong rain to wash away the wrongs of humanity. Thank you, Lord, that my folks never led me on this path."

The auctioneer's runner led two young women away from the platform, their steps limited. Quen stared. A vision of children she'd taught in Nigeria flashed through her mind. They'd skipped, laughed, chased butterflies. Mothers watched from the doorways of their huts where they pounded flour, smiling at the antics of their children.

A child cried out, banishing the picture.

Quen's gaze fell on a whip, coiled and draped over a fence post. She shuddered.

The utter contrast between the two worlds sickened her. She swallowed hard. The hopeless slump of the women's shoulders broke her heart. How did these men live with the pain they caused? And now she and Jonathan had to pretend to be part of them. Could she have done this on her own? *Thank you, God, for him.*

The woman with the child passed by, led by a man who'd just purchased her. Quen studied her face. Nora was a stranger to her, and Caleb couldn't describe the daughter he hadn't seen for almost fifteen years. Did the elder sister have familiar features? Would Quen recognize Caleb's smile or Missouri's eyes?

A man pulled the barn door open and waved roughly at the people inside. Four Black men emerged and climbed the steps to the small stage. The owners' attention sharpened. The snakes prepared to strike.

Quen ignored the proceedings and took a step toward the woman with the child, who glanced at her, eyes full of fear. Quen knew her immediately. She turned to Jonathan, excitement raising her voice. "That's her. I'm positive. She has Missouri's eyes, and Caleb's freckles." The boy, who appeared about three years old, clung to her hand with both of his, cleaving to her as if a ferocious tide tugged at him, and she was his lifeline. Freckles stood out like a ladybug's dots on his lighter-colored skin. He had to be Nora's son.

The woman's drawn visage told the story of her world crashing around her, but she forced a smile for the boy, encouraging him. Quen hadn't believed her heart could break any further, but Nora's brave love undid her. Tears flooded her eyes.

The ringman's helper approached, holding up a cautionary hand. "Hold up, Mr. Johnson. You signed a promissory note only for the woman. The boy will cost you more."

Quen took another step toward her. "Nora?" She whispered the name. Did anyone watch?

The woman's eyes widened. She faltered.

The man yanked the woman. "Git along. I don't have all day." He glanced back. "And get rid of that boy. I'm not payin' for your litter."

Panic washed over Nora's face. She gripped her hands together as if in prayer. "Please, sir. He won't be any trouble. You won't even know he's there."

The child began to cry.

The helper grabbed the boy's shoulder and pulled. "Come away, now."

Nora begged. "He's only three years old. Please don't do this." She groped at the man who'd purchased her. The child cried out. The auctioneer snapped at him to shut up.

Utter sorrow tore at the air. More clouds blew in, dimming the sunshine. The sky turned gray.

Anger flowed through Quen, curling her fingers into fists. She struggled to breathe.

A different man stepped forward. "Stop. You're frightening him." He peeled two bills from a roll in his hand and thrust them at the auctioneer. "I'll take the boy." Reaching down, he encircled the child's torso with his arm. "Come, child." He pulled him away and walked toward his wagon. The child cried out, kicking, writhing, reaching for his mother.

Nora followed him with her eyes. "Isaac!" Her hands reached toward him. The man yanked again.

Quen stood frozen. What to do?

For such a time as this.

She darted over to the man, who stared angrily at his wailing property, his face filled with disgust.

"Pardon me, good sir. You appear to have made a questionable acquisition. My employer sent me here to find a young woman to work in her kitchen. I could take her off your hands and perhaps you could choose another, one who suits you better." She raised her voice over Nora's pleas. "I heard the auctioneer mention a promissory note. I'll pay what you owe, plus $200 more." She held out her hand, bills clutched in her fist.

How much had the man promised to pay? Did she have enough?

The man's brows shot up.

"Please, sir!" Nora cried harder. "Don't let them take my boy."

With an abrupt motion, the man turned away. "I'll get the auctioneer. Don't know why you're so all-fired up to pay $200 extra, but I'm happy to part a fool from her money."

Quen met Nora's gaze. Tears streaked down the woman's face, cutting shiny lines through the dust on her skin. "Everything will be OK," she murmured.

Jonathan approached, a key in his hand. "Move over, Quen." His voice rough with anger, he kneeled and freed Nora.

The woman hiccupped through her sobs. She grasped Quen's forearms. "My boy. Please buy my boy too."

The urge to pull the young woman into her embrace was almost more than Quen could stand. "I will, Nora." She promised automatically.

"We may not have the money." Jonathan hissed under his breath.

The auctioneer returned and stated an amount that made Quen's heart sink. She counted the bills Mrs. Lancaster had given her and handed them over, then gave $200 to the man. Only twenty dollars remained.

Quen placed her hand on Nora's arm and led her to the buggy. "Jonathan, will you get the papers?" She squeezed Nora's hand. "We'll find the man who took your son."

The child's sobs lifted above the hubbub in the yard. He had to be nearby. Quen stood on a wagon wheel spoke and peered around.

Jonathan returned with papers clutched in his hand. He tugged at Quen's arm. "Get down. You're drawing attention." He glanced around. "I watched the man who took the boy return to his wagon."

"Do you have any money?" Quen whispered.

"No. You, of all people, know that." Sadness cloaked his face. "I'm sorry."

Lord, help us.

"We can't just drive off and leave her son behind." Quen paced a small circle around Nora and Jonathan.

Nora's tortured gaze jumped from Quen's face to Jonathan's.

"What do you plan to do? Kidnap him?" Jonathan scrubbed his face, then drew a deep breath. He set his jaw. "I'll go find out the man's name. We can track him down and buy Isaac back later, just as Mrs. Lancaster did with Nora."

Nora gasped. "Mrs. Lancaster? Tara Lancaster?"

"Yes." Quen nodded. "She's been looking for you." She gripped Nora's hand. "She sent me to bring you home."

"Oh, praise Jesus."

Jonathan walked to the man's wagon. Placing a hand on his shoulder, he turned him away from the noise in the yard and spoke with his mouth near the man's ear.

The auctioneer's rattle carried on in the background, punctuated by men making bids. Despair filled the air like the clouds covered the sky.

Quen's gaze followed Jonathan. Would he be able to convince the man to return Isaac? From the corner of her eye, she spied the child clambering from the back of the man's cart. He pelted across the yard to his mother, bare feet puffing up small clouds of dust. Nora kneeled and gathered him to her bosom, wrapping her arms around his thin body as if to absorb him into her very skin. He buried his face against her neck. She closed her eyes. "Jesus will keep us safe." Her murmur quieted him.

Quen glanced to where Jonathan talked with the man. Straightening, she whirled around and yanked the quilt from her carpetbag. She shook the cover out, then spread it across the back seat, creating a tent. "Let's air this out, shall we? It's damp from the morning dew."

She turned her back, casting her gaze around the yard. Had the men seen Isaac's dash to freedom?

Jonathan returned to the buggy. "His name is Mr. Moses Brown. I said nothing about buying the boy. We'll let Mrs. L's investigator handle that end of things once we get back. I can't extend a promise in her name that she may be unable to honor." He paused. "He's a Puritan from up north. I believe he'll treat Isaac well."

A sudden shout pulled their gaze. Mr. Brown strode toward them. "Where's the child?"

Quen pulled on every resource she had to keep her face neutral and clamped her mouth shut.

The auctioneer's assistant followed. "What's going on?"

"The boy's missing." Mr. Brown seemed more worried than angry, but he had handed over cash for the child. Quen didn't trust his concern.

The assistant glared at Nora. "Where'd you put the boy?"

Tears still streamed down her face. She held her hands up, claiming innocence.

The man stomped to the buggy and reached for the quilt. Quen gripped Nora's wrist and held her breath. She flinched as the man yanked the cover away and flung it to the ground.

She gaped. The seat and the space beneath it were empty. Schooling her features, she marched over. "I beg your pardon." Snatching up the quilt, she adopted an angry tone. "I laid that out to dry. How dare you trample it into the dirt?"

"Where's the boy?" The man glared at her.

Quen drew back, affronted. "I'm sure I don't know. What sort of place do you run that you can't keep track of your inventory?"

He squatted and peered beneath the buggy. There was no sign of Isaac. "Come on, Mr. Brown. He's hiding somewhere. We'll find him."

The men hurried away, pushing a path through the crowd.

"Jonathan, let's get out of here." Quen helped Nora into the back seat, then scrambled into hers.

He climbed up and grasped the reins, glancing over his shoulder at Nora, who had quietened. "We'll do everything we can to find your son."

The buggy jerked into motion, and the horses trotted out of the yard. A spatter of raindrops made tiny craters in the dust as a cooling breeze caressed Quen's face.

As they headed back down the road, a man's silhouette drew her attention. With a gasp, she twisted to peer over her shoulder. He turned away and vanished around a corner of the barn.

She was almost positive ... had she just seen ... was that Samuel?

Chapter Twenty-Five

Jonathan's thoughts ranged ahead. The buggy rattled along the road, eating the miles as consistently as a termite tunneling its way through a fallen log. When they arrived in San Antonio tomorrow, he would deliver Nora to the loving arms of her family, then he would sit down with Mrs. L and have a long conversation. Her goals were honorable. He would support her however he could in her ongoing efforts. But he took issue with her methods. What had she been thinking to send Quen to do this alone? Honestly, Mrs. L's secrets hurt his feelings. Was he not trustworthy enough to bring into the fold?

Quen twisted around at his side.

"What are you looking for?" He snapped, his frustration boiling over. "You've turned around about a hundred times since we left."

"Nothing, really. I thought I saw someone back at the ..." She trailed off.

"Who? How would you know any of those people?"

She gave a shake of her head and faced firmly forward. "It was nothing, I'm sure."

He cut his eyes sideways at her, but let the argument go. He glanced back at Nora. Quen had explained how Missouri and Mrs. L worked to find her, gave assurances Caleb was hale and hearty, and promised all eagerly awaited her arrival. "Did you have any idea your family still lived?"

Nora shook her head. "I prayed for God to protect them. After I said my prayers each night, I talked to them. I hoped they were somewhere, staring up at the same stars I saw, thinking of me like I thought of them."

Jonathan opened his mouth to ask about Isaac, then thought better of it.

"How old were you when they separated you from your family?"

"When Mr. Lancaster sold me, you mean?" Bitterness soured her voice. "Eight. Mama died, and Mr. Lancaster sold me and Papa. I watched out the back of the wagon, waving goodbye to my sister as my new owner drove me away. Mrs. Lancaster held Missouri to keep her from chasing us down the road." Nora fell silent, gazing at the passing fields, the only sound the clopping of the horses' hooves.

She drew a deep breath. "I got used to my new life quickly. I shared a cabin with an old woman who took me in and taught me how to survive. My first few years there, I worked in the kitchen, learning to cook and bake."

Quen turned back again. "You share that talent with Missouri."

A forced smile flashed across Nora's face, disappearing as quickly as it came. "As I grew older, I drew the attention of the master. His wife didn't like it, and she banished me to the fields. That work took some getting used to." Her tone turned dry. "Of course, moving me outside didn't do any good. In fact, he was freer to do what he wanted out from under her watchful eye at the house."

Jonathan caught Quen's glance. Heat creeped up his neck. Did Quen understand what Nora meant? Shame for his fellow man engulfed him.

Nora's words grew quieter. "But God blessed me. He gave me Isaac. Having my child made anything they could've thrown my way worth the pain and suffering they caused me. He is my sun, moon, and stars. Isaac gave me a reason to get up every morning. And God knew I needed one."

Bile pressed up the back of Jonathan's throat. What must she be going through right now? "I promise we'll do everything possible to get him back. Mr. Moore, the man who took him, seemed a considerate, honorable man, if such a thing can exist at an auction block. Isaac is safe."

"I agree." Nora's calm voice held a smile.

Jonathan frowned. What had brought on this one-hundred-eighty-degree change in her demeanor? Quen remained silent, staring pointedly down the road. Had they stashed the boy somewhere on the property while he talked with Mr. Moore? If so, how did they plan to retrieve him? How would he fare on his own?

The morning had spent itself as they traveled to the deceased man's plantation, then to the auction block. The sun now followed its path toward the western horizon. Quen's stomach growled loudly enough for Jonathan to hear.

"Why don't we pull over and make camp? I'll start a fire, then I'll find some game for supper." He tossed a grin over his shoulder at Nora. "How do you feel about tea?"

She raised her brows.

Quen turned her gaze from the road long enough to narrow her eyes at him. He chuckled.

"Shouldn't we keep going?" She darted another quick glance down the road they'd just driven.

What was up with her? "I can hear your stomach from here. And the horses need rest."

She seemed as if she wanted to say something else but subsided. He couldn't help looking behind them himself. What had her so spooked?

They stopped near a grove of live oaks. He unharnessed the two mares and hobbled them, then turned Cisco loose to graze. Quen and Nora had a pile of downed twigs and broken branches gathered by the time he finished with the horses.

"Let me show you how to use flint to start the fire. You can do the job yourself next time." He pulled a flintstone from his saddlebag.

Within moments, flames crackled. He stood and reached for his rifle. "I'll have to range out. We've probably scared everything away."

Both women seemed primed for something, as if they would spring into action the second he turned his back. His gaze bounced between the two, but no answers appeared. "I'll be back soon."

Quen held her breath as Jonathan disappeared through the trees. She walked to the road and peered back the way they'd come. No one appeared. Hairs prickled on the back of her neck. Had she seen Samuel? If he'd been there, did he see her?

She turned back to the buggy and froze. Isaac sat up in the carpetbag, rubbing his eyes. When the auctioneer had snatched the quilt away and no Isaac was found, she'd surmised Nora stashed him away. She never would've left him behind. But in the carpetbag? *Thank God I brought such a large one.*

"Mama, I need to pee."

Nora lifted him from the satchel. "Come with me, sweet boy."

Quen checked under the back seat. Nora had removed the teapot, mug, and few remaining supplies. She tucked the lot into the corner of the buggy floor, pushing the carpetbag against them, trapping everything behind its bulk. What sort of terror must a child live through in order to understand the seriousness of staying quiet and hidden for so long? She shook her head. He could never go back. She wouldn't allow it.

Nora returned, holding Isaac's hand. Quen crouched to his level. "Hi, Isaac. What a brave boy you've been to hide so well."

Isaac stuck his thumb into his mouth and leaned against Nora, his arm wrapped around her leg. Nora rubbed her hand against his head.

Quen stood and pulled jerky from Jonathan's saddlebag. "Are you hungry? Want something to eat?"

He glanced up at his mother, a silent question on his face. She nodded. He reached for the piece Quen offered.

"Will you tell Jonathan? About Isaac?" Nora asked point-blank.

Her no-nonsense approach appealed to Quen. "I think we should. We'll need his help if confronted, and he deserves to know what he's up against. The auction block made him angry. I know he wouldn't return Isaac to that life. We've traveled far enough to be closer to home now. We'll figure out what to do once we arrive."

A twig snapped within the shelter of the trees. Both women stood stock still.

"Someone is watching us." Nora whispered the words, pulling Isaac close.

"It might be an animal," Quen said.

"Wrong, Quen. Only me. I'm here to collect, counting my next paycheck." Samuel stepped through the trees, a pistol in his hand.

Nora made a sound like a growl. Quen moved to stand between them.

"How quaint." Samuel's voice mocked. "She's protecting them." He waved the gun as if shooing away a fly. "Out of the way, Quen. You're in over your head. I'll take the boy—that you stole—and return him. No questions asked. I'll keep you out of trouble with the law."

"They din't steal me." Isaac's young voice pierced the tension. "I hided."

Nora pushed Isaac behind her. He peeked past her hip, thumb back in his mouth. "You're not taking my son." Her voice rang with authority.

Samuel appeared to consider. "OK. Fair enough. I'll take you. Leave the boy with Quen. You'll bring more money, anyway."

Fear tightened Nora's face, but she stared him down. Quen crossed her arms.

"Quen, be reasonable." Samuel spread a conciliatory hand. "Helping a slave escape is against the law. You'll go to jail. Even hang."

Quen swallowed her unease and lifted her chin. "You're not taking Nora. We paid her price. She's a free woman now."

"Says one piece of paper, easily destroyed."

"And says the auctioneer and everyone in that yard." Quen shot back.

"They've all gone home by now. Do you know anyone's name? Know who to ask? Besides, the auctioneer is a friend. He'll scratch through that line in his register if I grease his palm with a little extra cash. Face it, Quen, you can't manage this. Out of my way."

"This is wrong." She squared her shoulders. "Samuel, do the right thing."

He sniggered. "Aw. She thinks she can talk me into being a good guy." Hunger crossed his face. "All right, I'll make a deal with you. I'll turn around and go right now, leaving the two of them behind. But—" his gaze sharpened "—you come with me."

Quen snorted. "Me? What on earth do you want with me?"

Samuel stepped closer. "You don't know what a man wants with a beautiful woman? Are you that innocent?" His ugly laugh settled in Quen's stomach like hot acid. "All the better." He reached out and gripped her chin.

Nora moved sideways, taking Isaac with her.

Quen leaned away, but his fingers tightened. She flinched.

Samuel's gaze lingered on her mouth, his heavy lids half closing over his gaze. "Maybe I should get a little taste before I seal the bargain. Make sure I'm getting my money's worth."

Quen gripped his wrist and pushed. Fear fluttered, waiting for the slightest invitation to pounce. *God, help!* He tucked his pistol into his waistband, then gripped her wrist, twisting her arm behind her back. She arched, and the movement pressed her chest against his. The pressure threatened to snap her bones. "Let go of me." Her voice shook, weakening the power of her demand.

Samuel's mouth hovered over hers. "Make me."

Quen turned her face away, evading his kiss. She leaned as far back as possible, and he bent toward her, seeking like a hawk striking a mouse.

"No." She stepped back toward the fire, creating space between their bodies. She kneed him, tugging her wrist from his grasp.

He grunted at the impact but was undeterred.

A loud thump penetrated Quen's growing panic. Surprise and pain flashed across Samuel's face, then he crumpled, falling face down onto the grass. Quen staggered back. Nora stood behind him, gripping a large branch from the firewood pile in her hands. Samuel's horse snorted, tossing his head at the unexpected movement.

"Animal." Nora spat on his back. "He's not taking anyone."

Quen clapped her hands against her mouth. "Did you—? Is he—?"

"Dead?" Nora nudged him hard with her foot. "The world'd be a sight better place if he was, but no. He's not."

Rustling from the trees had both women gasping. Samuel's horse leaped back, then trotted away through the trees. Quen whirled to face their new attacker.

Jonathan appeared.

"Light's fading, and I didn't want to be gone—"

Mouth agape, he eyed Samuel's body, then faced the women, eyes wide. "What in tarnation?" His gaze fell on Isaac, then popped back to Quen's face. "I knew something was up." He moved closer, eyes narrowed. "What happened here?"

Nora dropped to her knees and gathered Isaac against her, ignoring Jonathan's question.

Quen filled him in. "Let's go. We can stash Isaac at Mrs. Lancaster's home until we find Mr. Moore and reimburse him what he paid. Everything will be Samuel's word against ours. He has no proof."

"And if he wants to go to the sheriff with a complaint about why the back of his head is stove in? Will we say he fell off his horse? Tripped?"

"We acted in self-defense." Quen lifted her chin and stared Jonathan down, but her eyes flooded with tears.

"What?" Anger darkened Jonathan's face. He brushed a fingertip along her chin. "Explain these red marks." The words snarled.

Forming the words in her mind to relate what happened made the incident a reality. The weight of the evil possibility

Nora had interrupted hit her. Her teeth tugged on her trembling lower lip.

Nora spoke up. "He told her he'd let me and Isaac go if she'd leave with him. Then he decided to help himself to a kiss."

"He kissed you?" Jonathan's chest swelled, and he took a step toward the prone body.

Quen stopped him, her hand gripping his forearm. "No. Nora saved me."

Jonathan studied her face. "Are you OK?"

She nodded.

He pulled her into his embrace. He buried his nose into her hair, pressing the side of her face gently against his chest. "You promise he didn't hurt you?" His words whispered into her ear.

Quen melted against him. Safe. So safe. She never wanted to be without him again. "He did nothing but grab my chin. Please, Jonathan. Can we go? Let's leave him here. I can't bear to be close to him."

"We should kill him." Nora's voice was flat, her face expressionless. "What if he comes after us?" She pulled Isaac closer.

Quen blinked. She considered ... Her better sense took over. "We can't do that."

"No one is getting killed tonight." Jonathan's answer was emphatic. "Get the horses, Quen. Nora, get your son back in the buggy. I'll tie Jenkins's hands behind his back. That'll keep him here a while. I'll send the sheriff back for him once we're home." He turned to Quen. "Why would Isaac be safe at Mrs. L's house? Won't that be the first place they look?"

She smiled—the expression grim. "I'll explain on the way."

Chapter Twenty-Six

Jonathan rotated his shoulders, stretching tension from his muscles. Quen's chin touched her chest as her head nodded. Nora lay on the quilt on the floor of the buggy, under the back seat, curled against Isaac. Her motionless body appeared sunk in a deep sleep. Probably the best rest she'd had in days.

He eyed the position of the stars. What time was it? The horses walked now, heads drooping, coats lathered with sweat. He'd been unable to catch Jenkins's horse, so they'd finally left him, the women's anxiety to be away overcoming his determination. Everything would be OK. Jenkins couldn't catch up on foot.

They passed familiar countryside. "Almost home, girls." He spoke the encouragement as much for himself as for the mares. Weariness dragged heavily on his arms.

Though the nighttime sky offered a quiet canvas, his thoughts churned. Viewing events from the past months with his new awareness, Jonathan marveled at what Mrs. L and Caleb had accomplished. "God, you protect your own. The fatherless and the sojourner have cried out to you, and you have surely heard their cry."

The escapees' courage was extraordinary. Running away was only the beginning of the danger they faced. They had so far to go, across hostile land. How could he aid them? Mrs. L snuck people to Mexico like he wanted to sneak his cotton.

An idea drove the slump from his shoulders. Days ago, he and Manny had discussed the cotton bales piling up in their barns. Both had sectioned off an acre for cotton—all they could handle without slave labor—and now they each had five or six bales moldering in their barns. At eleven cents a pound, a bale was worth about fifty dollars. Jonathan's bank account screamed for that money.

"We've got to find a way to sell this crop." Manny had leaned against the corral fence. "Those blasted Union soldiers have made shipping bales from Galveston impossible, and the army doesn't appear to be leaving anytime soon. What if we haul them across Texas in wagons instead? We can ford the Rio Grande and sell the harvest in Mexico."

Jonathan considered. "That's a good idea. But who can be gone that long? The trip'll take weeks."

Manny turned to face him, humor creasing the crow's feet surrounding his eyes. "Grady'd go. He's feeling his oats."

Jonathan pictured the teen who'd come to Texas with Abby two years prior. Calm, good-humored, loyal. At seventeen, the sap would be rising. After surviving that adventure, the young man would be antsy for new excitement.

Now, as he rode through the darkness with only his thoughts for company, the conversation from the previous week took on new meaning. What if they delivered those bales with the help of Black men? Pretending to be slaves, they could actually be on their way to a new life. Mexico had outlawed slavery in 1830.

A surge of excitement thrummed through Jonathan's veins. "We could stack the bales, creating a hiding place for any young ones, like Isaac." He slapped his hand against his thigh. "This could work!"

Quen stirred. "What?" Blinking, she lifted her head.

"Just thinking out loud. I'll explain when I've chewed on my idea a while longer."

She stretched her arms above her head, yawning.

As she twisted from side to side, her slim torso caught his attention. His heart rate sped up, and he admired the view. She would be his wife soon. If she wasn't already convinced, he'd do his best to bring her around.

"Are we there yet?" Quen rubbed her eyes. "Has there been any sign of Samuel?"

"Haven't seen anything." Jonathan pointed toward a field on the left. "We're almost home. We just passed the easternmost boundary of old Mr. Thornton's place. That means we're coming up on Mr. Garner's farm."

"Do I know Mr. Thornton?" Quen mumbled. "I don't think—"

Jonathan jerked, slashing the air with his hand. "Quiet!"

Her mouth snapped shut, mid-yawn. "What?" she whispered.

As dawn approached, the horizon's edge glowed, outlining the intersection of ground and inky black sky with a pale line. A faint rumble, barely discernable, floated across the early morning air. The whole world seemed to slumber except for that ominous pounding noise.

"Galloping hooves." Jonathan slapped the reins against the horses' backs.

Quen gasped. "Samuel?"

"Come on, girls. Give me whatever you have left." Jonathan leaned forward, urging the animals to speed.

Quen reached over the seat, waking Nora.

The horses stumbled into a lope. Moments later, their breathing became labored.

"They can't continue, Jonathan." The speed of the buggy slowed. Quen peered through the darkness behind them. "Let us out. We'll run across Mr. Garner's field and head to Teddy's new house. You can keep going. Samuel won't know we got off, and he'll follow you."

Nora sucked in a quick breath. "He's back?"

"I won't leave you alone." Jonathan slapped the reins again.

The horses wheezed.

"Jonathan, stop. We need time to hide before Samuel comes."

Growling, Jonathan thought furiously, stacking up the various scenarios, but she was right. He raked his hand through his hair. Hauling on the reins, he pulled the buggy to a stop.

Nora scrambled down, holding a drowsy Isaac in her arms.

Jonathan pulled Quen against him, pressing his lips to her temple. "Be careful, Quenby Martin." His words were for her ears only. "I'm pretty sure I'm in love with you."

"Jonathan!"

Nora hissed. "Let's go." Setting Isaac's feet on the ground, she grasped his hand and rushed from the road.

After a quick glance at Jonathan, Quen hurried after her.

"This way." She grabbed Isaac's other hand, and they ran to the fence.

The moment Quen's foot hit the lowest rail of the fence, Jonathan slapped the reins again. Time to play the decoy.

A form appeared at the side of the road. Jonathan jerked, startled.

"Jonathan? Is that you?" He called softly, waving his hand. "What are you doing out here?"

Jonathan pulled the horses to a stop once again.

The older man jogged to Jonathan's side. "The Holy Spirit woke me, gave me a real twitchy feeling to be out and about, praying." He seemed to notice the horses for the first time. "Why do you have Mrs. Lancaster's buggy?" His voice went up an octave. "Where's Quen? Why ...?" He paused. "What do you know?"

Jonathan set his jaw, his knee bouncing with impatience. "I'm not blind. I figured out what Quen was up to." He glanced back down the road. "I dropped them off at Mr. Garner's fence line. Jenkins is on our trail. I'm leading him away."

"Them?" Caleb paused, grabbing at the reins before Jonathan could leave. The horse tossed her head at his sudden move, snorting. "You found my girl?" Emotion thickened his words, and his eyes shone.

"Yes. We have Nora. Quen's taking her to Teddy's place."

Caleb stepped back, his face glowing like the moon shining on the water. "My girl." He breathed the words like a prayer. "God be praised." He slapped the rump of the mare closest to him. "Go. I'm gonna catch up to them." Darkness swallowed him as he turned away.

Quen led Nora and Isaac through brambles, fighting to gain shelter behind the thicket. "Once we cross Mr. Garner's field, we'll be on Jonathan's land. Teddy, a hired hand, is building a house in the back corner. We'll shelter there."

A shout pulled them up short.

"Quiet!" Quen gripped Nora's wrist. They froze, poised like fawns.

Nora looked down at Isaac and held a finger to her lips. *Hide or flee, God?*

"Quen?" The call came again.

Quen sagged against Nora. "That's Caleb's voice."

Nora gasped, hope brightening her eyes.

"Mama, I'm scared." Isaac tugged her hand.

"We're here." Quen called toward the road. Pressing branches away, she peered through the receding darkness.

Caleb crashed through the hedge like a wild boar.

"Nora."

He rushed toward them and grasped Nora by the shoulders. Holding her at arm's length, his gaze roved up and down. He clasped her tightly to his chest, wrapping his arms around her like he never meant to let go again.

"Papa." His shirt muffled her endearment.

Isaac clung to Nora's leg, eyes wide, still as a possum playing dead.

"Praise Jesus!" Caleb's voice rang with joy. "God has restored my precious girl to me. Oh, how I've prayed for this day."

He stepped back, fingers skimming her arms, studying her through a shimmer of tears. "Oh, child, you are a sight for sore eyes." He glanced down, his grin so wide Quen smiled in reaction despite her fear. "And who is this?" He rested a gentle hand on Isaac's head.

Nora laughed through her tears, dropping her fingers to the back of the boy's neck. "This is my son, Isaac."

Caleb bent on one knee. "Isaac." Reverence softened his voice. He laughed. "One who rejoices." He pulled the child into his arms and stood, wrapping Nora in a hug. They clung to each other for a moment, seeming to breathe in each other's presence.

Vision blurring, Quen swallowed past the lump in her throat.

Caleb faced heaven. "Lord, sustain me. I'm gonna die of joy." He pressed a kiss onto Nora's forehead. "But you must get to safety." He turned to Quen. "Jonathan said you were heading to Teddy's place."

"Yes."

Holding Isaac, Caleb grasped Nora's hand. He turned toward Jonathan's farm. "This way." He glanced at the sky. "We'd better hurry. Morning'll be here soon."

The foursome hurried across the pasture, leaving behind the road that held danger. With each passing moment, Quen's skin itched more.

Finally, the fence separating the two farms appeared in the dawning light. The tree where she'd stashed the bundle stood dark against the sky.

"Come on." Quen jogged to the crisscrossed rails, climbing over into Jonathan's pasture with a sigh of relief. "Teddy's house is in the eastern corner." She turned toward the small homestead, and they started along the boundary between the farms, walking swiftly.

Emotion throbbed in Caleb's quiet voice. "I have so much to tell you, Nora." He beamed. "Mrs. Lancaster has searched for you all these years. I never stopped praying for you."

Love radiated from Nora's smile. "Nor I you."

"I have a small farm. You can live with me for now, with Isaac." He jogged the boy on his hip. Isaac slipped two fingers into his mouth—eyes wide as he studied Caleb. "My life has been good. You were the only thing missing." He gazed heavenward again and stopped. "Thank you, Jesus. I am complete." He stopped.

Quen glanced at the increasing glow in the east. She urged them to continue. "Let's go."

Caleb passed Isaac to Nora. "Y'all go on. I'm going back to the tree to get the pistol I hid there yesterday."

"Papa, no." Nora reached for him. "Come with us."

He pulled her into his arms. "Child, I have prayed for this moment every morning of the world since they took you from me. I won't let that rotten scoundrel harm one hair on your head." He pressed another kiss on her cheek.

"God willing, I'll be with you momentarily." He gripped Isaac's shoulder.

"Come on." Quen tugged at Nora's arm, nerves crawling under her skin like fire ants.

Casting a glance over her shoulder, Nora allowed Quen to lead her away.

"Stay close to the trees where there's cover." Quen kept a hand on Nora's back, almost pushing her. She looked back, fearing the specter of Samuel rising behind them like Ichabod Crane.

Uneven ground gave way beneath her feet, sending a wrench of pain through Quen's ankle. Her palms struck the acorn-littered ground and her knee collided with an exposed root. She groaned through gritted teeth, biting back the cry lodged in her throat. Pushing to her feet, she winced as her ankle took her weight.

Waving her hands, she hissed toward Nora. "You go on. Follow the fence. You'll be there in a few minutes. Samuel doesn't know Teddy's building back there. He can't find you."

"Come with us." Nora's voice trembled.

She shook her head. "I don't think Samuel will hurt me. But we know that isn't true for you or Isaac. Go. Everything will be all right."

"Mama?"

Isaac's scared voice seemed to make the choice for Nora. Her worried frown smoothed into determination, and she pulled Quen into a quick, fierce hug. "We'll go. Promise you're coming."

Quen nodded. "I'm right behind you."

Within moments, Nora and Isaac vanished. Quen hobbled along, hopping with each step, her foot barely touching the ground. A rustle sounded behind her. She whirled. Now what? Phoenix approached, stretching her nose toward Quen's hand.

"Oh." A breathy sigh escaped her. "It's you."

The donkey drew close, and Quen leaned against her. "Just in time. You can help me walk."

The horizon, slowly lightening with streaks of tangerine and pink, introduced the smallest sliver of the sun. The trees would soon no longer hide her.

"I think we're almost there, girl." Quen's pounding heart slowed.

Once again, Jonathan urged the animals forward. The rhythmic sound of hooves behind him steadily increased.

He'd removed the gun Samuel pointed at Quen and stored the weapon in his saddlebag back at the campfire. He checked the bounty hunter's body but hadn't seen another one. Jenkins probably had one in his saddlebag, but the horse had run off. *Be strong and of good courage.* God was with him.

A shout hailed him. He glanced over his shoulder. Apparently, the horse had returned. Samuel was close enough to see in the growing light of dawn. The game was up. He slowed the buggy.

Jenkins hauled on his mount's reins, his face savage. "Where are they?"

Jonathan squinted through the dimness. Did he hold a gun? "Why would I answer that?"

The man kneed his mount, urging the animal forward. He reached for the quilt puddled on the floor of the buggy and yanked. Seeing nothing, he threw the cover to the ground.

"This isn't over, Campbell. You stole that boy. You're going to pay." Samuel's voice vibrated. "One way or another." Snarling, Samuel whirled his horse around, digging his heels into its sweating, heaving sides.

"Jenkins!" Jonathan shouted after him.

Within seconds, the darkness swallowed him. "Dear Lord, protect them." He considered the spent mares. Hauling on the brake, Jonathan leaped to the road and dashed to the back of the wagon. He untied Cisco's reins. With a grunt, he pulled himself onto the back of the horse. Kicking hard, he pounded down the road after Jenkins.

Where was he? The noise coming from Cisco's hooves drowned out any sound Jenkins may've made. Leaning over the animal's neck, he urged him on. A flash of orange fire birthed a blast of gunfire, then searing pain sliced him. He jerked, the move instinctive, and his hands flailed, scrabbling for a hold on the saddle horn.

No! The ground rushed to meet him.

Chapter Twenty-Seven

Quen froze when a gunshot rang through the early morning air. Heart in her throat, she turned and headed back the way she came. Moving as quickly as her twisted ankle allowed, she hobbled. Her hand gripped the bristly mane on Phoenix's neck, using the donkey as a crutch.

What would she find? *Please, God, let everything be OK.*

Voices alerted her as she drew nearer. She slowed.

The creeping light of dawn illuminated the scene. Caleb stood with his back against their stash point. He faced Samuel, who pointed a pistol straight at Caleb's chest.

She crept closer, eyes narrowed as her gaze ran over Caleb's body. He appeared unharmed.

But that gunshot.

"Quen, you might as well stop hiding. I heard you a mile away." Samuel turned, training the barrel on her.

He wanted her. Samuel wouldn't kill her. Would he? She stepped from the cover of the trees and edged a step closer to Caleb. "How did you find us?"

Samuel laughed. "I track runaways for a living, Quen. I know what to look for." He waved the weapon toward Caleb and sneered. "And what to my wondering eyes should appear?"

"Did you shoot Caleb? He's done nothing to you." Quen moved closer.

"How disappointing. Your expectations of me are so low. No, I didn't shoot your little darkie pet. I did, however, shoot your lover."

The world went gray, and sparkles glittered in Quen's vision. Releasing Phoenix's mane, she lurched one step toward Samuel. "You ... you shot ..." The words to speak that possibility into truth wouldn't come.

"You're nothing but a snake." Caleb snarled. He twisted and reached into the hole in the tree trunk. His hand withdrew a pistol.

Another gunshot exploded, leaving Quen's ears ringing. Phoenix bucked and darted toward the fence, braying.

Caleb fell back against the hollow tree, one hand pressed against his chest, the other dangling at his side. Quen moaned. Ignoring Samuel, she stepped to the injured man's side. Her heart thudded so hard in her throat, nausea threatened. Emotions careened. "How can I help you?" She touched the wet spot on his shirt. Slick, warm blood coated her fingertip, and tears threatened. "Please, God, no."

Samuel stepped closer, his voice sharp and clipped. "Stop whining. He's nothing."

She turned on him, fury and grief narrowing her eyes. "You're vile." She spat the words. "You've harmed two kind, decent men. And for what? Your own greed?"

"Easy there, sweet thing. It was him or me. You saw. He pulled on me first." He twitched his mouth sideways and spat. "I have too many loose ends now. I need to finish this." The hard glare in his eyes softened with regret for a moment as his gaze passed over her, then he shrugged, turning the barrel of the pistol in her direction. His gaze flicked to a spot over her shoulder. "I know you've stashed them somewhere nearby. I'll find them."

Quen's breath caught in her throat. No. she had so many things—

A boom of sound deafened her. She shrieked, covering her ears.

Did Samuel shoot her? Was she dying?

Samuel stumbled back and collapsed to the ground—eyes wide.

Quen clapped her hands over her mouth.

Caleb coughed again. He slid down, his back scraping along the tree trunk until his bottom met the ground. "Made a trade. My life for hers." He paused. "And yours." His hand lay limp in his lap, a gun cradled in his fingers.

Quen gasped, and lightheadedness threatened. His life? She kneeled beside him and pressed her palm against the darkening patch over his chest. A surge of red gushed over her fingers. And another. His life ebbed away with each heartbeat.

"God, no. How can you let this happen?" Tears flowed down her cheeks. "Caleb, tell me what to do."

Caleb's chuckle faded into a gurgling cough. "First, you're gonna praise God for his blessings today."

"Praise him?" Quen's breath caught on a sob. "How can you say that? He let Samuel shoot you. And Jonathan may be dead."

Caleb's eyes shut, but a beatific smile lit his face. "Yes, praise him. First, we're gonna trust the Holy Spirit's care of Jonathan. Second, the good Lord in heaven answered a plea today I've prayed every day since they took my baby. He brought my firstborn child to me. I saw her. Held her." His eyes opened, shining with tears of happiness. "He kept her safe. Returned her to me. No joy could be greater."

Quen latched on to the hope that Jonathan was unharmed. She struggled to understand Caleb's peace. "But Caleb, you just found each other."

He nodded, a tear slipping down his cheek. "Yes'm, and we'll find each other again." He struggled to catch a gasp of air. "At the gates of Heaven." Raising a hand, he touched her cheek. "Though he slay me, yet will I trust in him." He drew a ragged breath. "God'll never forsake you, Quen. Simply follow him."

Quen absorbed the certainty of his words. A kernel of assurance nudged against her grief. Could her newly budded faith be that strong? She gripped his hand and squeezed. "Caleb, don't leave me. I need you to teach me ..."

He shook his head, the movement small. "You got everything you need. I'll be waitin' for you on the banks ... of the River Jordan." His voice weakened. "Take care of my girl."

His hand grew heavy in hers. "Caleb!" Quen bowed her head. Tears dampened their clasped fingers. "Father, I don't understand. But I ask you to lead him home." She flattened his palm and cupped his hand against her cheek, the skin rough and warm. "He was so happy to see Nora again. Thank you for giving him that." Unexplainable comfort filled her heart. She slumped back against her heels and wept.

Phoenix brayed again. Jonathan appeared and gathered her against him.

Quen wrapped her arms around his waist as tight as she could. "Jonathan." The word was a gasp, a prayer of thanksgiving. "You're here."

His embrace tightened. "Only death could keep me from you."

She leaned into his chest. Too many emotions flooded her heart. She clutched him, a lifeline in the middle of the torrent.

Nora ran to them, tugging Isaac by the wrist. "Papa. Papa, no." She flung herself to the ground at his side, tracing her fingers across his dear face, wiping away the wetness on his cheeks. Gripping his other hand, she pressed a kiss on its back, then buried her face against his shoulder. "No, no."

Quen leaned into Jonathan's embrace. "What do we do without him?"

Jonathan swallowed hard. "We carry on." He tucked Quen's face against his neck and rocked her. She clung to his strength. "But we don't go alone. God promised to never leave us, and we'll see each other again. His presence is the great hope Jesus left us with."

Jonathan lifted his head at the sound of approaching footsteps. Teddy and Ernest appeared.

"Sounded like a shoot-out was happenin' over here." Ernest called out as they drew near. "What in the blue blazes are y'all up to?"

Shock froze the men's faces. "Boss, you OK?" Teddy blanched at the sight of the bleeding wound on Jonathan's arm.

"*Ach du lieber.*" Ernest's eyes widened when he saw the two bodies on the ground. "We really did hear a shoot-out."

Jonathan sent Teddy back to the house to fetch the wagon. He described where Ernest would find Mrs. Lancaster's buggy and asked him to drive it to Caleb's.

Teddy returned with the wagon. Quen bandaged Jonathan's arm using a napkin from the carpetbag. They placed Jenkins in the wagon and lifted Caleb in with care.

"I'm taking y'all to Mrs. L's house." Jonathan spoke to the women, sending a worried glance to the sky. "Time's ticking. We could pass anyone on the road. All three of us have blood on our clothes, and I'd rather not meet our neighbors with two bodies in my wagon. We've got to get Isaac behind closed doors. Teddy, Ernest, y'all head back. Keep this close to your chest, OK?"

Nora climbed to the wagon's bench and sat next to him, her body twisted at the waist as she leaned over and rested her hand on Caleb's head. Isaac curled against her torso, thumb stuck in his mouth.

Caleb's body stretched out next to Samuel's, Black touching White. Jonathan had dug deep to resist the urge to toss the bounty hunter into the wagon like a sack of potatoes. Let him spend his final moments sharing this space with someone he held in contempt.

Forgive.

He blew out a breath, expelling the anger on the puff of air. He would try.

Quen rode Cisco, sticking close as if loathe to let him out of her sight. Her shuddering sighs broke Jonathan's heart, drawing his gaze. Tears welled in her eyes over and over, but her face remained stoic.

Jonathan resisted the urge to hurry, forcing himself to let the old mare walk. The hour was still very early, though a lifetime had passed since he'd left the buggy and raced back to the spot where he'd dropped the women.

At Mrs. L's house, he drove down her driveway. He helped Nora from the wagon, then assisted Quen as she dismounted. They presented quite a bedraggled picture. Quen had small leaves snagged in her hair, and Nora had pressed her skirt into the mud when she kneeled next to Caleb. Jonathan scratched the two-days' growth of whiskers on his face and slapped his hands against his rumpled and dusty dungarees. Isaac looked like he hadn't bathed in a week. All were weatherworn and exhausted.

As they headed toward the back porch of Mrs. L's house in a tight clump, the door wrenched open. The widow and Missouri peered into the yard. Missouri rushed outside and flung her arms around Nora's neck. "They found you!" The joy in her voice brightened the morning.

"Oh, praise God." Mrs. L's voice shook as she followed.

Concern replaced joy as she took in the blood on Quen and Nora's clothes. "Are you harmed?"

Tears flooded Quen's eyes again. "We're both fine. Jonathan was shot."

Jonathan held his breath as awareness stilled Mrs. L's face. Her examination shifted to him, lingering over the bandage. The question formed in her eyes. Why was he there? Her gaze left them and darted over his shoulder, searching. The sudden pain in her eyes told him she'd spotted Caleb's well-worn boots sticking out the back of the wagon. Grief blanched her skin.

"Caleb?" She swallowed hard, her gaze shifting back to him. She pressed a fist against her mouth. "Oh, no. How was Caleb involved?"

Missouri stepped away from Nora's embrace, confusion crossing her face at Mrs. Lancaster's grief. "What's wrong? What happened?"

Nora turned and nodded toward the wagon. Missouri gasped, then dashed to Caleb's side. "No!"

Quen stared at the ground, her shoulders slumping. "Samuel was there ... he followed ..."

Unexpected anger flooded Jonathan. Mrs. L had sent Quen, alone, to do a job she was unprepared to do, and now Quen acted as if she was responsible for Caleb's death. Before he could form the words to say on her behalf, Mrs. L moved forward and wrapped her in an embrace.

"Oh, child. Please forgive me. I'm so sorry to have laid this burden on you. I prayed every moment you were gone that God would protect and lead you." Her gaze lingered on those motionless, muddy boots. A wrenching sob hiccupped from her chest. She bit down hard, turning away. She drew a deep breath, wiping her eyes with her sleeve, then pressed her lips tight, a forced smile tipping the corners of her mouth.

"I'm sorry too." Quen's words slipped out with her tears, dampening Mrs. L's shoulder.

"Shh." Mrs. L patted her back. "God answered our prayers. You're home, safe and sound, and Nora has been rescued." She glanced at Jonathan. "And it appears God sent us some much-needed assistance." Gulping through tears, she continued. "Though he apparently used a method I hadn't anticipated, God knows best. We'll trust that every outcome from this adventure will turn out as he wants."

Giving Quen a final squeeze, she stepped back, sniffing. She turned to face Nora. "My dearest girl, let me see you." She placed her palms on Nora's wet cheeks and smiled, love pouring through her gaze. "This day is a long-awaited answer to uncountable prayers. God is good indeed."

"And who is this?" She squatted in front of Isaac, tucking her hands against her middle. "You have the look of Caleb about you. He must have been so proud to meet you." The last word caught, and Mrs. L cleared her throat, then blinked rapidly. But not before Jonathan caught the wet sheen in her eyes. The widow stood and walked to join Missouri, wrapping her arms around the girl's shoulders.

He shot a glance toward the road. "How about we all get indoors?" He stretched his arms out, herding them in like a flock of ducks.

Once the door closed behind them, he pulled Mrs. L to the side. "I'm taking the bodies to the sheriff's office. Quen and Nora can fill in the details. I have an idea to share with you when I return."

He followed her into the parlor. He led Quen to the hallway for a kiss before he left. They held each other for a long moment in silence, his head bent over hers. She'd become so important to him. He shuddered. The morning could've ended very differently. "Make sure no one leaves. The less notice we bring to this situation, the better. I'll be back as soon as I can."

Leaving Quen behind took all Jonathan's strength. The urge to hold her in his arms, to protect her from the ravages of her sorrow, was almost too much to withstand.

On the road, his thoughts circled like a dust devil. He ran the scenes through his mind again, searching for an alternative ending.

Would the outcome have been any different had he arrived sooner?

Phoenix had announced their location as he passed. Finally earned her keep.

Jenkins made a mistake shooting him and then Caleb. Had taken his hatred one step too far. Caleb was—had been—a free man. With Quen standing there to witness his act, Jenkins'd backed himself into a corner. And for all he knew, he'd left Jonathan lying dead in the road.

No, things would've ended the same. Caleb would've killed the man regardless, to protect those he loved.

Grief at losing his friend overwhelmed Jonathan. He wiped his own tears away as he headed to the sheriff's office. The conversation at Mrs. L's home had been as difficult as he'd imagined. At least Nora's presence tempered the grief of the women.

The Lord gave and the Lord hath taken away.

"I don't like that verse." Although he agreed God gave good things to his children, he didn't believe God had taken Caleb. Samuel had. Bad things happened in a sinful world.

Jonathan steered the wagon to a stop in front of the jail and swallowed nerves. No actions from this morning should land anyone in trouble. Caleb had acted in self-defense and had also protected Quen. He drew a deep breath. Would the sheriff be of the same mind? He climbed from the wagon. "Here we go, Lord. I place this in your hands. Let's get this done and over with. I need to see Quen." He had something to say.

Chapter Twenty-Eight

Jonathan debated whether to stop at Caleb's farm to tend to the animals or go straight back to Mrs. L's home—to Quen. Concern for his love overrode his worry for Mrs. L's mares or Caleb's mule. He knocked on the door to the widow's house. The sound of merriment took him by surprise. What were they doing?

The door swung open to reveal Quen, her face shining. She wiped tears from her eyes, but her cheeks glowed with laughter.

"Come in." She reached for his hand and tugged.

He allowed her to lead him, resisting the urge to pull her into his arms. His attention zeroed in on the touch of her warm palm against his. Though he nodded a greeting to the others sitting around Mrs. L's table, his focus remained on the woman he loved.

Could he make her happy? Would he be able to bring that smile to her face on a day-to-day basis?

"Come, Jonathan." Mrs. L patted an empty chair. "Join us."

Empty China cups littered the table. A tin of Missouri's biscotti lay open, crumbs scattered across the tablecloth, crumpled napkins in front of each chair. Where was Isaac? Jonathan peered around the room. The child lay on Mrs. L's sofa, snoring softly, a crocheted throw tucked around his shoulders.

Jonathan pulled out the chair and sat. Quen placed a hand on his shoulder as she moved to stand behind him.

"We never ate breakfast this morning." She leaned down and spoke quiet words into his ear. "I'm sure you're hungry. Would you like some tea? Some biscotti?"

The warm puff of Quen's breath sent a trail of goose bumps across his skin. Hungry? Yes, he was. But he didn't suffer from the hunger she imagined. His gaze met hers over his shoulder and he smiled at her. Redness rimmed her puffy eyes, but her voice had calmed. Tamping down the baser emotion, he covered her hand with his. "Thank you. That'll be nice."

Mrs. L spoke quietly. "What did Sheriff Moore say?" All eyes focused on him.

"My conversation with him took far less time than I expected. I explained Samuel followed us, trying to steal Nora away. He said it was a cryin' shame about Caleb. Called his death downright criminal. Then he said Caleb served us all a great justice by taking care of Quen the way he did. Called him a hero."

The women relaxed.

"He seemed disinclined to investigate any further than our conversation. I left him and drove the wagon to the mortician's. I left the remains in his care."

The vision of what that entailed brought everyone to a standstill. Mrs. L jumped into the silence—her voice falsely bright.

"The girls are regaling us with tales of Caleb as a young father. Perhaps you'll have a story to help Nora reconnect with him as a man grown."

Nora turned to him. "Tell me of the Caleb you knew."

Jonathan leaned back against the chair. Memories of his good friend and neighbor flooded his mind. He chuckled to cover the burp of pain in his heart. "Where should I start?"

Quen set his tea, a fresh plate, and napkin before him. "Start with the one about how he helped me bring Phoenix to you."

Stories, tears, and laughter flowed. The ache in Jonathan's heart eased.

Sleepy-headed, Isaac stumbled to the table and sat, feet swinging back and forth. He crunched a cookie, his gaze bouncing between the two sisters, a look of wonder on his face.

Finally, a satisfied silence settled, similar to the glow that appeared after Jonathan's family had stuffed themselves with Ma's chicken and dumplings.

Missouri drew a deep breath. "I have an idea. As soon as it's safe, Nora, let's move into Papa's house."

Mrs. L blinked rapidly, and a stiff smile crossed her face.

Missouri gripped Nora's hand. "I've just found my sister. She's my only family now." She shot an apologetic glance at Mrs. L. "Well, you know what I mean."

Mrs. Lancaster dipped her head in a bow. "Of course. I understand."

She grinned at Isaac. "And I have a nephew to spoil." Missouri paused. "But, ma'am, who will help you?"

Mrs. L scoffed, waving a dismissive hand. "I can take care of myself."

Missouri frowned. "Keeping this house and caring for your animals is quite a job. The work is more than you realize. It would be a lot—too much—for anyone to do alone."

Quen jerked. "I can stay with you."

Four heads swiveled around, staring at her in surprise.

"Really?" Doubt rang in Jonathan's voice.

Quen darted an annoyed glance at him. "You don't think I can do the job?"

Jonathan held up his hands. "I never said that. I'm thinking of the conversation we had on the way to get Nora is all. You're the one who said—"

"You told me I could do anything I wanted." Quen shrugged. "And I want to do this for Mrs. Lancaster. If I take Missouri's place, she can focus on helping people gain freedom."

Mrs. L turned pink and cleared her throat. "That's a very generous offer, Quenby, and I appreciate you. Your mother may not agree, though." She pulled a wry face. "I'll just have to put on an act and seem quite feeble. Ask your parents. If they give their consent, this will provide a fine solution."

"And I can remove Hans and Phoenix from under your feet, Jonathan." Quen pressed her lips, containing a smile. "Mortimer might enjoy some company."

Jonathan shook his head. "The only way I knew to stop racing down the road is because Phoenix alerted me to where y'all were with her noisy braying. She's earned a place to stay for as long as she wants." One eyebrow raised. "Monster Hans, on the other hand, might make an excellent Christmas feast."

"He most certainly will not." Quen's amusement faded as quickly as it came.

"Whath a hans?" Isaac spoke around the cookie in his mouth.

Jonathan leaned close. "It's a big, scary white bird who chases people." A conspiratorial tone entered his voice. "And he bites."

Isaac's eyes widened.

"He doesn't bite me." Quen's clipped voice ended the discussion.

"I need to go get Mrs. L's buggy from Caleb's place." Jonathan stood.

"Let's go with him, Nora." Missouri's voice grew somber again. "We can go through Papa's things. Decide where we'll sleep, things like that."

"That's not a good idea." Mrs. L stood, gathering cups to clear the table. "We're keeping a low profile, remember? You go." She nodded at Missouri. "I'll stay here with Nora and Isaac."

"Yes, go without me." Nora's gaze roamed across the comfortable parlor, and she breathed deeply. "We'll stay here and rest. Freedom feels good. This is the first day of my life I don't have to hurry and do something for someone else."

Mrs. L patted her hand. "Let's get you into a warm bath and some clean clothes." Sadness filled her eyes as she glanced at the stains on Quen's dress. "New clothes for you too, Quen. Missouri can loan you a dress while we wash yours." Determination strengthened her voice, and she lifted her chin. "You won't be well served to show up begging favors from your mother looking like that."

Jonathan drove the wagon down Caleb's drive, with Missouri and a cleaned-up Quen seated next to him on the bench seat. Mrs. L's mares watched them approach from their place in the corral with Ol' Blue. The mule stretched his neck over the top rung of the corral and brayed.

"Oh, dear." Quen's eyes filled with tears once again. "Caleb's animals won't understand why he isn't here. Do you think they'll be sad?"

Jonathan covered Quen's hand and squeezed. "Most of them are concerned with one thing only—getting fed. Ol' Blue might miss him, though."

"Maybe we should bring Phoenix here instead of leaving her at your farm. She can be company for him."

Missouri nodded. "There's a sight more room. In fact, Mortimer can join 'em." She scrunched her nose. "Can't believe I'm offering to take him with me. But his care would be one less chore for Mrs. Lancaster."

Jonathan steered the wagon toward the cabin and hauled on the reins. "Why don't y'all check inside while I hitch the mares to the buggy?"

Momentarily, the women joined him behind the house. The mares were in their traces, and Jonathan pointed the buggy toward the road. "Missouri, you want to drive the buggy back? I'll follow in the wagon."

Quen climbed up and settled herself in the wagon's seat. She cleared her throat. "Now I have my task to complete. I must talk to my parents and convince them to let me move in with Mrs. Lancaster. My assistance with the underground railroad will be so much easier if I'm not living under their watchful eyes."

Jonathan met her gaze, and his heart gave a big thump. *You can present this idea if you want, but I have a different solution.* Hers wasn't the only plan that required parental approval.

Chapter Twenty-Nine

Quen opened the door to Mrs. Lancaster's home for Missouri, whose arms were full of things she'd found to share with Nora and Isaac. Among the items were a worn Bible and a buckskin coat.

"Oh, I remember this coat." Nora slipped the garment on, pulling the collar up around her neck. She burrowed in like a turtle, as if seeking to absorb Caleb's essence. Quen sat on the sofa beside Jonathan, and they listened as Nora thumbed through the Scriptures and read aloud the verses Caleb had underlined.

Finally, Quen stood to head home, and Jonathan walked her to the door.

"Sure you don't want me to come with you?" He faced her, tender concern creasing his brow. "You might need backup."

Quen stood silent for a moment. "I should go alone. Mother may think we're ganging up on her if you accompany me. Plus, your presence may give her the idea the only reason I want to live at Mrs. Lancaster's is to be nearer ..." Heat flushed her cheeks. What if Jonathan thought the same?

He placed a crooked knuckle under her chin and tipped her face up. "To be nearer to me? So, we can do this?" He pressed his mouth against hers, his lips firm and warm.

She should pull away. A proper young woman would not allow this.

He straightened, and Quen groaned softly at the loss. So much for being prim and respectable. She fought the urge to grip the front of his shirt in her fists and pull him back for more.

"All right." His low, warm voice melted her. "I'll head back home as well. I'll drop by later to see how everything goes with your mother. But if she says no, which I expect, I have a Plan B." A curious mix of defiance, pleasure, and nervousness overtook his handsome face.

What else could he have in mind?

Quen practiced her argument all the way home from Mrs. Lancaster's house, muttering under her breath.

"I'm a grown woman now. I'm eager for my independence, and I'd like to step out on my own. Plus, taking care of her home will be good practice." She strode down the sidewalk, oblivious to the people she passed.

Quen twitched her mouth sideways, various iterations of the mysterious Plan B running through her mind. What did Jonathan mean by that?

She turned down her street. Ruminations would have to wait. The moment had arrived to face her parent. She paused on the porch, smoothing a hand over her hair.

Pushing the door open, she called out. "Mother?" Her voice rang down the hall. "Where are you?"

"Is that you, Quenby?" A reply came from the rear. "We're back here." Mother stepped through the kitchen doorway, wiping her hands on the ruffled apron tied around her waist, dusted with flour. "Prissy and I are preparing bread. Join us. How is your friend Abby?"

Abby? Frowning, Quen paused. The memory of her deceit hit hard. So much had happened since Quen walked out with her carpetbag. That morning felt like a lifetime ago.

"Er, she's fine. Thank you for asking." Quen entered the kitchen, where bright sunlight streamed through windows. The yeasty smell of bread in the oven wafted through the room, setting her mouth to watering. Prissy looked up from the batch she worked, puffing a strand of hair from her face. "Just in time. You can help us."

Quen unbuttoned her cuffs and rolled up her sleeves. Having Prissy here might be a good thing. One could always count on her to be an enthusiastic supporter of adventures. She washed her hands, then stepped to the table. "Pass me that bowl."

Prissy studied her. "Where'd you get that dress? I've never seen it before."

Mother gave her a quick once-over but remained focused on her task.

Quen struggled to keep her face neutral. "I borrowed it. Mine got stained."

As her fingers kneaded dough, her mind raced. *Please help me, God. But your will, not mine.* "Mother, a situation has come up. Turns out, I may be the solution to a problem. I'd love to help my friends."

Mother turned from peeking into the oven, placing a quilted potholder on the counter. "Oh?"

"A friend of Mrs. Lancaster has died." Emotion clogged Quen's throat. A friend? *Caleb, please know you were so much more than that to all of us.*

Mother made a sympathetic noise in her throat, but scarcely took her gaze from measuring flour into the next bowl.

"His two daughters are moving to his house. One has been living with Mrs. Lancaster all these years—remember

Missouri?—acting as her maid, cook, general helper. Now, Mrs. Lancaster will be alone."

The frown on Mother's face revealed skepticism. "And you provide a solution how?"

"They've asked if I could take Missouri's place." Quen studied the dough beneath her hands. To say she volunteered was probably more accurate. But everyone benefitted if she did this.

"By doing—?" Mother's sharp voice slashed her confidence.

"By moving in. With Mrs. Lancaster."

Mother drew back, eyes widened. "To be a maid? Absolutely not."

Quen sucked in a steadying breath. "Not a maid. A companion. Jonathan, Mrs. Campbell—they're all concerned about leaving Mrs. Lancaster alone. They can drop in to check on her, but with harvest coming soon, and butters to make and sell, they fear they won't have time."

"How do you know so much about these people?" Mother propped a fist on her hip. "Harvests? Butters? Whatever have you been up to?"

"Remember, I told you about Mrs. Campbell a while back. She loaned me the basket and the book about wildflowers."

"Yes, of course. But how have you progressed from borrowing a book to knowing every detail about this family's farm and working life?"

Prissy's eyes widened as she followed the unfolding conversation.

Quen swallowed, focusing on the dough. "Actually, I've been helping them. With their finances." She dropped the words on the table, offhanded, as if involving oneself in the financial details of a family all summer was no big deal. "Abby introduced us. And Mrs. Lancaster knows them well."

"Helping them?" Mother parroted her words and her voice rose an octave. "As in, you've had a job?"

Did one actually have a job if one wasn't paid for one's labors? Yet? "Not exactly." Quen risked a glance at Mother's face, forcing a casual smile. "Just being a good neighbor. I know how to keep books, and they needed assistance. That's all. I enjoyed giving back."

"Quenby Martin. Accountants are *tradesmen*. We are most certainly not a tradesman family. And you are a young woman. Keeping the books for our own family is one thing. This is outrageous."

"Mother, you misunderstand. I did nothing so formal as that. I simply provided support. The way you raised me to do."

Mother snorted, the sharp, inelegant sound a sure sign of her discomposure. Quen's hope withered.

Prissy raised her eyebrows, her glance jumping back and forth between the two.

"You are to cease *assisting* at once. If they need an accountant, I'm sure there are men in town they can hire. Clearly, you've had too much freedom these past weeks."

If she only knew.

"All right. I won't help with the accounting anymore. But may I stay with Mrs. Lancaster? I'll get good practice for keeping my own home—for when I marry." Toss that bone in. Talk of marriage might soothe Mother's ruffled feathers.

Prissy scoffed. "You? Marry? Since when have you wanted that?"

Quen turned her attention to her sister. "Attempting to manage my time so all my chores are done will be quite fun. Mother makes the job seem so easy. I wonder if I can do half as well."

"Daughter, you're ridiculous." The flattery Quen had shoveled on her mother had no apparent effect. Snatching up the potholder, Mother turned back to the oven. "What on earth will the ladies at church think? You absolutely cannot become a maid."

"Companion." Quen slid the word in. "If I do this, I'll not only help Mrs. Lancaster, but will also relieve her friends of a time-consuming responsibility." A begging tone entered Quen's voice. She clamped her mouth shut. It wouldn't do for Mother to know how important this was to her. The way she'd described the task didn't warrant such emotion.

"I'm sorry, Quenby. This is unseemly." Mother didn't bother to look at her.

"Won't people think highly of our willingness to love our neighbors?" Quen forced an even and measured tone to her voice. Come on, Mother. Say yes.

Prissy, bless her heart, chimed in. "I think the job sounds fun. You'll be playing house. I want to join you."

Mother slapped the potholder down onto the table. "Prissy, you'll do no such thing." She narrowed her eyes at Quen, then gave an aggrieved sigh. "I'll speak to your father. But I fully expect him to dissuade you of this nonsense."

Prissy took the bowl of measured flour and stirred in yeast and water. "Won't you be scared staying in a house without a man around? What if a coyote gets after your chickens?" She gasped, a delicious note of fear creeping into her voice. "What if an Indian comes?"

Quen darted a quelling glance at her sister. "Don't be silly, Priss. Indians rarely come this far south, and the chickens have a henhouse. Besides, Mrs. Lancaster lives in town. Everything will be perfectly safe." She turned to her mother, the kneaded bread in her bowl now resting under a dish towel. She dusted her hands together. "When will Father be home?"

"In time for supper, I imagine. Now, let this matter be."

After they finished eating, Quen pushed her chair back and stood. "I'll clear the table, Mother. Give you some time to talk with Father. Prissy, you can help me."

Prissy pouted.

"Now, please." Quen sent her sister a challenging glare. With a sigh, Prissy joined her.

In the kitchen, she heated water for the dishpan. Prissy lurked near the doorway.

"Don't you want to listen?" Her sister's grin was broad. "You need to hear how she puts the proposal to him, so you'll know what to say if you have to argue your side."

"It's impolite to eavesdrop." Quen moved to stand near Prissy, then paused, stretching an ear toward the door.

Prissy snorted.

Quen straightened. "Come away. Mother will be upset if she catches you." She marched back to the pile of dirty dishes and dunked a plate into the warmed water. "Here, rinse and dry."

The murmur of voices in the dining room remained too low to understand.

"I forbid it." Father's harsh tone came through loud and clear.

Prissy stamped her foot. "Drat! Sounds like he says no."

Quen's heart sank. Staying with Mrs. Lancaster was a perfect solution to everything. And, of course, there was the small matter of being closer to Jonathan's farm. *God, please change their minds.*

A knock sounded at the front door. "I'll get it." Prissy tossed the dish towel on the counter and skipped out of the room.

A male voice drifted down the hallway. Quen paused, her hands dripping water into the pan. Was that ...?

Prissy bounded back into the room. "The visitor is for you." Her eyes shone, and she practically hopped from one foot to the other. "I'd forgotten how handsome he is." She pulled the dishrag from Quen's grip, tossing the cloth into the water with a splash. "Come on. See what he wants."

Quen brushed her hands across her skirt, smoothing the wrinkles. She patted her hair, then huffed. He'd seen her wake up on the other side of a campfire after sleeping in her clothes. Why bother primping now? And yet, she pinched her cheeks as she bustled from the kitchen.

She stepped onto the porch and shut the door firmly behind her, closing off Prissy's inquiring face. "Hello." She smiled. His appealing grin set her heart pounding. "Is everything OK at Mrs. Lancaster's?"

Jonathan stepped close and reached for a silken lock of Quen's hair. He rubbed the strands between his finger and thumb. "I think so. But I'm more interested in you. I came to see if you got the go-ahead to stay with her."

She gave a defeated shake of her head.

"They said no?" Acceptance rang in his voice.

Quen shrugged. "I haven't received the official word yet, but I overhead my father declining the possibility. They're not going to let me."

A strange smile crossed his face. Quen squinted, attempting internal guesses at his plan.

Jonathan tugged at her hand, leading her to the wooden porch swing hanging a few feet from the door. "Sit, please. I have something to ask you."

Quen plopped onto the swing. "What?"

Jonathan slid his hand into his pants pocket, then withdrew something, going down on one knee. He stretched his hand toward her, palm up. A small opal brooch glinted in the rays of the setting sun.

"Jonathan?" Quen's trembling hand covered her mouth. "What …?"

"Quenby Martin, will you do me the honor of becoming my wife?"

A muffled squeal of delight came through the window behind the porch swing.

"Are you sure?" Quen's fingers twisted, and a flush of warmth crept up her neck. "You know how irritating I can be. In point of fact—"

"I know everything I need to know, Quen—every irritating, loveable detail. It's all part and parcel. I want all of you." He reached for her hands and pressed his lips against her knuckles. "What do you say? Marry me?"

Joy exploded in Quen's chest like a sunrise.

Her mouth pressed into a line when a stifled "Say yes" floated through the air behind her.

Jonathan quirked an eyebrow and cocked his head toward the window. "Sage advice. I think you should listen to her."

She cupped her palm against his cheek. "Of course, I'll marry you. You've become quite dear to me this summer."

Jonathan stood and pulled Quen to her feet, then slipped the brooch into her hand. He tilted her face up toward his. "Quite dear?" he murmured. "That's all I get?"

Quen's face grew hot. Her gaze jumped around like a hopping sparrow. "You know what I mean."

"Say it, Quen. Say the words." His breath caressed her cheek. His mouth was so near.

Quen's muscles went weak. She focused on him. Blue eyes stared, gripping her with intensity. When had he become so important to her? Spending the rest of her life with him was the most natural thing now. "I love you, Jonathan Campbell. With my whole heart."

He leaned down, sliding his hands around to encircle her ribcage. His warm lips pressed against hers, and she melted against his chest. The sound of muted clapping pierced the fog in her brain. A laugh escaped her, and she straightened. "Prissy's making enough noise in there to raise the saints. My parents are sure to investigate."

"Are you telling me you don't want to be in my arms?" Jonathan's smile convinced her she was the most important person in the world.

Smothering a chuckle, Quen stepped back. Seconds later, the door swung open. Father scowled from the doorway. "What's the meaning of all this?" Prissy's glowing face peered past his shoulder.

Jonathan turned and stepped toward her father, his large hand outstretched. "Good evening, sir. May I have a moment of your time?"

Chapter Thirty

The crowd drifted away, leaving Jonathan standing at Caleb's graveside with Quen, Mrs. L, and Missouri. After much tearful debate, Nora had stayed at Mrs. L's house with Isaac. "I won't risk my son's safety. I'll remember Papa the way I held him in my heart. My goodbyes were said in the pasture."

Now Jonathan swept the area with a careful gaze. "We've got to decide what to do next." He pitched his voice too low for eavesdroppers to overhear, worry circling in his mind like a hungry vulture. "Isaac is in danger until we get payment to the man who purchased him. We don't know if Jenkins talked with anyone about his plans to take the boy back. Others could follow." The sideboard covering the entrance to the hiding place flashed through his mind. "And we certainly can't expect a three-year-old to live in the cellar." He drew a deep breath and faced Mrs. L. "I have an idea, but we'll have to bring a few more people into your operation, namely Grady."

She frowned. The idea obviously did not enthrall her. "Why? What do you have in mind?"

Jonathan recounted the conversation with Manny regarding selling cotton. "Nora and Isaac can be his passengers on the first trip to Mexico."

Mrs. L copied his action, shifting her gaze from his face to their surroundings. "This sounds like a dangerous undertaking for a small child." Her voice was quiet.

Missouri shook her head. "Staying here could be even more dangerous for him. Abby's group had children almost that young on their trip to Texas, so it can be done."

"Grady fits into this how?" Mrs. L asked.

"He'll lead the trip." Jonathan shifted. "We'll send one wagon so that forces Grady to make another trip with a second load of bales, giving him an excuse to return to Mexico. Hopefully, we'll have answers for Nora by then. So, what do you say? May I tell him your secret?"

Mrs. L's focus seemed to turn inward before she gave a sharp nod. "I believe Caleb would want us to continue. His girls are being so brave. They're willing to move forward with their lives, no matter the threat of evil men. I'm sure they'll proceed with courage, trusting their futures to God. We should offer that opportunity to as many people as we can."

She dabbed a handkerchief-wrapped fingertip to the dampness in the corner of her eye. "Yes, you may tell Grady. But only share the parts he needs. For now, we focus on getting Nora and Isaac to safety. Try not to mention the fact others will follow. As Mr. Benjamin Franklin once said, 'Three people can keep a secret if two of them are dead.' We want everyone involved to be as safe as possible. The fewer who know, the better."

"Is Grady going by himself normal?" Quen's worried gaze pierced Jonathan. "You're transporting a lot of money in those bales. Should we be more concerned about that?"

Jonathan sucked his teeth. "Good point." He turned to Mrs. L. "Can we send Manny's father, Gabe, along? Two men, two wagons. The enslaved people can drive, and Gabe and Grady can ride their horses. They'll carry their rifles, looking like they're guarding the cotton. But they can keep our friends safe."

"Yes." Resignation underscored the answer. "The operation will appear very ordinary." She nodded to Missouri. "I believe this is a fine solution for your sister and nephew. God undoubtedly planted that idea in your mind, Jonathan."

Jonathan continued. "If we get word in the meantime your detective has found Moses Brown and completed the transaction, they can turn around and come back."

Mrs. Lancaster jerked to attention. "Moses Brown? Did he mention where he lives?"

Jonathan blinked at her intensity. "No. I only know he's a Puritan from up north."

The widow clasped her hands. "Is he about my age? Tall? Reddish hair?"

Jonathan traded a wide-eyed glance with Quen. He nodded. "You know him?"

She waved her hands in the air. "Oh, praise the Lord. I know him well. He's the person who set me up with connections to extend our portion of the underground railroad to Texas. We have no reason to worry about any further prosecution. All we need do is send Mr. Brown word, explaining where Isaac is. Assuming he hasn't left his home in Tennessee, I know where to direct my investigator." She pointed at Jonathan. "However, I think we'll still use your plan with the cotton bales and the wagons. This deception gives us a safe way to escort people to freedom."

A week later, Quen pressed her back against the open door to Mrs. L's recently vacated spare bedroom, her home for the next six months, allowing Jonathan to pass. Missouri and Nora had taken Isaac to live at the farmhouse, leaving the room available. Jonathan had presented his suit for her hand to her parents, and they had, amazingly, acquiesced, but with reservations. Quen was uncertain whether to classify their blessing as a miracle.

Jonathan heaved her trunk from his shoulder to the floor at the foot of the bed with a huff, his face red. "Good grief. How many books are in here, anyway?" Straightening, he groaned. "Are you planning to bring these with you when we marry?"

Quen peered at him with mock disdain. "Of course. In point of fact, the trunk contains only my favorites. The others can wait. Part and parcel, you said."

Jonathan reached for her hand and tugged gently. She resisted but fell against his chest with a laugh when he pulled. "Part and parcel, indeed. Right now, I'm interested in this part." With a fake growl, his mouth landed on hers.

Her haughty demeanor dissolved in a puff against his lips. "Unhand me, kind sir." She squirmed out of his reach, smoothing her hand against her hair. "Just because we're engaged doesn't mean we can run amok."

Jonathan's head tossed back with a loud guffaw. He leaned closer, one eyebrow cocked with a rakish slant. "Darlin', the running amok is the fun part."

Heat torched Quen's face, and butterflies exploded inside her belly. The reference did not escape her. She knew about the birds and the bees.

But knowing a fact and *knowing* it were two different things entirely.

Jonathan smoothed a strand of hair behind her ear, then trailed his fingertip around her earlobe.

Goosebumps rose on her skin. Why had she insisted they wait six months? Of course. That was Mother's request. Could she be that patient? Did they *have* to wait?

She stepped closer to Jonathan and tiptoed her fingers up his chest, following the path of his buttons. "Let the countdown begin. One-hundred-eighty days until amokness may commence."

The look of amazement on his face threatened to destroy her composure. She turned and swept from the room.

He followed on her heels. "What did you have in mi—"

"There you are, Jonathan." Mrs. Lancaster stepped from the parlor, waving a piece of paper in the air. "Please read this and see if I've missed anything."

Jonathan stared as if she'd spoken Latin. Quen covered her amusement with a cough.

Mrs. Lancaster cocked her head. "Jonathan?"

Clearing his throat, he moved past Quen toward the parlor. "We'll finish this conversation later." His muttered promise held a fervent tone.

Quen snorted a quiet laugh, admiring his long-legged stride. Oh, Lord. Had she ogled? *Jonathan, I'm going to love being your wife.*

Mrs. L handed Jonathan the paper. "I've written a pass giving permission to travel. We'll pretend our enslaved friends belong to the brother of my friend, Mr. Brown, who owns property in Louisiana. Our story will claim he hired out his workers to assist with the cotton delivery. It's a common enough occurrence among plantation owners."

Jonathan frowned, his lips moving as he stared at the paper.

Quen stepped forward. "May I? I might have to write one of these myself one day. I'd like to learn how Mrs. Lancaster phrased things."

Holding the paper so Jonathan could see, Quen read aloud, tracing sentences with her index finger.

Jonathan's hand curled around her waist and squeezed.

When she finished, she lowered the page.

"Well? Will the letter pass muster?" Mrs. L's brows knitted.

He took the paper back from Quen, glancing at the page once more. "I think it'll work fine so long as they don't run into anyone who knows Mr. Brown, or our two friends."

"Very well. I'll make a second copy, one for each man." The widow hurried from the room.

Jonathan pulled Quen close. "That was a very sneaky thing you did, covering for me." He pressed his lips against her temple. "I do love you so, Quenby Martin." The quiet words dropped like pearls.

She gazed up at him, smiling. "Whatever are you talking about? I merely read the letter." She kissed her finger and pressed the tip against his lips. "I love you too, Jonathan Campbell."

Mrs. Lancaster returned. "Behave yourselves. Jonathan, are the wagons loaded?"

He stepped away from Quen, leaving a void where his presence had warmed her. "Yes, ma'am. Manny loaded his rig too. He'll bring his after he finishes in the field tonight. I'm meeting him here." Jonathan glanced toward the buffet. "Are our travelers ready?"

Mrs. Lancaster drew an enthusiastic breath. "Yes. They're eager to go."

Thoughts played on his face, obvious to Quen. He was every bit as concerned for the escapees as her partners. His kindness and patience, honor and trustworthiness all combined to create this man—this dear, sweet, handsome man—and he'd promised to cherish and protect her.

He loved her.

The realization humbled her. She was like a dandelion puff, teetering. One strong gust of wind would send her sailing. And he'd sworn to cup his hands around her, shielding her from what came. The idea she might need someone that way had always been unwelcome, threatening her independence. Now, she yearned for their partnership, the sharing of a life. She wanted this.

A knock sounded at the door. "That'll be Grady." Jonathan left.

Mrs. Lancaster gave Quen an arch look. "Are you quite sure, my dear, you want to get married at Christmas? Not sooner?"

Quen's cheeks burned. "If the plan was *only* up to me, I'd marry him today. But my parents gave their blessing begrudgingly. They fear this is too sudden, that I'm leaping without looking. I agreed to this getting-to-know-each-other period to honor their wishes."

"You could always elope, you know. People do."

Quen shuddered. "I'd never hear the end of it."

"Well, you could confess and tell them you've been getting to know him all summer."

"I'm unwilling to incur their wrath should they ever realize just how well." Quen grimaced. "No, we'll carry on as we are. Besides, we also need time to find someone to stay with you." She raised her finger. "Speaking of, I have an idea. Let's ask Sarah's younger sister, Coral, if she'd be interested. The girls and their brother, Frank, live with Pastor Green. From what Sarah says, Fannie Belle, his wife, doesn't welcome them completely. She's quite clear they remain because keeping them is her Christian duty."

Mrs. Lancaster gave a sharp shake of her head. "I know Fannie Belle Green. Christian duty, indeed." She sniffed. "Wouldn't Sarah be the more obvious choice? She's older, isn't she?"

Quen nodded. "But she's started working for Mrs. Carter at her boarding house. Mrs. Carter invited Sarah to live there with her. She's getting older and needs help. I'm afraid if Sarah leaves, Coral will feel abandoned. I think she'd enjoy staying here."

"The brother doesn't offer any comfort?"

"Frank helps with cattle drives. He's gone more often than he's home." Quen shrugged. "Let's ask her. She's a helpful girl."

"OK. I enjoy having young people around," Mrs. Lancaster said. "Keeps my mind agile."

The men walked into the room. "Evenin', ma'am." Grady swept his hat from his head.

Mrs. Lancaster shook his outstretched hand, her gaze traveling up his considerable height. "I believe I can lay my worries to rest. You'll hold your own against anything you encounter on this trip."

Grady nodded. "Yes, ma'am. I don't expect this to be more challenging than our trip here on the wagon train. We'll be fine."

Jonathan gripped Grady's shoulder. "You understand your task?"

"Think so. Just need the details."

"This is a service we can provide for other farmers in the area. You'll lead our maiden voyage, so to speak. Work out the kinks. The plan is to haul cotton bales through Texas, crossing the King Ranch. At the Rio Grande, we float the wagons across and sell the cotton in Tamaulipas. Captain King buys longhorns from Mexico, so there's a route to follow." Jonathan raised and lowered his hands like a scale. "The farmers sell their crops, and we earn money by taking a cut. Two enslaved men from Louisiana will travel with you to drive the wagons and care for the oxen. You and Gabe keep everyone and everything safe until you get there."

Grady frowned. "We're using slave labor?"

Quen and Jonathan exchanged a glance, then turned to Mrs. Lancaster. The widow closed her eyes briefly, then straightened. "No." She smiled at Grady. "But that's what we want everyone to think."

Grady cocked his head. "Is something going on I should know about?"

Mrs. Lancaster clasped her hands. "Are you aware Mexico outlawed slavery in 1830?"

"No. But won't they be upset with us when we show up using slave labor to drive the wagons?"

"A reasonable conclusion." Mrs. Lancaster's eyes twinkled. "*If* we were using slave labor."

"I don't understand."

"We agree with Mexico." Quen moved to stand by Mrs. Lancaster. "We think slavery should be against the law."

"Then ... why are we using slaves?" Grady's gaze jumped from Quen's face to Jonathan's.

"We're not." Jonathan interrupted. "But we want people to think we are. Another fact about Mexico is this—if an enslaved person steps their foot onto Mexican soil, they're considered a free man. No questions asked."

Grady's eyes widened, then a brilliant grin split his face. "Interesting. What a shame if my ... helpers ... took advantage of that once we arrive. Gabe and I would have to drive our wagons home by ourselves."

"A shame, indeed." Mrs. Lancaster added.

Grady's brow wrinkled. "You mentioned taking a second load after we return. I'm guessing we'll need new ... helpers?"

"That we will." Quen pointed her finger at him. "As many times as necessary. There are hundreds of bales stored all over this area thanks to the Union blockade. Transporting them all will take months."

Mrs. Lancaster sobered. "This task won't be easy, though. Comanches do come this far south occasionally, and they don't like the White men taking their land. And several Mexicans feel the same way about us claiming Texas. Your rifle may well see some action."

Jonathan gave Grady a sober look. "You don't have to do this. The job will be difficult."

Silence filled the room. Quen held her breath as Grady chewed his cheek.

"Welp, I see things this way. I coulda died on that trip to Texas. Heck, half my family did. I don't figure God saved me so I could rest on my laurels. People deserve to be free. I'd like to help folks gain a better life." He paused. "That's why Jesus came, right? To set us free? And freedom's worth dyin' for. At least, Jesus seemed to think so."

Quen blinked away tears. Grady put things so simply. Sacrificial love. God had shown her time and again examples of sacrifice offered with no strings attached, only for the sake of love. A picture of Caleb filled her mind.

All she had to do was accept Jesus's gift. Her heart swelled.

Quen slipped her hand into Jonathan's. His fingers closed around hers, and he smiled down at her, love glowing in his eyes.

Mrs. Lancaster cleared her throat. "Grady, accompany me to the kitchen. Missouri baked provisions. You can load them on the wagon." As she walked away, she shot a mischievous look over her shoulder at Quen.

Quen faced Jonathan, but lowered her gaze, fighting unexpected shyness. She reached for his other hand, rubbing her thumbs across his knuckles.

Jonathan bent, peering into her face. "What're you thinking?"

She opened her mouth, shut it, then tried again. "The first thing I noticed about you was the love you share with your family. I envied you so."

"You didn't notice my devastating handsomeness first?"

She yanked on his hands. "Be serious. I'm trying to tell you something."

"I'm sorry." He wiped the smile from his face. "I'm ready. Please speak your mind."

She drew a deep breath, searching for words. "One would think moving with my family to Africa and spending my childhood as the daughter of a missionary, I would live and breathe Jesus and the Bible. But that's not how I felt. If anything, I experienced the opposite. My father's devotion to the *mission* took all of that. Instead of loving me, he loved them." She paused. "Or he loved the idea of loving them. And my mother ... well, she suffered heartache while we lived there, and there wasn't much left for me. Frankly, I resented God."

Jonathan's thumb stroked her bottom lip. "I can't imagine someone not loving you."

"After being around you, Caleb, and Mrs. Lancaster, I saw a different side of God. You showed me—in the way you live, not the words you say—what God can mean to a person, how he influences lives. You showed me something I wanted. And bit by bit, I began to trust him that way too."

Jonathan's heart shone in his eyes. "That makes me happy."

She swallowed. "My mother thinks being a good Christian means you follow the rules correctly. That you've done enough to earn your place in Heaven." She shook her head. "That responsibility was a cage for me. A burden I couldn't bear. I was clearly incapable of living that perfectly. So, I rejected that life. And God."

She gazed at him. "But being with you has shown me I had it all wrong. You never act as if you fear God will abandon you or grow weary of your failed efforts. I've lived with that my entire life, almost expect God's rejection."

His brow furrowed. "You see yourself that way? Quen, you helped me get rid of my shame at my inability to read. You complete me. That was a gift from God."

The corners of her mouth tipped up. "See, you're doing it now. You simply accept God's love and grace and try to act like Jesus did."

Her praise obviously made him uncomfortable. Humble as always.

"It's exactly what you do, Jonathan. I never learned that until now."

Awareness filled her soul. By demonstrating how to follow Christ, he'd taught her how. He'd shown her a person she could accept to lead her. Someone she could trust with her love. Caleb's dying words drifted through her memory. *God'll never forsake you, Quen. Simply follow him.*

She stood on her tiptoes and pressed a kiss to Jonathan's lips. "Yes, God wanted to set us free. All of us. And love is the only thing that ever truly has."

Author's Note

Thank you, Dear Reader, for spending your valuable time with me and my story. I am humbled and grateful that you did so.

If you enjoyed Quenby and Jonathan's story and would like to read more from the San Antonio series, go back to how it all started in Book One—*Protected*. Discover how Abby and Manny met. Then look for how their story continues in the Christmas novella in *Christmas Love Through the Ages*, both available on Amazon.

And be watching for book four, which will share the story of Grady Strong as he joins the Texas Rangers. Subscribe at paulapeckham.com to get notifications of all my upcoming books.

And, if you believe reading this book would bless others, please leave a review on Amazon and/or Goodreads and share your thoughts. A quick sentence or two will let your friends know you recommend the story. Your word-of-mouth is the most effective advertising I can ask for.

About the Author

A fifth-generation Texan, **Paula Peckham** graduated from the University of Texas in Arlington and taught math at Burleson High School for nineteen years. She and her husband, John, divide their time between their home in Burleson and their casita in Rio Bravo, Mexico. Her debut novel, *Protected,* was an ACFW Genesis semi-finalist in 2020, and won the Global Book Golden Award in 2022. Book two in the San Antonio series, *A Father's Gift,* was a finalist in the 2023 Selah awards. She also writes short stories, novellas, and poems. She had contributions in the 2021 release *Christmas Love Through the Ages*, and *Texas Heirloom Ornament*. She is the president of ACFW DFW and is a member of Unleashing the Next Chapter. She has spoken at ACFW, Unleashing the Next Chapter, and the Carrollton League of Writers. For more about Paula and her books, follow her at paulapeckham.com.

Paula's Books

Protected

San Antonio Series
Book 1

PAULA PECKHAM